HOUSE OF BELLS

HOUSE OF BELLS

Chaz Brenchley

This first world edition published 2012
in Great Britain and in the USA by
SEVERN HOUSE PUBLISHERS LTD of
9–15 High Street, Sutton, Surrey, England, SM1 1DF.

British Library Cataloguing in Publication Data

Brenchley, Chaz.
  House of bells.
  1. Horror tales.
  I. Title
  823.9'2-dc23

ISBN-13: 978-0-7278-8156-4 (cased)

All Severn House titles are printed on acid-free paper.

Severn House Publishers support the Forest Stewardship Council [FSC], the
leading international forest certification organisation. All our titles that are printed
on Greenpeace-approved FSC-certified paper carry the FSC logo.

Typeset by Palimpsest Book Production Ltd.,
Falkirk, Stirlingshire, Scotland.
Printed and bound in Great Britain by
MPG Books Ltd., Bodmin, Cornwall.

ONE

She had never really believed in the guru.

She was a firm believer in herself, in all her guilt and grief.

And in the noble art of running away, geographical distance, that too.

It had seemed enough, once. Behind her, back in London, where everything was loud and immediate and unbearable. *Get away, get far away, be somewhere else. Somebody else.*

It had seemed all too wonderfully attractive, if she were honest.

She could be honest, sometimes. If she was paid enough.

'Money's not an issue.'

Well, of course he'd say that. For him it was not, it never had been. He'd been born to it: the Honourable Anthony Fledgwood, son of his father, junior lordling and news-paperman. Editor to one of his father's rags; entitled to appear in the very social pages that he published. Entitled? Determined, rather. Which was how Grace had bumped into him tonight, as it happened: at that kind of party where one only went to be noticed.

For him, it was his stock-in-trade; for her, a professional engagement.

Those weren't quite the same thing, though it was easy sometimes to confuse the two. Confusion was something that she traded on.

Had traded on, in the past. No longer. The cost was too great.

That night her host Dr Barrett was her employer, though he was too polite to admit it. Certainly he was far too polite to call her a hat-check girl, though really he might as well. It wasn't that kind of establishment, but even so.

By her own definitions, it was a bell, book and candle night.

She and the other girls were there to answer the door, serve drinks, listen to the conversations – and contribute too, in a wide-eyed admiring kind of way – and then go home with anyone who wanted them. It was a literary party – hence the book in 'bell, book and candle', coming handily between the doorbell and the night light: she could still amuse herself with her own bitter wit, even if she found little enough to laugh at any more – so there was likely to be a queue of hopefuls. In her own case, it was likely to be a long one. Notoriety will do that to a girl.

Notoriety will fill a room, too. Fill a party. She was one of the reasons the place was so hot tonight. A better reason – she thought – than the Soviet poet whose new book was being launched, whose embassy watchdogs stood four-square on either side of him in bad suits, glowering. In a spirit of perversity, she had ignored the poet and tried to charm the watchdogs. Having achieved nothing but a more severe glower, she was devoting herself now to their torment: sashaying by with a sway of miniskirted hips at every opportunity, trailing literati and gossipmongers at every step; bringing them the virtuous and regular orange juices they had demanded, spiked with lethal quantities of vodka they knew nothing about; sending anyone she could to murmur bright nothings into the poet's hairy ear, just a little too softly for his minders to overhear.

The vodka might be wasted effort – they were Russian, after all, and built like brick outhouses: so far they were showing no effects at all, despite the heroic quantities of Stolichnaya they were innocently imbibing – but she thought she was winning on all other fronts. Even outhouses had libidos, seemingly. They watched her come and go and come again. They watched everyone, of course; it was their job, just as it was her job – a part of her job, one of her jobs – to be watched. But even so. They watched *all* of the girls most of the time, which probably wasn't their job at all. But even so. She didn't think they did it indiscriminately. She thought they discriminated absolutely. In her favour, if it was a favour to be so coldly lusted after. She could feel their chill hunger follow her around the room like the eyes of a sinister portrait in some cheap Hammer Horror flick: dark and empty and meaningless and deadly.

Deadly to her spirits, at least, if she would let it be. But, of course, she wouldn't. She'd go on goading them, however she could manage it, for whatever mean pleasure it might give her. Already they were eyeing their charge askance, frowning after the purveyors of those whispered messages, half inclined to whisk him swiftly back to the embassy. Or else to durance vile, if life in the USSR wasn't already vile enough. A little more of this, a little more purpose to it, and she thought she really could make them believe that MI5 was trying to seduce him. The game was all the more enjoyable because they didn't know the rules. They didn't even know they were playing.

She had decided, quite some time ago, that all of life was a game. It was how she got through. She had lost a couple of rounds, quite catastrophically – but how could that matter in the long run, or the short run, or at all? It was just a game. She could be a good loser and start again. Nothing left to lose now, after all . . .

'Grace, girl! Amazing Grace. Still strutting your stuff, then? Of course you are. I'd be proud of you, if I had any right to be. If you were mine.'

'Tony.' His hands were on her hips, his voice was in her ear; he was here, then. Well, of course he was here. He was a player too: on his father's behalf, and his own. If those were different. Neither man – nor any of their newspapers' avid readers – would have the least interest in a Russian poet, but there were other attractions tonight: the Beautiful People, the buzz of fashionable London. And herself. The Honourable Tony's readers were very much interested in her. Likely, he'd have a photographer stationed in the street outside. No matter. She knew a back way, if she was leaving with company, if she wanted to keep it a secret. Or she could be bold, leave by the front door, keep her face on the front page. If she chose to play it like that.

She leaned back against the familiar comfort of his body and said, 'You wouldn't want me, darling. Your dad would disapprove.' She was fine on the front page, selling papers at 6d a time; not so good on his son's arm at a nightclub. Appalling across the dinner table in the family home; worse across the breakfast table next morning. Unthinkable within the family, permanent, married.

Just as well that had never been on the cards, then. Not a legitimate move.

Tony made a noise that was obviously meant to mean *bugger Dad*, but it wasn't very convincing. Everything he had – money, position, access: that last particularly, every open door – he owed to his father. There had never been any question of a split between them. Even before she disgraced herself utterly, finally, irrecoverably.

She was still a player, but the game was different now. All she had to play for was survival. He was out of her reach. He probably always had been; it was just that she knew it at last.

Still. He had a tight grip and a firm body. A tight grip *on* a firm body, which was hers. His father wasn't here. If anyone was watching – apart from the Russian goons – she didn't care, and apparently neither did he.

Of course, people were watching. People were always watching. There was probably somebody here who was being paid to watch her, and not by Tony or any of his rivals. When once you've been a trouble to the government, they don't ever quite let you run free. Mr Wilson would be keeping an eye on her, she was sure.

She still didn't care. She tried not to think about it much; it was too strange, knowing that the Prime Minister read reports on what you did, who you saw. Who you slept with.

She tipped her head back on Tony's shoulder, so that she could squinny sideways at his face. 'Love the moustache, darling.' No doubt Daddy would disapprove of that too, but he shouldn't. It suited the shape of Tony's face, and made him look older at the same time. Not too much older; not too old for the velvet suit she stroked her cheek against. Not too old for her, either. Just old enough. Responsible. A newspaperman. Son of his father . . .

Oh, bugger the old man. She could say that – or at least think it – with more vehemence than Tony. Remembering that particular, dreadful breakfast.

She wouldn't let him spoil this evening too. Besides, she was here to work, not to lament past losses. Nor, strictly speaking, to tease the embassy bulldogs. Tony was legitimate, exactly the kind of man she was here to amuse. If she could play him somehow to her advantage in the doing of it, then she'd be well ahead. Scoring all down the line, both ways from the middle. If that made any sense at all. She didn't know much about sports. Her games were more complicated, and mostly played in the dark.

He seemed entirely willing to play along. His hands wanted more than a cuddle, but that was minor; there were cuddles and more for the asking, all through the flat. Presumably, he was hoping to play her too, looking for a score on his own behalf. She'd expect nothing less.

She'd best show dutiful as well as willing, in case mine host was watching. She did still want to go home with her pay packet in her handbag. That at least, whatever else she took with her, whatever detours she made on the way. She peeled herself determinedly out of his hands and smiled up at him. *Hat-check girl*, she reminded herself, but he wouldn't be parted from his trademark Nehru jacket, nor his cap. These days they were everywhere, since Lennon had appeared in one, but Tony had his first. It was absurd to be so defensive on his behalf, but she still was. 'Can I get you a drink?'

'Yes, why not? And fetch yourself a glass of whatever coloured water the good doctor is allowing you, and then come and talk to me. In here –' with a sideways jerk of his head towards a closed door – 'where we can be private.'

'Tony, it's a *party*. There's no such thing as private.'

'That's Barrett's study. There's a reason why he shuts the door.'

'There is. I know. He thinks it'll keep people out. Which would technically include you too – but, as it happens, what I also know is that there are at least half a dozen people in there already. *They* think closing the door will keep the smell of dope in, but it's a party. There's no such thing as private. Everyone knows.'

'Grace. Fetch the drinks. Leave the people to me.'

So she did that, coming back with one bottle of Pol Roger and two glasses, because she was damned if she would let Tony or anyone catch her drinking a hostess cocktail. He was absolutely right, of course, that was exactly what she should be doing; but if she got tipsy and misbehaved, it would only add to her legend. People would talk, *The Daily Messenger* and other papers would gossip, and Dr Barrett's party would be discussed all over. Even more than it was going to be already. It would be epic; he'd be thrilled.

And one thing was for sure, certain safe. Whoever she went home with tonight, it wouldn't be Tony Fledgwood. So it didn't really matter, did it? If she got sozzled?

She found the study door ajar, the corridor outside more of a squeeze than it had been. Someone pinched her bottom as she wriggled by, but that was only to be expected. Almost to be played for, it almost counted as a score. Bruises only rise on living skin; she was a survivor, she could wear them with pride. *See me? I was there, and now I'm here. I had that, all of that; now I have this. These. I fell a long way, but I'm still alive, still breathing. Still bleeding. See?*

Someone had thrown a chiffon scarf across the desk lamp; she slipped through the door into reddish light, the colour of sunsets. And the smell of bonfires, that too: a harshness in the air, a texture like tweed as she breathed it, rough and outdoorsy and scratching at her throat. A roach still burning in a brass incense-holder, the rising twist of smoke almost deliberately ironic.

All those people in the corridor must have been the people in here before. Somehow Tony had chased them out. He sat waiting for her, solitary and almost imperial in this dusky light, on a white leather couch with his arm along the backrest. It wasn't an invitation so much as an expectation. She would sit there beside him, and his arm would come around her shoulders as a matter of course, and—

No.

It was his right arm that lay flung along the sofa-back, and he was devoutly right-handed. She held out the bottle to him, and of course he reached to take it with that hand. She stood waiting while he fussed with wire and foil and cork, while he cast the odd amused glance up at her, while neither of them said a thing. When the bottle spurted foam, she was ready with a glass to catch it as he tipped. When both glasses had been filled and topped up as the froth subsided, she dragged a worn red pouffe out from under the desk and sat on that. Deliberately at his feet, to let him feel even more like an emperor dispensing favours; deliberately not within the ambit of his arm. Giving herself a little leeway, space for some feelings of her own.

He said, 'Well, then. How've you been, Grace?'

She shrugged. 'Oh, you know. No, wait – you *do* know. If you read your own paper, you do.'

'I know what we've been saying about you. That's not the same thing.'

'Well,' she said. 'Thanks for admitting that, at least.'

'Be fair,' he said, worrying at his moustache with his finger. That was new, of course. Previously, he would have taken his cap off and worried at his hair. 'If you don't talk to us, we have to take what we can get from other people. And we haven't been as hard on you as the rest of Fleet Street is. Have we?'

'No, Tony. No, you haven't.' Small mercies, something to be grateful for: a paper that was almost on her side. That would listen to her, at least. If the lawyers would only let her talk. She could have sold her story and made some real money, if she'd been allowed to. *The Dentist, The Arms Dealer and the Diplomat: Jailed Call-Girl Spills All.* Or: *'It Was Only A Game,' Says Playgirl.* Or: *The Chink in Her Amours*, if they wanted to be clever.

Instead – well, this. Hat-check girl, trading on her notoriety. And snatching the chance to sit at Tony's feet, just for ten minutes, when she should have been working the rooms, fetching drinks and laughing at jokes she didn't think funny and dancing with oily strangers, waiting for one of them to grip her wrist and claim her for the night. It was understood, even by those who didn't know she was being paid for it, that was what she was there for. She and all the other girls, but herself particularly. She was that kind of girl. Everyone knew it.

Still, that kind of girl was sure to be flighty and unreliable, not always where she should be or doing what she was paid for. And besides, Tony was a guest here, and a significant one. Barrett couldn't complain if she spent ten minutes closeted alone with him. Or if she spent an hour. Or if he was the one who took her home . . .

No. Not that. Never again. She'd been quite clear about that, and so had his father.

'So. How are you, pet? Really?'

That shrug was becoming automatic, apparently. She stilled it, and found herself staring down at the bubbles in her glass. At least something was light and frothy and on the rise, the way she used to think life was. Her life, especially: she hadn't ever thought much about anyone else's, until that was all she had to think about, when it was gone.

It was hard to talk, apparently, even to him. The longer she waited, the more her shoulders hunched under the weight of all that silence, all those words unsaid.

He outwaited her, which was just mean. At last – talking to her knees, because she could, apparently, still not talk to him – she said, 'I hate it. All of it. All of this,' with one wild champagne-spilling gesture which might as well have been a gesture back through time to the girl she used to be, when she used to spill champagne for the sheer gorgeous hell of it. 'I hate being the party girl that people pay for, because it gets their parties in the paper. I hate being so desperate I'll go to bed with anyone for a hundred quid and a kind smile – and, actually, don't bother about the smile. I *hate* that. I hate the way everyone thinks it, and I hate the fact that it's true.'

'Actually,' he said, 'what everyone thinks is that you don't care what you do now.'

'That's true, too. At least, that I'll do anything for money. Why not?' After these last years, why would she even hesitate? 'But no, I do still care. I just try not to show it. You won't give me away, will you, Tony?'

'Never,' he said. 'Not give you away, and not sell you either. I will use you, though, if you'll let me. If you'll do anything for money, will you do a job for me?'

That shrug was becoming harder every time. She really, really wanted to say no. *Not for you, Tony love. Not you. Please don't ask me.*

But it was too late, and so she managed to shrug at him with her poor overburdened shoulders, and she managed to say, 'Yes, sure. Why not, if the money's right?'

'Money's not an issue,' he said.

She snorted. 'Speak for yourself, love.'

'No, I'm serious. You can have all the resources of Fledgwood Enterprises at your back, if you need them.'

She blinked, sipped, said, 'What is it, then? This job?' Not hat-check girl at one of his father's parties, that was for sure.

'It's for the *Messenger*. Undercover work, an investigation.'

'What? You're bonkers. I'm no bloody journalist.'

'No – but you are a girl who needs to hide. Or you could be. It's the perfect cover, sweetheart. If you're blown, it's just all the more convincing. And you'd be out of London, a long way away from all of this. No one's going to forget about you, I'm not saying that – but, well. Nine days' wonder, you know?'

'More like nine months,' she said; and then heard herself, realized what she'd said, started to cry. It wasn't at all what she'd meant; she was just trying to be bitterly clever, the way she did when she was trying to keep up with Tony. But that was a hopeless enterprise in any case, and it had led her to walk flat-footed into the heart of sorrow. Nothing new there. She despised herself for many reasons – every good reason, and quite a few that were no good at all but she used them anyway – and this was one of the best: that she tried to be slick and tripped herself every time.

She wasn't clever enough to be any use to Tony. She couldn't save herself, let alone help anyone else. Or expose them. She wanted to say so, but talking was all manner of hard, too much to manage while she wept; and when he passed her a hankie that only made her more incoherent because she'd never been any good at gratitude.

'Oh, keep the sodding thing,' he snapped, when she tried absurdly to hand it back to him. Or maybe he'd said 'sodden'; she really wasn't sure. And then, 'Keep it,' he said, 'and go home. Meet me for oysters at noon, and I'll tell you what I want.'

'I can't,' she said, gulping. 'I can't go home. Dr Barrett's paying me to be here . . .'

'How much?'

'What?'

'How much is he paying you? A hundred, did you say? Here.' A sheaf of folded notes, thrust into her fingers, uncounted by either one of them. 'Just go home, Grace. Or do I need to take you?'

No. No, not that. Never that. He needed not to see where home was now; that was suddenly rather urgent.

As she hurried downstairs, she realized that she'd left her coat behind, but never mind. Also that she hadn't actually said thank you. Oddly – for someone who was no good at gratitude – that seemed to matter rather more.

As she left, she heard her name called from across the street. Stupidly, she lifted her head to look, and the camera's flash caught her full in the face like a blow. That would be Tony's tame photographer; that would be her all over tomorrow's front page, then. She'd meant to slip out the back way, and forgot.

Tony never forgot anything, and never missed his chance. Whatever he asked for tomorrow, tonight he had just what he wanted: a notorious good-time girl with her mascara smeared down her cheeks, scuttling out of a trendsetter's party unusually early and unusually alone. Of course there was a story in that. Rampant speculation was the same thing as news. Friendship was a tool like any other. He would lend her his handkerchief and offer her the hope of escape and still send her out of the front door looking like this, still use her face tonight to sell his paper in the morning. Of course he would. She would never expect anything else.

It wasn't even betrayal, when he was so upfront honest about it. Tony used people without a second thought; everyone knew. If he liked you he'd be kind about it, in person and in print, but he'd still tell the story. Sell the story. He'd use his own wife, if he had one. He'd use his child, if . . .

Oh. Damn. Now she was crying again, and that photographer

was still on her heels and flashing away. Tony would be seeing his own hankie on his own front page, then.

The sound of her own footsteps underlay all her dreams these days. Walking and walking: sharp heels on city streets, rapid and determined, getting her there. It was all she knew how to do, to keep moving. She always walked when she could. Head down, hood up, on her way. Sometimes she would walk all night, sooner than go home.

Home meant stopping, stillness, quiet. Bed. All of those were terrible to her. And no more than she deserved, her punishment. She always did have to go home in the end. Just as she always read the papers, sooner or later. They were her punishment too.

Tony was her affliction, the one sorrow that she didn't think she'd earned. There always had to be something extra, the free gift at the bottom of the cereal packet. She still dug her hand in to grope for those, like a little kid. He was like that, like the aching tooth that your tongue couldn't keep away from.

Oysters meant Soho. Soho meant putting on a face; you never knew who you might meet, only that you were sure to meet someone. Which would be why Tony had chosen it, to get more mileage out of her. Yet more. To some people she was poison, but it never did a young man any harm to be seen out and about with poison on his arm. Nor an editor, nor an heir. With Tony you never knew quite which game he was playing, which hat he wore beneath his trendy cap. Which face he was showing to the world, or why.

Herself, she had only the one face to show. It took an hour to paint on, even after she'd done her hair; and then a headscarf went on to hide the hair, and she did what she could to hide her face too, head down and walking briskly, always moving, not even pausing at a light. If the traffic was against her she'd just carry on, miss her turn and go out of her way, walk further than she needed to. She'd cross three sides of a square rather than stand still and be trapped in the world's stare, feel that moment of recognition happen, wait breathless for whatever might come next. The crow of triumph or the impertinent questions or the savage accusations, they were all equally unbearable, though she did in fact bear them all when she had to. Even the silent cold shoulder hurt, even while she welcomed it: the best of everything that's awful.

Mostly, people just stared. She'd been through the range of responses – she'd tried staring back; she'd tried, 'What are you staring at?'; she'd tried a V-sign and a vicious tongue and a regal mocking wave – and nothing worked to her comfort. Now she ignored them stoutly, eyes on the middle distance once she'd been spotted. Hide until they found her, yes, head down and scuttle onward, but never let them see her try to hide thereafter. Never gift them an easy victory, never show her shame.

In Soho, for oysters – well. No hope of hiding there. She'd just have to be brazen, the way everyone thought she was anyway. Shameless.

She could hate Tony for doing this to her, except – well. He was Tony. What was the point?

It was one of those days that London did so well, warm spring and a clear light; so of course the streets were busy, and the little park was full of lunchers and loafers, and she was sure they must all be watching her. Head up, then, girl; sunglasses on, eyes front and just keep moving. Dean Street, Frith Street, Greek Street: all in alphabetical order, the secret knowledge that helped her navigate the heart of Soho.

Oysters was easy. There was only one oyster bar Tony deemed acceptable; she could find her way to Tarsier's in the dark, in the rain, in extremis. And frequently had.

Just as well, because gazing into the middle distance was useless for finding her way. Pretending to look stopped her actually looking to see where she was. She supposed that must be ironic or something.

But here was Tarsier's, all barrels and sawdust and bare wood. Here was Tony, perched as ever on a stool in the open window, exhibited to the street. Looking unfairly lovely, the dark tumble of his hair snaring the sunlight while the wide lapels of his jacket only showed off the breadth of his shoulders. Oozing self-content, that too. *See me: here I am, the most fashionable man in London, waiting to eat oysters with the wickedest girl in England . . .*

'You're late,' he said as she hoisted herself on to the high stool he had somehow kept for her despite the crush.

'Darling. Of course I'm late.' *Sorry, Tony, sorry.* But it was a rule now, never to apologize to anyone. She'd done too much of that, and it didn't help at all. People liked to see you grovel, but that was all about punishment, not forgiveness. She'd been punished enough. She had that in writing, from a lord. 'So were you, I expect.'

He grinned. 'I was, but you win in the lateness stakes. I should know never to compete with a pro.'

Damn. She'd flinched at that, which made him twitch a little in his turn. Sometimes they played sensitivities like ping-pong. 'Just a talented amateur,' she said quickly, as if it didn't matter at all. Trying to cover up too late, as usual. 'What shall we drink? Is it a Guinness day or a champagne day?'

She had seldom felt less like celebrating, but that wasn't the question. There were only the two alternatives with Tony, when oysters were in the case; and the choice hung somewhat on his mood, somewhat on the needs and intents of his day, but mostly on criteria that she'd never quite managed to pin down. She no longer tried to guess which way his choice would fall. Fifty-fifty gambles were no fun at all when you always, always lost.

'Champagne, of course,' he said, as though she should have known that. 'Guinness is for workdays.'

'Aren't we working?'

'Not at all. I'm seducing you. That was never work.'

No, she thought wearily. *I was always too easy, wasn't I?*

This time she was careful not to let any of that show on her face. Wearing masks was second nature to her now, and she could swap one with another at a moment's notice. She gave Tony her bright glad smile, and never mind if he saw clean through it; he wouldn't say a word. He was a collaborator through and through, when it suited his convenience. He practically laced her masks up for her, caught them if they started to slip. They both conspired to keep raw emotion under wraps. Her pain embarrassed him, she thought. He shouldn't have to deal with that.

She said, 'Seduce away. If you can keep your hands

to yourself while you're at it.' That was their agreement: no touching now, or not with any serious intent. And being jocular about it, that was in the agreement too. Making like it didn't matter. She could do that. 'What's this mysterious job of yours?'

And why would you offer it to me? I'm not qualified.

Except that she was, apparently, if having her cover blown was a part of her cover.

He said, 'There's a house up in the north, border country. Old place, big grounds, you know the sort of thing.'

She did. She said, 'Tony, I'm hardly – what is it, persona grata? – on the country-house circuit any more.' And never wanted to be, no, never again.

'No, but that's what I'm building up to.' He gestured towards the waiter in his long apron. No need to order – just a flick of the thumb to suggest a cork removed from a bottle and all was understood. 'This place isn't on the circuit either, and it ought to be. For some reason your country-house set abandoned it way back, before the first war. It's been half a dozen things since, but never a home.'

'Never till now, are you going to tell me?'

'Not even that, not quite. Someone's making a commune there, unless it's an ashram, unless it's a cult. I don't know; there's no information. We sent a man in, and he hasn't come out again.'

'Oh, so now you want to send me in to be murdered as a spy? Thanks, Tony, but no thanks.'

'Don't be daft, love. I don't think he was murdered. I think he was swallowed up by all the love and butterflies. I think he was converted. I think he's chanting mantras and eating lentils, or making love and growing onions, or expanding his inner consciousness and waiting for the end of the world.'

'Making love sounds nice,' she said, because they both expected it of her. She could be as brittle as hard plastic, but she did still have to shine.

The waiter came over with bucket, bottle, glasses. Tony poured. Little rituals: the touch of rim to rim, 'Cheers, then,' the first sip. Froth, chill, bite. Something seemed to have happened in her head since last night, so that just the taste and touch and tingle of it on her tongue made her want to cry again.

She needed him to say something quickly, so he did. He was probably worried he might lose another hankie. Today's was raw peach silk, peeping from behind that broad lapel, an exact match for his shirt.

He said, 'OK, Grace, it's like this. You've had enough of London, way too much. You can't leave your flat without being followed by photographers, you can't go to a party without being cornered by hacks and gossipmongers, and you can't walk down the street without being hissed at.'

'Tony . . .'

'Basically,' he went on remorselessly, 'you can't live your life. Everything you see, everything you do reminds you of what you've done, what's happened to you, what you've lost. You need to get away – and that doesn't mean Biarritz or St Tropez; it doesn't even mean Jamaica. Those are just London with better weather. Everyone there is someone you know, someone who knows all about you. What you want, what you're desperate for is a whole new way to live. You want to be someone else, someone who doesn't have a court case and a dead baby and a cruel kind of fame to live with.'

She wasn't going to cry, and she wasn't going to interrupt again. He was telling her story entirely, but he thought it was a fiction, a cover story he was composing on her behalf. Or at least he was pretending that. She owed it to him to play along. She nodded solemnly, clung to the weight of her glass, looked around to see if oysters might be on their way yet.

'Something you overheard at a party seemed to offer you the chance. The world's full of retreats, of course it is, but this was the one you heard about just when you were desperate enough to do something about it. You were buzzed on dope at the time so you're hazy on the details, but you remembered the name of the nearest station; so when you got home at dawn you just chucked some clothes into a suitcase and lit out. Maybe you were still stoned; maybe you made a conscious decision to be impulsive for once, after way too long trapped in the machine. You choose. Whatever, on the train you're going to change your name. You get on at King's Cross as Grace Harley, and you get off in Leeds as Georgie Hale. Same initials: people always do that, and it's convenient, because I bet half your things have your initials on them.'

Tony, you know half my things have my initials on them. Or are we pretending you don't? Half my other things have your initials on them. Do I need to change your name too?

'At Leeds you change on to the local line. Drop me a postcard while you're waiting, so I know you've got that far at least. After that you're on your own.'

Tony, love, I've been on my own for a long time now – but here came the oysters, a great platter of ice and shells and lemons and shimmering flinching vulnerable flesh. Squeeze and swallow.

TWO

Sometimes Grace felt squeezed herself, squeezed like a lemon – all the juice wrung from her – and swallowed whole. Sometimes she felt the other thing: chewed up and spat out.

Mostly, she tried not to feel anything. Actually to *be* as remote and untouchable as she could seem, with her face perfect and her eyes on the far horizon, statuesque. Literally that, like a statue: heartless and bloodless, cold marble all through.

Today – well, any day, really – she wasn't doing so well at that. She tried, she did try, but it was never easy. Like making herself unhuman, by a simple effort of will. Today was harder yet, as wheezing clanking engines dragged her further and further into the north country.

She should be glad, to be out of the Smoke. She *was* glad, in every way that counted. Almost every way. It was just . . . she had made and lived all her life in London, all her adult life, the one that mattered. Even when it had shattered between her hands like a glass bubble, lethal and gone in a moment: even then she had stayed, stubborn or determined or desperate. Living in the ruins, refusing to run away. Keeping her name in the papers, her face in the public eye, because anything else would have been an unthinkable surrender.

This, now: she wasn't surrendering, no. Nor running away. She was *working*. Which felt better on the inside, at least. If anyone – or everyone – else thought she'd slunk away from London in a funk, that was a part of the job, and she could feel good about it.

She could try.

Nothing was easy, but she didn't expect that. She had no right to.

She didn't deserve even this much, this journey, and on the face of it this was no blessing. To sit hour after hour in uncomfortable trains, crowded shoulder to shoulder with strangers; to keep her headscarf and sunglasses firmly in place and her face averted, staring blindly out of the window; to endure the surge and suck of her thoughts, that constant tidal reach from unbearable guilt to dreary desolation. And to wait, of course. To wait and wait for that moment of recognition, the shrill voice, inescapable in these cruel closed carriages . . .

But she waited and waited, and that moment never came. Probably nobody could actually believe that the actual Grace Harley – The Third Woman, they liked to call her in the press – would be travelling north out of London in a second-class carriage. She could have gone first class, Tony would have paid for that – *money's not an issue*, he'd said, and he meant it. Only, if she wore these same dull clothes and sat in first class just like this, headscarf and sunglasses and all, everyone would look at her and see Grace Harley running away. Here in second class, they looked and saw Georgie Hale: a look-alike, perhaps, or an attention-seeker, a young woman who'd like to be mistaken for the infamous Third Woman if it wasn't so ridiculous.

She was doing her job here, thinking it and thinking it. Being Georgie Hale; being Grace Harley being Georgie Hale. Ready for anything. Dreading everything. Feeling the long cord of her life thus far stretching behind her, stretching and stretching as she tugged it tighter and tighter, as she moved further and further away. Maybe she could cut it, cut loose and start again. Maybe she should. Everything that mattered to her was back there, and it was all dreadful.

Maybe it would snap of its own accord, if she just got far enough away. If no one knew her, if she really could live as Georgie Hale.

Maybe it would snap her back, like elastic. Maybe she wouldn't be able to stand life in the deep country, so very far from the bright lights. But then Tony would be disappointed and everything would be just that little bit worse.

Really, there was no telling. Only this: the past at her back in vicious, painful clarity; nothing but fog ahead; and this moment of stillness, sitting and watching the countryside unreel beyond the window. Farmland went to moorland, slowly yielding place. Cattle went to sheep, hedges to rough stone walls, fields to broad open rocky heights. No wonder no one recognized her. She barely recognized herself, in this alien landscape.

Maybe she could shrug Tony away, with all that he implied. All of London, all her life just gone: that could all go with him. Then she'd just be Georgie.

She might like that.

Really, it wasn't so bad, chuntering into the unknown this way. New name, new life. Nothing to carry with her, nothing worth keeping. Nothing to look back on, except Tony—

Who held the purse strings, maybe, but not the strings of her soul. *Money's not an issue.*

Maybe she could find a way to make that true.

One station after another, and at last this one was hers. Grace Harley had boarded a train at King's Cross; an unknown, uncertain creature had changed at Leeds; Georgie Hale stepped down on to the dusty platform of a country station that Grace Harley had not heard of a week earlier, where she could surely never be expected to appear.

Nobody, of course, was expecting Georgie. You didn't wire ahead to a commune, if that's what this place was. You followed a rumour, or your need led you, or the yogi drew you, or the spirit brought you. She didn't really know; she'd never been a commune sort of girl.

Never till now.

She was fairly sure of this much, though, that you didn't announce your arrival and expect to be met. Oddly, Tony had almost lost his nerve when she said yes. He'd offered to run her up in his two-seater and drop her off at the door, more or less: 'Just to be sure you arrive safely. Not literally at the door, I'll be discreet, but—'

She shouldn't have laughed at him, probably, when she was so dependent on his kindness; but honestly. 'Tony, love, you're about as discreet as . . . as . . . as I am!' She had been trying to be, but it didn't come easily, after so long the opposite. She'd need to try harder. She knew that. 'And that car of yours is worse. How many pink E-types are there, anyway? Just the one, I'm guessing, made specially for you. And what, you think no one's going to *notice* . . .?'

'Robbo's Mini, then. We could use that.' Robbo was his flatmate, his manager, his ally: his fag, the public schoolboys said. That seemed to mean things she didn't quite understand. So did factotum and major-domo, at least when Tony's father used the words, with that nasty little wrinkle to his lip.

'Still no, Tony. You're not getting this. People talk. In the country, they talk about strangers; what else is there? It's not like London, where everybody's a stranger and there's so much going on.' She didn't know much about the country, but she did know this. 'E-type or Mini, somebody's going to see it. And if they see the car, they'll see us. And talk about us, and that's the last thing you want. You let me go my own way, the way you said. The way Georgie would go.'

And so he had, and so here she was: stranded, abandoned, footloose and regretting everything. Regretting the train above all, as she heard it strain and creak at her back, carriage wheels clanking and banging over points as it pulled away. She did miss steam engines – there was no romance to the modern diesels – but either way, it really was better to be travelling, hopefully or otherwise. She'd left all hope behind her – and not in London – but even so. She'd rather still be sitting in her cramped corner than standing here. She'd enjoyed it, almost, the helplessness of being taken, nothing to do but sit and wait and watch the world unreel.

Now she had to walk, find her way, go to work.

She went out on to the station forecourt, case in hand. It felt strangely light, but she was Georgie Hale; she didn't own much, and most of what she had she'd left behind her.

If that was true of Grace Harley too . . .? Well, never mind. She was Georgie Hale now, pro tem. A temporary pro.

Grace had been a different kind of pro, sleek and greedy. A little desperate. Perhaps a lot desperate, but never mind. Grace was like everything else: left behind. Pro tem.

She liked that phrase. There was shelter in it, both ways. Everything had changed, but not even change was permanent. She had choices; she was moving on.

She walked out of the forecourt, past a waiting taxi. The driver was a young man; she could feel his eyes on her as she passed. Looking for a fare, or else just looking, the way young men do. Grace Harley would have stopped without thought, without question; taking a cab was as natural to her as breathing. Or it used to be. Not recently, but still. Here, where she didn't know the ground and couldn't walk? Grace Harley would take a cab.

Georgie Hale wouldn't even think of it. She couldn't afford to. A young man might turn her head, but not when he was touting for custom. She'd blush, he'd misunderstand, that way trouble lay. Young men were always trouble. It's why she was here, with all her life left behind her.

The road behind the station ran one way into town, the other up the valley. Unsure, she turned towards civilization, what passed for it around here. At least she should find someone who could help her with directions. And it would add credence to the story: a girl fresh off the train and ignorant, not briefed, not spying, no.

Only she'd barely gone fifty yards towards the town before she was crowded to the roadside, almost into the wall, by a car coming in the opposite direction. There was no pavement but also no traffic, plenty of room for both of them, it should have passed her with a margin of comfort on either side. The reason it didn't was the long ladders lashed rather haphazardly to the roof rack; they'd either been strapped on at an angle or else they'd shifted in transit, so that rather than pointing fore and aft they slewed diagonally across the car and across the road both sides, a throat-height threat to anyone not fast enough to dodge.

Rather than stopping to make them safe, the driver was forging forward intently, while their passenger leaned out of the side window yelling a warning that sounded almost like a scold, as though it were Georgie's own fault that she was having to duck aside to avoid decapitation.

The car was a Morris Traveller estate, what her father would have called a shooting brake, what Tony liked to call half-timbered; its vintage might be uncertain, but its paintwork had most certainly not come from any Morris garage. The doors – on this side, at least: Georgie wasn't at all willing to swear to the other – were purple, while the bonnet was orange and the body between was a green unknown to Cowley. The wooden frame and its panelling had been decked out like proper half-timbering, in black and white. Another day she might have laughed at that. Today she was more inclined to cut loose with the vocabulary that a childhood in suburban Essex had bequeathed to her, in the cut-glass accent that she'd so painfully acquired.

No, wait – that was Grace's story, not her own now. Georgie's accent came to her by nature, and her language was as shyly decorous as Grace's could be foul. All she did was glower, then, at the frizzy-haired person hanging from the window as the car careered by. Once they were safely past, she worked out – almost on her fingers – that it had been a male person yelling; the driver she really wasn't sure about at all.

Also, there were sigils painted in white on the car doors. They were probably supposed to mean something, but neither Grace (secondary modern, left school at fourteen to work in a haberdasher's and dream of discovery and fame) nor Georgie (grammar school, A levels, only didn't go to university because her dad was old-fashioned and didn't approve of college for girls) could decipher them in the brief seconds they were visible.

The car swerved dangerously around a corner and was gone. She stood still until she was sure; and then changed her mind abruptly, and went back into the station yard and straight up to the taxi.

On the driver's side, walking in the road, determinedly not looking like a passenger.

The driver had lost hope of any fare until the next train came in, and had unfolded a newspaper to read while he was waiting. He glanced up, a little startled, as her shadow fell across his page. For a moment, he looked hopeful; but she shook her head quickly, and then tapped on the glass as he turned away.

When he wound the window down, she said, 'I'm sorry, can you just help me out here? I'm trying to find my way to Hope's Harbour, and I think I just saw some people who might belong there –' *hippy drop-outs in a crazy car* – 'and—'

'Hope's Harbour?' he repeated doubtfully.

'Um, that's all I know to call it. It's a commune, I think, but . . .'

'You must mean D'Espérance.' Now he sounded firm and certain. 'It's over in the next valley. Just follow the road, where it rises; go over the top and you can't miss the place. Big house, big grounds. But – well, it's a long haul on foot,' he said, with an eye to the main chance, though actually she thought his hesitation had started with some other motive, some variation on *you don't want to go there, they're all weird there*, 'and you with a case to carry . . .'

'Oh, I'll manage, thanks,' she said, determinedly in character. Never mind her sinking heart. Or let him see her sinking heart – that would be in character too.

'Tell you what,' he said, measuring her obvious poverty against her obvious exhaustion, 'I can't run you there myself, because I need to wait now for the five twenty –' *as you're obviously not a paying fare* – 'but if you go to the Golden Lion in town and ask for Mr Cook in the public bar, he's safe to be there this time of an evening, and he'll take you out when he's ready to go. He's the janitor, see.'

It seemed odd that a commune should have a janitor. Still, if there was the chance of a ride and someone to talk to, a way to avoid that solitary walk, she'd take it. She thanked the cab driver as prettily as she knew how, which made him blush beetroot-red; and then she followed the road down to the cobbled market square.

There as promised was the Golden Lion, a typical country hotel, white frontage with small old-looking windows and a black door that stood ajar. It reminded her of a hundred Sunday jaunts in one car or another, with one crowd or another, or a single man. Or a married man . . .

No. She wasn't going to think like that. She was Georgie Hale, and she didn't do that kind of thing.

She probably didn't go into pubs much at all. Certainly not on her own: that was so loose it was almost fast. Still. Nice country hotel, she could do this much.

Over the threshold, and a narrow passage faced her: off-sales to the left, public bar to the right, another door ahead. She turned right. Through the door, and a bell jangled above her head, startling her into stillness. After a moment, she decided that it made sense in a hotel, where it wouldn't in a pub. The staff might be anywhere, and would certainly want to know that someone had just stepped into the bar.

Never mind that she hated bells, with their old cold summoning clamour. It wasn't hung there for her.

Nor for these other people, who were lifting their heads and turning in their seats at the sound of it. That was another reason to hate the thing – that it drew all eyes to her – but she wasn't really here to hide, however much she wanted it to seem so. Hiding in plain sight, full exposure, that was the trick of it . . .

So she dropped her head like a shy girl, but still took note of the middle-aged couple taking tea and scones in the window, the three witches in the corner with their shopping bags heaped about them, the solitary man at the untenanted bar smoking a roll-your-own and nursing a pint of mild as he read the evening paper.

'I'm sorry, miss: if you're not a resident I'm afraid I can't serve you, not till six thirty, unless you were wanting a cup of tea. That's the law. Or is it a room you're after?'

The landlord had surprised her, coming in at her back, jangling that damn bell again. Surprised a gasp out of her, too: which irritated her mightily, but was probably all to the good in the long run. He'd seen her first and then her case, and was trying to work her out. He was a big man, burly but kind-seeming; it'd do no harm to have him think she was frightened of him, a little.

'Oh,' she said, 'not a room, no. A cup of tea would be lovely.' Especially as Grace would never think of it, at this time of an evening; she was cocktails all the way. 'But I'm really looking for Mr Cook. I was told I might find him here . . .?'

'Cookie? Aye, he's right there.' His head jerked towards the lone man at the bar, while his eyes reassessed her again. She deliberately didn't look like a candidate for any commune, but likely she wasn't the first to turn up in civvies and reappear in tie-dye and beads. Or whatever the uniform was. The car had been there too suddenly and gone too fast: bright colours and long hair, that was all the impression that she'd kept.

She nodded her thanks, doubted that she'd get that cup of tea now, and went to the bar.

'Mr Cook?'

He looked around from his paper and cocked his head at her. An elderly man, grey-haired under his country cap, dressed in worn tweeds that looked too good for him: hand-me-downs, perhaps, from a landowner older yet. She might have tagged him as a gamekeeper or a tenant farmer, rather than any kind of janitor. Still, the right man in the right place. And his eyes were bird-bright, curious, expectant. Unsurprised.

'A young man at the taxi rank said that you might be able to run me out to . . . to . . .' What had he called it again? She didn't want to say 'Hope's Harbour' to another local, if they used another name. That was too much like taking sides, and possibly the wrong side. She might need these people later, one way or another. And Georgie would be eager not to repeat a mistake. She'd come so far, she was so much in need; she'd be desperate, almost, not to stumble now.

'To D'Espérance?'

That was it. She nodded with a weary enthusiasm that she was rather proud of, if only because it was entirely the way she actually felt. She really had come far and was very tired, and only wanted to get there.

'Yes, I can take you there. Give me ten minutes,' he said, with a nod towards his drink.

'Oh, thank you! And of course, yes, all the time you need. Don't hurry on my account. I'll just . . .'

She'd just drop into a chair, slide her case beneath the table, and sit. Just sit: as she had been all the day, almost, but it was suddenly needful. Relief, she supposed, more than rest. She was almost there. The last contact made, first hurdles jumped. Better, she'd found someone to take her in. She didn't need to go alone. That was priceless.

And here was her cup of tea, a pot of tea with a scone besides, all unexpected; and when she took her purse out to pay for it – Georgie's purse, which had been Grace's purse when Grace was a teenager, long long ago: a first clumsy reach for style, almost before style was there to be reached for – the landlord wouldn't take her money.

'You keep that,' he said, 'for when you need it more.' Which was perhaps meant to say *when you want to leave that place and go home like a sensible girl*, but she thought the truth of it lay somewhere else, between the landlord and the janitor. If they had so much as glanced at each other she hadn't caught it, but even so: the older man's stillness at the bar was as telling as the other's rough, awkward refusal of the coins she had fumbled for. And she couldn't have a drink but he could, although he was no resident either. Something lay between the two men, some history that made her almost incidental.

She still had her gloves on, she realized. Of course she did; they were instinct, in London. They should go. She needed to show willing to the commune.

She'd take them off when she got there, perhaps. Make a point of it. That would work.

She waited, then, gloved hands in her lap, suddenly too sick to eat a scone. Grace Harley had no nerves, that was widely known and commented on: but Georgie Hale? Sick to her stomach, poor Georgie, any time she had to face the unknown. She'd make it through, she always did – but she never had to diet, and she often had to chuck up privately beforehand.

Not this time. She drank tea, and didn't excuse herself to the ladies' even to check her make-up. Grace would have done that without even thinking about it; Georgie didn't even think about it. At last Mr Cook drained his glass and folded his paper, stood up and glanced around for her and said, 'If you're ready, then?'

It was strange: he looked like one thing, was apparently something else, and sounded like a third thing altogether. His voice was educated, refined almost, in defiance of his dress and his position. She might have tagged him for a teacher or a college lecturer, by the way he sounded.

Not by what he drove. He had an old Bedford van, an ugly pug-nosed vehicle in grubby beige, decorated with dents and patches of red oxide around the wheel arches and seals, anywhere that rust might have attacked it. She couldn't quite see why even rust would want to.

Now she might believe him as a janitor, seeing what he shifted from the passenger seat to make room for a passenger. A galvanized mop-bucket handily filled with cleaning things – Ajax and dusters and floorcloths and a scrubbing-brush poking out jauntily over all. A wooden box of tools and jars and tobacco tins and blue paper packets. He was of an age and type with her grandfather, she thought: which meant that the jars would be full of meths and turpentine while the tobacco tins and packets would hold screws and nails and useful hooks and such, some salvaged and some bought new by the half-ounce. She used to love visits to the ironmonger with Grandad. It was a memory Grace and Georgie could reasonably share: the mops and hoes and axes hung from the ceiling like weaponry on display; the ranks of wooden drawers behind the counter, each with its paper label; the smell of steel, as it seemed to her. And the way the assistant in his brown overall would fold a crisp flat sheet into a paper carton, weigh out the near-liquid flow from one or another of those drawers, seal it with a wafer and write down the contents: *2" nails* or *½" screws*. She'd have one packet of her own to carry home, marvellously impressed by the weight of it and the way the contents shifted if she squeezed, that sense of sharpness even through unpunctured cartridge paper, sharpness and light, bright things contained . . .

Somewhere beyond that thought lay a sadness, which again Grace and Georgie shared. She didn't want to follow it down. She'd rather just stand here, mute and a little desperate, watching this other old man make space for her. His tools were used, his tins were battered, but everything else was new and looked clean. And it all lay on a sheet of fresh newspaper, not on the seat directly; and the seat itself might be worn almost through the leather, but it looked clean too when he whisked the paper away. And the cab smelled of nothing worse than Golden Virginia, not the petrol fumes she'd half expected; and he did her the courtesy of rolling down his window before he lit the thin twist of paper and tobacco in his mouth.

He didn't try to talk. She thought he was probably the silent

type in any case, solitary by nature and quiet even with his
friends, what few he had. She hadn't known many like that;
they didn't come to Soho, by and large. Her grandfather,
though, yes. One or two boys at school, one or two boyfriends
since. *The ones that didn't last*, she liked to say, except that
no one really lasted. Even before . . .

Even before.

She tried to draw him out, in any case. 'This place, this
Hope's Harbour – D'Espérance, did you call it? Tell me what
it's like.'

But he just smiled, shook his head, said, 'No one can tell
you about D'Espérance. You have to find out for yourself.'

She was a fool; she thought he meant the commune, the
strangeness of it, how ill its hippies fitted into this rural life.

A little later she still thought that, all of that. It was, quite plainly,
true.

He drove her up and away, out of this valley and over a
bleak moorland rise where nothing flourished, it seemed, but
sheep and gorse and rocks amid the scrubby soil; and then
down into dark woodland, and eventually through a gap in a
tumbledown stone wall that seemed to be losing its eternal
battle against the trees. There had been gaps all the way along,
but this was more formal. It must once have been a proper
gateway, with a proper drive beyond. The gate was gone, and
one stone gatepost too. Atop the other was perched a guardian
both ancient and modern, a young man dressed all in green,
with flowing hair and beard. He had folded his legs beneath
him and played a wooden flute as they swung by. He might
have stepped straight from the pages of mythology, a wood
spirit, a faun; he might have stepped straight from her imagination, her vision of what a hippy commune must be like. Or
from the pages of Tony's rag, his readers' prejudice.

He was, presumably, what she had been sent here to report
on. A symptom, the pure essence. *Everything that's wrong
with youth today*, blustery colonels would mutter into their
moustaches.

Was he really watching the road, guarding the gateway?
There might have been an acknowledgement as his eyes met

Mr Cook's through the windscreen: a lift of his eyebrows, a lift of his flute. Licence to pass. But there was nothing he could do, surely, if the van had been a stranger: no gate to close, no way to turn a vehicle away. Perhaps he had a walkie-talkie and could warn the house that it was coming?

A radio wouldn't sit too well with Lincoln green. Perhaps he was neither myth nor modern; if it weren't for the flute, he might have stepped from the pages of her Robin Hood book instead. His clothes looked authentic enough, hand-sewn rough stuff, maybe even hand-woven. Maybe even the flute was right. They might have had flutes in the green-wood. In which case he'd probably lay it down and pick up a bow from behind a tree and shoot an arrow up to the house in signal . . .

She wasn't usually this fanciful. Grace wasn't. The opposite thing, rather: professionally down to earth. Grace would be looking for the walkie-talkie. Maybe this was Georgie, taking charge. Taking possession. Being herself, dreaming of a better time: when she was a little girl, reading books and dreaming of outlaws in the forest.

It was Grace's book, but never mind. That copy had been lost long since. No one could confront her with the evidence, her name on the flyleaf in childish schoolgirl script.

Besides, they wouldn't need to. She wasn't here to deny her past, not really. Just in seeming; and then to be caught out, and then . . .

Well. Then she didn't know. Then she'd play it by ear. Amazing Grace.

In the meantime, Georgie was daydreaming about outlaws and arrows and a forest that was almost magic but never quite – and Mr Cook was slowing the van suddenly, here in amongst the trees, where a sudden rutted track ripped itself away from the drive.

'I go that way,' he said with a jerk of his head, leaning on the wheel and gazing at her. Monumentally patient, and not budging. Not going to budge. Not even going to say it, but *you go the other way*: it was written in the moment, absolute.

'Oh! Um, won't you take me up to the house . . .?' *I thought you were my way in.*

'No,' he said. *No*, he meant. He wasn't unkind about it, just immovable. She could no more wheedle him than push the van with him inside it.

She wasn't delaying the moment; she honestly couldn't quite work out how to open the van door from inside. He had to lean across and pull the hanging cord for her, lean a little further yet to push the door open. She wriggled out, stepping into deep leaf-litter on the verge; he passed her case down to her, slammed the door, put the van into gear and drove away.

Left her standing. In the late sun of a northern summer evening, in the shadow of a strange wood, in the grip of what should perhaps have been a storm of temper – what she wished would be a storm of temper – but was really not.

Nor a storm of tears, not that. Just a surge of self-pity that was not quite enough to lift her and carry her on along the drive, nor quite enough to suck her back to the road. It bogged her down, rather, held her here in the gloom of the trees, unnerved. She'd be jumping at shadows, except that it was all shadow in all directions: like standing in a photograph, in black and white, which really meant a thousand shades of grey. That was her mood, as much as her surroundings. She wasn't even frightened, nothing so extreme: only weary to the bone of her, depressed, unwilling. And—

This little piggy went to market.

—she had that damn nursery rhyme in her head again, and couldn't shift it. Sometimes she thought it was her punishment, except that it never seemed enough. *You've been punished enough*, but not with this.

Sometimes she thought it would drive her mad, except that that might be a kindness. The mad didn't suffer, did they? If she'd been sure of that, she might have run to madness long ago.

This little piggy stayed at home.

She wished she'd stayed at home. If she'd stayed at home instead of going to the doctor's party, she wouldn't have seen Tony that night, wouldn't have let him or the champagne – say it was the champagne – make her giddy.

Wouldn't have said yes to this stupid, stupid adventure.

Maybe.

She wanted to go home right now, but she had no way to get there. Not till the morning. If she walked back to the station, there wouldn't be a train.

She should just go on up to the house, then. Just for tonight, and see how she felt in the morning.

Besides, she was hungry now.

This little piggy had roast beef.

She was hungry, but apparently not hungry enough; she still wasn't moving.

The breeze was cool, but not cold or strong enough to move her. Apparently.

She stood until the last glimpse of the van's tail lights was lost between the trees, until the last sound of its engine was lost beneath the soft sounds of a wood in evening. She wasn't really imagining that he might relent and come back, no. She wasn't imagining anything, really. Only standing here, with her case at her feet and the road dim before her in the failing light and absolutely no desire to pick up the case and set her feet on that road and go forward.

Except that she couldn't go back, not now. Not from here.

So really she might as well go forward.

Except . . .

Except that somewhere she could hear a great bell tolling, somewhere ahead, and she really did hate bells. So maybe she would just stand here for a little, until it stopped.

Except that she was standing here, peering, listening – and there was no sign and no hope of the van coming back, but *something* was certainly coming.

She could hear it like a beast between the trees, between the strokes of that damned bell, pressing through the undergrowth, coming.

Except that what she heard was the undergrowth it pressed through, the leaf litter it trod in, the noises it made in the world around. Not itself, nothing of its own sounds. She thought it had none. She thought it was woven of silence, nothing there.

She could see it like a shadow among the shadows, a darkness drawing in, local twilight compacting into night. A shape made of absence, a nothingness so solid it made all the world seem hollow else.

Coming.

Light goes away; darkness doesn't come. Darkness is just there, all the time, like silence. Waiting.

This, though: this was coming. Personal, intentional, here for her.

Imagination didn't bend the world, push shrubs aside, snap twigs and crush rotten fallen boughs beneath its weight. She wasn't imagining a thing.

She wasn't screaming, either. Wasn't running away.

She hadn't ever been punished enough, and it was a monstrous lie to say so. Everything she did was punishment, everything she did to herself; none of it ever measured up.

Maybe she'd just stand here, let this thing come. *This little piggy.*

The voice in her head, chanting nursery rhymes to the slow rhythm of a distant bell—

—was her own voice, which somehow didn't seem fair. If she was going to be sucked down into nightmare, she thought at least she might have hoped for one last echo of someone else chasing after her. Something to snatch at, if not to hold on to. Not company, not comfort, but something. That, at least. Tony's voice, perhaps. Or the light gurgling laughter of—

No. Not that. She didn't deserve that.

This, now. She deserved this. Let it come, then.

She stood and waited, and almost called it on.

THREE

Apparently, she'd closed her eyes. Not *that* brave, then, to stand and watch it come.

She only realized when she started hearing something else, over the relentless sounds of its approach, over the thudding impact of the endless bell.

There was music somewhere in the wood, drifting through the trees: low and plaintive, haunting almost, a breathy melody that seemed as right as moonlight, as natural as wind song. And utterly impersonal, heedless, unattached: the very opposite of what so threatened her. Close, perhaps, but remote. Like someone standing by her and looking at the stars.

Close, though, and coming closer. And the shadow . . . wasn't. At least, all she could hear now was music. No crashing, blundering progress as that weight of silence surged towards her.

No bell.

This little piggy stayed at home.

She might almost open her eyes now. Almost.

One more breath, and she could smell – oh lord, the whole country of England, all the damp dank buried wonder of it, what she went to the city to forget. To escape, along with everyone else.

Nothing coming. No reeking threat, no monster; no mysterious emptiness, vacuum, absence. She wasn't quite sure what that would smell like, but not this.

With an effort, then, she did open her eyes . . .

A man stood in the roadway.

Unless he was a faun, unless he had goat's legs beneath his trousers.

But no, even in this fading light she could see his feet in sandals, no hooves. Dressed all in green else, with long brown hair caught back in a ponytail and as much beard as he could manage: he was, of course, the man they'd passed at the turn-off, sitting on a gatepost keeping watch.

Young man, younger than that beard made him look – or else, now that she was looking properly, it was the straggly sparseness of the beard that emphasized how young he was, despite all his efforts to seem older.

He wanted to be Pan, she thought, in his forest. Playing music to his trees.

It was his flute, of course, that she had heard. Cutting through the bell-strokes, turning away the silence. Like a statement, *I am here*, and so she wasn't alone, and so that absence could not come to haunt her. She kept it at bay with company, always, when she could.

Except that it had never been physical before, never made noises in the world. Never broken a path on its way to reach her.

He lowered the flute from his lips and said, 'Hullo.'

His voice was as sweet as his music, soft and husky and irredeemably young. She thought he probably practised that. Well, not the young part; that he only had to live with. For a while. It would pass.

What she had to live with was eternal. Still, she could manage this much. She took a breath, licked dry lips and said, 'Hullo.' And then, because she had to: 'Did you . . . did you hear anything? Moving, I mean, in the wood just now?' *Not the bell.* She didn't even want to think about the bell.

'Oh, has Big Bertha been scaring you, crashing about in the undergrowth? I was wondering why you were stood here all alone in the middle of nowhere.'

I'm standing here all alone because your janitor abandoned me. In the middle of nowhere. Aloud, she only said, 'Big Bertha?'

'She's our pig. Well, not ours: she is her own pig. Entirely feral. I suppose she or maybe her mother escaped from a farm hereabouts, and she's been living wild and free ever since. We see her occasionally, but mostly she's just noises off. Just as well, really. You wouldn't want to get too close; she's not safe by any measure. But then she doesn't want to get too close to us either. It works out. Everything does, you'll find, here. Welcome to Hope's Harbour, by the way. My name's Tom.'

Tom, Tom, the piper's son. That wasn't fair.

Except that it was, of course: more than fair, generous even, against what she deserved. Nothing could ever be punishment enough. If nursery rhymes were going to run through her mind like streams of scalding water, she wouldn't try to dam them up in seething pools, no. Better to let them run, dabble her fingers in the fierce sting of them, take off her shoes and paddle.

She said, 'Georgie. I'm Georgie Hale.' Nervous and fanciful, standing frozen in the middle of the road because she didn't dare walk on, because she thought their pig was a ghost of absence, a haunting hollow shaped like a boy who never was. That was Georgie all over.

More than once Grace had thought she might run mad. Wished for it, almost. Perhaps it was happening at last. Perhaps this was Tony's last gift to her: to rip her in two and let the two halves torment each other crazy.

Not his plan, though. Not deliberate. Not to say *he wouldn't be that unkind, he didn't think that way* – of course he did, of course he would if it benefited him, his paper, him – but this, out here? No. He wouldn't see the benefit.

He might still make it happen, regardless. Let it be.

He might not care.

She hoped he'd care.

It might be easier to fight, if she thought he was doing it deliberately. She might want to fight it, then.

'Georgie. Georgie . . .' He rolled the name around his mouth as though trying the taste of it. Then he lifted the flute back to his lips and tried a brief phrase, a sudden trill of notes. Tried it again, seemed to like it; he put more breath behind it, let it dance out into the wood. From his mouth to the pig's ears; she thought about silk purses and sow's ears and grew a little confused, decided she was too tired to reach for a joke. Besides, there had been nothing funny about her mood a minute ago, and there was nothing funny in it now. It was lighter, a little; men did that to her, the company of men, it lifted her. Even hairy young men in the half-dark, whose faces she couldn't really see.

And the sense of imminent danger had receded. The pig in

the wood. Yes. She would believe that entirely. She could do that. No little-boy-lost, no sucking shadows, just a feral animal crashing about in the undergrowth.

She was still afraid, but of normal things, what loomed ahead: encounters, people, secrets. Work. Everything had that shadow now, of dread until it happened; nothing was ever quite as bad as it might have been. That was something to hold on to, maybe.

Her case was something to hold on to, something to carry. Tom was walking up the lane, and she was following. Apparently. She had after all found someone to take her in.

He played as they walked – sometimes he skipped, or danced a few steps in the beechmast – so that she felt like a child at the heels of the Pied Piper, following the soft thread of his music through the dark.

It was almost dark enough to be true, under the shadow of the trees. But the trees had to end at last; not even the deepest forest goes on for ever. They stepped out into light again, and here was a dark stretch of water contained between straight lines and stony banks. Beyond that rose a wild tangled garden; above that, the house.

She had seen houses, grand houses, many of them. Seen them, been through their doors and welcomed, slept in four-poster beds as though she belonged there. Played with their luxuries like a little girl dressed up and playing princess.

Learned the truth of them – or no, she had always known the truth of them, had been a part of it herself; only that she had seen it ruthlessly exposed, their truth and her own – and did not ever expect to be invited back.

This wasn't the same, but even so. There was always this moment, where she stood in the shadow and knew that she didn't belong. She used to brazen it by, because that was what a princess would do; now she was daunted, because of course Georgie would be.

Of course she showed it. That was what Georgie would do. She stood here by the lapping water's margin – Tom wanted to walk on the grass now that he'd slipped his sandals off, so she'd gone with him, a few steps to the side of the stony roadway, that much closer to the lake – and stared up at the house where it loured against the darkening sky, and could apparently not move at all.

As soon as he'd caught on, Tom stepped back to stand beside her, with her. Not waiting for her, in any sense she knew – not impatient, not visibly or determinedly or effortfully patient, not mocking, not any kind of manly – but simply there. Keeping her company, until she was ready for the next step and the next and the one after that.

Nice boy. She could draw comfort from that, perhaps, a little. And mock herself, perhaps, a little; be impatient on her own account, with her own anxiety.

Draw a nervous little breath and say, 'I hadn't . . . I hadn't expected it to be quite so big.'

'No,' he said. 'No one does. And it always is that big. You don't get used to it, I mean. Familiarity doesn't shrink it down to any contemptible size. Just as well, really. I mean, you wouldn't want it to, would you? Who'd want to get used to that?'

Tony would. The thought was immediate, unbidden. It was the scale that he thought in, the sort of house that came natur-ally to him.

She needed not to be thinking about Tony.

She said, 'I don't get it. What's it *for?*'

'Well,' he said, 'at the moment, it's for us. What comes next, what we build here, what we make of it – that's for the future to show. For us to decide. For you, maybe, if you stay.'

'I don't belong in a place like this.' That was more than honest, it was absolute. Said in two voices, to contain every-thing that she was or could be.

'No one does,' he said again. 'How could you? But here we are, and I think the house is getting used to us.'

'How many of you are there?' She wasn't sure if she wanted the house to be full or empty. Two dozen souls, or two hundred. Lose herself in a crowd, or make herself known to a handful.

'Not enough,' he said. 'Yet. One more now.'

'If I stay.'

'Of course. That's up to you; don't let me bully you into

it,' he said with a smile and that little trill on his flute that apparently meant her. Meant Georgie. Meant who she was meant to be.

Meant a lie, then, but she didn't want to think about that either.

'Is it? Up to me, I mean?'

'Of course.'

'Isn't there a – I don't know, a test? Probation, something? Don't you get to watch me for a while, see if I fit in?'

'What, you think we should take you on approval, like a stamp?' He wasn't faking it, that baffled amusement, scratching at his head with the end of his flute.

'Yes,' she said, not faking it either. 'That's exactly what I mean.'

'Well. Not really how it works here. I mean, if you don't fit in, you're the one who'll know it first, aren't you? You'll feel it. And then I suppose you'll just go. I don't think anyone has, yet. Just gone, I mean, and not come back. Of course, you could, if this didn't feel right to you. But then, if it didn't feel right to you, you wouldn't have come, would you?'

I was desperate – which was true and not-true, and she didn't need to say it either way, truly or otherwise. She let it lie between them, unspoken, and said instead, 'I didn't know what I was coming to. Still don't, come to that. Who are you, what are you, why are you here?'

'I'm Tom,' he said. 'I grow vegetables and play the flute, and I'm here because I wouldn't be anywhere else right now.'

'That wasn't what I meant.'

'No, I know – but it's what *I* meant. What I mean. I can't speak for anyone else. I won't. If you come on up to the house –' *when you're ready*, his body said in its stillness: no gestures, no urgency, *no pressure* – 'I'll take you to Leonard. Then you'll see.'

'Leonard?'

A smile, a nod. Unforthcoming.

'Will he tell me what this place is all about?'

'You'll see,' he said again; and then: 'He'll probably want to talk about you.' *Tell you what you're all about*, she heard, unless it was *wait for you to tell him*.

She couldn't lose her nerve, even now. Grace had no nerves

to lose, and Georgie had lost hers long ago and was here anyway, because a girl had to be somewhere, after all.

She said, 'Come on, then,' and took that step, one step forward through the tangled grass; and as she started, so she heard that bell again, rolling down the terraces and over the water, slamming into her, slow and sonorous and cruel beyond measure.

'What's the matter?'

Apparently, she'd gasped aloud. It had to be that. She wasn't crying, and she was still walking, somehow. And the right way, too: along the verge, towards the house. Not into the lake, not back to the woods.

Something was stirring in the lake, she thought: some little hint of whirlpool, bubbles of mud.

Apparently, she could still talk as well as walk, even against the cold dull heavy beat of it. She said, 'What does it mean, that? That bell?'

He smiled. 'That means it's dinner time. Good time to turn up, actually. You get a chance to look us over, all together.'

You get a chance to look at me, you mean. All of you, together.

But she was still walking. And not in time with the bell, stubbornly out of step. That felt like a refusal; that was good enough. For now, for her. For here.

Stubbornly taking the lead, that too, positively marching up the road now. Properly on the road now, none of that kicking through the verge like a reluctant child. Let Tom hug the hedge if he wanted to, if the broken stone and gravel was too hard underfoot.

But the hedge was high and wild, throwing out bramble-runners to trip him by the ankle, and more to threaten his Lincoln green, his eyesight and his hair. Soon enough he was pulling his sandals out of his belt, slipping them on again, taking his place beside her on the road.

'I ought to have soles like leather by now,' he said ruefully, 'but they keep making me wear shoes and go to town. By the time my feet toughen up, it'll be all mud and frost out here and I'll want boots anyway.'

'No, you won't.'

'Well,' he allowed, 'not want, no. But I'll wear them. Anyone would.'

Inevitably, they were both looking at her own feet now, at the way she was struggling in court shoes that were entirely practical in London, on London streets, but the next worst thing to hopeless here. The roadway sloped steeply and was smooth nowhere: pitted and rutted, surfaced alternately with rough stone and gravel where it was surfaced at all, where it wasn't dried cracked mud with dark puddles lurking in the deepest ruts.

'You'll want to change those,' he said, brightly helpful.

'No, I won't,' she replied, immediate. This at least she could do, she was trained for it, bantering with bright boys.

'Well,' he allowed, 'not want, no. But you'll change them anyway.'

And then he smiled, pleased with himself, pleased with her for playing along. In honesty, she was pleased with herself too.

She said, 'They're my best shoes, these,' meaning *my most comfortable*, telling nothing but the truth.

He shrugged. 'Not to worry. We'll find you something better. Or make them. Or teach you how to make them, that'd be best.'

'Or you could mend the road,' she said, perhaps a little waspish as her ankle turned on a loose stone and her foot plunged into a hole and she almost lost that shoe in the mud at the bottom.

'Or that,' he agreed, 'but I don't think it's a priority. Hardly anyone drives this way, and we're fine on foot. Well, you will be, once you're used to it. Look, would you like me to take your case?'

Yes, of course I would, you oaf, I'd have liked that half a mile ago – but they were at the top of the slope now, right in the shadow of the house, and she was abruptly daunted again. Wanting something to hold on to.

She shook her head, and turned to walk along the paved terrace to the portico and the high door; and was stopped by his soft laugh, his unexpected hand on her arm.

'We don't use the front,' he said. 'We're in the country here.

The front door is for strangers and funerals. Family all comes around the back.'

She wasn't family, not yet. *Not ever*, Grace's voice in her head said as a reminder: she was undercover here, working, not joining in. Not signing up. So why did she get a warm feeling just from the way he said it, never mind the way he glanced at her sideways, conspiratorial?

It wasn't as if family had ever meant anything good to her. She and her parents weren't talking any more, and her son—

Well. If she talked to her son, he wasn't talking back.

She remembered an absence in the woods, coming at her. And might have faltered then, might have let the next heavy stroke of the bell stop her dead: only that it didn't come, and she sort of toppled forward into the silence of it and – well, just carried on.

Down the side of the house, then, and around the back: into a broad courtyard made by two long wings and a stable block. The arch through to the stables had a clock tower above; she glanced at the clock with a jaundiced eye but that was stopped at ten to three and surely couldn't have been striking. She couldn't see any other bell tower, any likely place for the kind of bell she'd been hearing.

Something to be grateful for, perhaps. Small mercies, and short-lived for sure. She'd hear it again tomorrow.

If she was still here tomorrow. If she didn't cut her losses and run. She might do that, she was tempted already – except that she had nothing to run to, nothing to go back for. Tony would despise her if she pulled out now, one night in. And she'd stuck worse than this, hadn't she? She'd stuck prison, and the trial. And all the press, before and after. And the funeral, her baby's funeral, she'd stuck that. And every day since, and . . .

And really this was nothing, walking over smooth cobbles to a back door that stood open, wide and welcoming. Parked there beside it was the car she'd seen in town, the Morris Traveller, confirming her suspicions. It still had the ladders lying slant across the roof rack. She wasn't going to ask; she didn't need to.

Tom said, 'Charlie and Fish. That's their car. We don't have

one, else; we don't really have one at all. They come and go.
But when they're here, they like to be useful round about.
Helping out the neighbours. And we've got these long ladders,
and of course nobody in town has any to compare, nobody
with sensible houses; so they clean out people's gutters for
them, and rescue cats from trees, and stuff like that.'

'And take people's heads off, near enough, the way they
drive that thing,' she said.

'There is that. They're not very good with knots.' He tugged
at the slack of a rope, and tutted, and did nothing to fix it
more tightly or to pull the ladders straight. 'But it saves little
old ladies having to call out the roofer or the fire brigade. It's
good to have a few voices on our side, to set against the gruff
old colonels who all think we should be called up or given
six of the best. Or both.'

She had some experience of gruff old colonels, and some
sympathy with them, if only because a few had shown her a
little disinterested kindness. She thought it might be better if
they could walk the streets of their own town without being
yelled out of the way by speeding hippies. But this was probably not the time to say so.

There was nobody about in the courtyard, presumably
because they had all been called to dinner. Where Tom was
now taking her. This would be her last minute alone with him,
then: she really ought to be using it to learn more about this
place, or Leonard, who was apparently leader here, or—

He must be hungry, or in a hurry to find his friends, or else
in a hurry to hand her over to someone else. Down below, he
had given her all the time she needed; up here, he gave her
no time at all. Across the courtyard and in at the door, no time
to linger and ask questions now, and that was suddenly almost
a relief. Even though it meant, it must mean, that the next
thing would be a roomful of strangers.

In at the door, then, and through a cloakroom, a chaotic
jumble of discarded shoes and boots and coats and jackets and,
yes, at least one actual cloak on a hook there; and into a corridor
beyond, long bare boards underfoot and doors leading off on
either side. Really, it was all very normal for a country house
and not at all hippyish, except that there was a little table just

at the side there as they came through, hung with a bright cotton tasselled cloth embroidered with tiny mirrors. It shrieked India at her, the hippy trail, girls come back with long loose hair and swinging skirts and cheesecloth shirts and gurus. Gurus above all, preaching meditation and peace and rebirth, ancient foreign wisdoms that sat impossibly awkward in an English landscape, as their clothes really didn't suit the weather.

Was that what she'd come to: a transplanted ashram, a little man with a vast beard teaching scriptures in an alien chant?

But on the table, on the cloth stood something else. No bizarre idol with too many limbs, no smoking incense, no sanctity. Just a polished wooden stand, a high frame with a bell hanging from it. Too big for a hall decoration, practical bronze: it was as out of place as the cloth it stood on, jarring both with that and the house around. Her mind labelled it a ship's bell straight off. She ought not to know that, unless she'd picked it up from those black-and-white war films her father used to take her to. She was still certain, though. Of course, it was possible to be certain and still wrong – oh, she knew: who better? – but she really didn't think so this time. If she looked more closely, that engraving around the bell's shoulder would no doubt tell her which ship it had come from.

But it was a bell, and she wasn't going anywhere near it.

But Tom was reaching out casually, unthinkingly, meaninglessly; gripping the white rope that hung below the mouth of the bell; swinging it once, twice and again.

Striking the unseen clapper against the inside rim: once, twice and again.

Making it sound, high and stern and penetrating.

Once, twice and again.

Only perhaps realizing that he'd done it after the thing was done, it was so unthinking an action. Turning then to her with a wry smile and a shrug, saying, 'We always do that to announce our arrival in the house. Leonard likes it. Once for each of us, twice for a visitor. First time, you count as a visitor, so— Hey. Are you all right?'

No. No, she really was not all right. She had dropped her case, just there by her foot, where she stood shaking.

Her wrist throbbed, in time with the hurried beating of her heart. It didn't seem enough to explain why she'd let go so suddenly, but that hand just felt too heavy and too remote; it couldn't hold on any longer.

Perhaps it was her who couldn't hold on, against the relentless resonance of the bell as it sounded through her skull like a knife; but really she thought it was her hand, all independent of her will.

She still hadn't taken her gloves off. They were fawn in colour, nylon, and she could see that one – the left, it was – darkening as she stood there, as it hung slack at her side.

Darkening all the way down, in a line from the invisible wrist towards the fingers' ends.

Darkening, filling.

Starting to drip.

She watched that first drip fall, straight down on to the clasp of her suitcase, where it lay splattered across the brass: not that dark after all, brightly red.

And another.

Once, twice and again.

'Here, let me see . . .'

Apparently, she was going to do nothing but stand there and watch it happen.

She needed Tom to take charge, as he did: gripping her arm and lifting it, tugging back the sleeve of her coat. Her dress beneath was sleeveless. There was just the glove, with that dark stain showing from the wrist down to the fingers.

Starting to spread the other way now, as he raised her hand. Little dribbles, rivulets of blood running down towards her elbow, tickling.

At least blood didn't make her faint. Not the sight of it, at least. If she felt abruptly giddy and sick, it wasn't girlish idiocy. Though she would quite like to sit down now, as that throbbing sharpened to quite a fierce ache as Tom struggled to peel the glove away from her forearm, trying to roll it back on itself like a stocking, not getting very far, so that in the end she did have to help him after all, showing him how to tug the fingers loose one by one.

They were quite wet now, the fingers. She watched them stain the fingertips of the other glove as she tugged, and made a little exasperated noise and wanted to tug that one off too, only she couldn't because Tom still had hold of that arm – and actually it was hurting quite a bit now, and she really did want to sit down even before he finally worked the glove away and there was her hand exposed, with its two cuts almost parallel across the inside of the wrist.

'Good grief, girl. Did you do that on the brambles? Why in the world didn't you say?'

No, she thought. *No, I did do that, but not on the brambles, no. And not today. Not recently. I thought that was all healed up now.*

That was a lie, of course, but she was quite used to lying to herself, silently, in the privacy of her head. She'd been caught out, apparently, by this one.

'I'm sorry,' she said, 'but I really do . . .'

And she really did. Right then, right there: she sat down on that convenient solid suitcase and watched blood drip on to the bare wood of the floor.

'Yes. Yes, of course.' When he was flustered, when she wasn't looking at him, Tom didn't sound anything like the hippy that he looked, hairy and mystical and remote. Just a nice English middle-class boy: the kind that she'd tried to overleap entirely, from Billericay to Cliveden in a single bound.

He had no idea, of course, of his significance. No notion of being a symbol for anything. His hair was just in the way suddenly, needing to be swept back – with the inside of his wrist, an oddly feminine gesture, as he had blood on his own hands now – while he crouched beside her to look more closely.

'Oh,' he said, 'I don't think it's that bad, actually. They're not deep. Only bramble scratches. Just, I suppose it will bleed if you cut yourself just there. Try to hold the hand up if you can, don't encourage it. Gravity's not your friend at the moment. Look, will you be all right if I leave you, just for a minute? Only, I think Mother Mary ought to have a gander at this . . .'

Of course she'd be all right. She didn't know who Mother
Mary was, she hadn't thought she was coming to a nunnery,
but she supposed it didn't really matter. Mother Mary and
Father Leonard, ruling their community with a rod of iron
and the stroke of a bell. Two bells. Two strokes, sharp as
a razor. Singing through her brain, singing through her
wrist . . .

This little piggy had none.

She didn't want anything, really. She never had, not really.
Even Grace at her greediest, her most immediately grasping:
even then, it had all been a cover story. Only that she was too
late, too slow to see through it. If she'd really cared about the
money and the status and the glamour, she'd have taken better
care of them.

That was what the unkind people had said about her poor
baby. Almost word for word, again and again, in print and
in her hearing: *if she really cared, she'd have taken better
care.* They didn't even think they were unkind. On the
contrary, it was the kindest thing they could think of to say,
which was why they didn't care if she read it, if she overheard it. Some of them would say it to her face. Thinking
themselves oh so kind, not to accuse her of worse. Being
generous, making allowances. Digging in their wilful
stilettos, needle blades that cut and cut, that made her bleed
and bleed.

Not like this. When she bled like this, it was because she
did it to herself. After she'd stood over her baby's little grave
in the parish churchyard with the great bell tolling above her
head, after she'd realized once and for all that she never really
did want anything else: then, well, why not? It had seemed
the least she could do.

She watched it come, this little blood, this gesture. Watched
it spatter on the floorboards. Didn't cry. Not any more, not
now. There had been too much crying already. Grace was
tougher than that, and Georgie was – well, too bewildered.
Out of her depth. You needed to know what you'd lost, before
you could weep for it.

Or bleed for it.

It was odd, to find herself sitting here bleeding. She really hadn't expected this. Hadn't anticipated it, in all her many imaginings. Well, how could she?

Here came footsteps. From inside the house, blessedly, not from the outside door and the cloakroom. Nobody else would be coming in to ring the bell while she sat here waiting, while she bled.

Here was Tom back again. She didn't lift her head but she recognized his green trousers, his bare feet.

With him – well. Mother Mary, presumably.

White robe, over the kind of sandals her mother might have worn. Seeing the two pairs of feet side by side, with the hems of those clothes at ankle height, she found herself thinking again of her Robin Hood book. Robin and the wicked abbess, who had drained his life away . . .

No. She shouldn't be thinking about that, while her own blood dribbled out to stain their flooring.

The woman gave her small chance to think about anything.

'Well. What's this, then? Just scratches, Tom tells me, but even so. They need looking at, he says. Hold your arm up, then, there's a good girl. No, higher than that. Hold it in the light, where I can see what's what. Besides, elevation will help to stop the bleeding. It's uncomfortable, I know, but keep it up. Above your head, yes, like that.'

'I did tell her, Mother.' That was Tom's murmur, somehow self-effacing and self-justifying, both at once.

'I'm sure you did. And then you had the sense to fetch me, so that I could tell her too. Hmm. These are actually quite shallow, despite all the dripping. No need for stitches. Tom, run and fetch me the first-aid kit. And you, girl, look at me. Yes, *look* at me. What's your name?'

Thus adjured, she did that: lifting her head to see the whole of the woman, rather than the fringes of her gown. Which was quite plain and practical, if white robes were the order of the day; and the woman inside it the same, quite plain and practical. In her forties at a guess, pushing fifty perhaps, with iron-grey hair done up in a bun; a pleasant face and a firm accustomed manner. Nothing hippy in her anywhere, except for that robe. But that was probably true for nuns too, that they seemed quite normal women except for the wimple and the habit.

'I'm Georgie,' she said, because she was now, she really
was. Nothing of Grace left in her: none of that bright glitter
jewel hardness, none of the angles, no resistance now.

'Well, Georgie. I sent Tom away because I do need my kit
– this needs a proper dressing; because he was being no help
at all, which is no surprise at all to either of us; and because
he may believe that these are bramble scratches, but I have
yet to encounter the bramble that can scratch skin that deeply
through a coat and gloves. I was a nurse in the war, and I
know scar tissue when I see it. These are old cuts opening up
again, aren't they?'

She nodded, helpless to deny it.

'So: do you want to tell me why you cut yourself?'

A shake of the head. Helpless to answer.

'Fair enough. You can keep your secrets if you must – though
this isn't a good house for secrets; they'll fester if you're not
careful of them. Still, never mind that for now. What have you
been doing, to open these up? They look like they had healed
before this.'

A shrug: she had no answers, except *it was the bell, the
sound of the bell that cut me, doesn't it cut you too? All of
you?* She could sound quite mad, if she tried. Better not to
try, then. Better to huddle in on herself and say nothing.

Here came Tom to save her, running back down the corridor
with a box in his hands, white-painted with a vivid red cross
on the top. Truly a first-aid kit, then: as unexpected as anything
in this house. But then, with a former nurse in authority, why
wouldn't it have a first-aid kit? Hippies could be as careful as
anyone, at need. A commune could be a community, and a
community could look after itself. It wasn't anything like the
world she was used to, but she'd always understood that other
people were different. Incomprehensible, but not necessarily
wrong. Better, maybe. That might be something to discover.

Iodine on her cuts, then, and a bandage wrapped around;
and as the older woman tore the end of the bandage and tied
it neatly off, she said, 'You'll do. No need to worry about
using the hand – you can hold a fork with it if you're that
way inclined. Come on through to dinner.'

She stood up a little warily, found Tom rather enchantingly

there to help if she needed it, too shy to offer if she didn't. Gave him a smile to acknowledge both, a little shake of the head at her own stubborn independence – and then thought of something, said, 'Oh, I should do something about my suitcase . . .'

'You should,' the woman agreed. 'You should leave it where it is. No one will touch it here. You don't need to be worrying about things.' She might have meant *your things*, but that wasn't what she said. 'Come along.'

Stalwart thing, her suitcase: something to hold on to, a weight, a weapon. Something to sit on, a support. She hated to abandon it, all alone in the corridor there. Also, she didn't quite believe that bland reassurance. One of Tony's reporters had disappeared here. Been swallowed up. Some of the stories she told herself about that, of course they would go through her case.

And find, perhaps, what they were looking for, traces of Grace; and then it would be a whole different story she was telling herself, telling them.

Tony might prefer that, actually.

She gestured awkwardly, just to draw attention to her hands. 'Please, is there a washroom . . .?' *Blood on my gloves, and I still have my coat on.*

'Yes, of course. I'm sorry, I'm rushing you, aren't I? Briskness gets to be a habit, I find; if I wasn't brisk, I'd never get anything done. Never get any of these to do anything, I mean.' With a little nod at Tom, who was apparently happy to stand in for everyone and be criticized. 'Time has a different measure in Hope's Harbour; no one hurries, but the clock does rush around.'

'There aren't any clocks,' Tom said.

'Hush. And don't tell Leonard, but I do still carry a watch.' A nurse's fob, on the inside lapel of her robe: she flashed it at them, tucked it away again. Briskly. 'Someone has to.'

'Yes, Mother.'

'And my *name* is *Mary*. Don't let them tell you any different, Georgie. I'm nobody's mother now.'

Neither was she. The bells were a constant reminder. She had to face down the ship's bell again, turning back in defiance of instructions. It was silent like a knife, heavy with potential, brooding. She walked stiff-legged, wary as a cat under a dog's eyes; scooped up her case and looked to Mary with her head cocked inquiringly. Of course she'd need her case in the bathroom. And time, that too. Time to catch her breath, scrub blood out from under her fingernails. Put her gloves to soak in cold water. Silly, useless gestures: they'd expect those from a new girl, her first day. It was important to seem inappropriate, not to be prepared.

FOUR

The lavatory they brought her to was a big square room, half a dozen basins, half a dozen cubicles. Seats and doors with the varnish worn from the wood; old heavy ceramics with cracks and chips in the glaze; taps that almost needed two hands to turn them, then hissed and gurgled before they spat water. The flush worked, though, and the water was scalding. That was something, an unexpected comfort. She'd stayed with millionaires and lordlings whose plumbing would have been a scandal to Victorians.

Washed, refreshed, not ready – but at least not bloody now, except beneath the bandage – she left coat and case together in a corner and came out to find Tom waiting on his own.

'Mother Mary went ahead. She'll let people know that you're here.'

Was that a good thing? Perhaps. She didn't know. She didn't really know anything, except that she was here now, committed. Engaged.

'She said you weren't to call her that.'

'She said *you* weren't. I'm a hopeless case; she gave up on me long since. Hungry?'

Oddly, she was.

'Me too. I hope you don't mind vegetarian. Not everyone here is actually veggie – we don't have rules like that – but a lot of us are, and it's good that we can grow most of what we eat. Some people are really evangelical about it, and they're the ones who do the shopping and most of the cooking, so meals tend to work out that way. It's safe, anyway. Something everyone can eat.'

'I don't really know,' she said. 'I suppose so.' Lentils and rice, then. What did it matter? She'd never cared that much about food. Dinner was an opportunity to be amusing, enchanting, available. Bright eyes, provocative manners, witty gossip. Eating only got in the way.

*　　*　　*

Here was a broad open hallway, stairs going up. Someone had started a mural, swirling patterns, meaningless to her eyes; also, she didn't think it was finished. Perhaps that was the point.

High double doors standing open, the buzz of conversation. Here it was, then.

It seemed dark in there, heavy shadows, compared to the house around. Oil lamps and candles: well, she was used to that. People liked to eat in the half-dark. Actually, she thought it came from the women, people like her, who weren't too concerned with what lay on their plates. Candlelight made big eyes lustrous, hid flaws, made up for clumsy make-up, drew the shadows in close like curtains around the table.

In other rooms, other houses, it did all of that. Not here. The room was just too big to be made intimate. It must have been the ballroom once, when this was a grand family house. Now it was – well, communal. Where they gathered, where they ate. The walls were hung with fabrics, which could hardly be safe with all those flames around. The candles were in jars and on tables, but even so. The house had electricity, which they weren't shy of using elsewhere. She thought she'd use it in here too.

The tables were all different shapes and sizes but more or less the same height, not high at all. Tables with their legs cut off, she thought, mostly. They were arranged like an echo of the house, three sides of a square, and she was walking in at the open end for everyone to stare at.

It's hard to set your chin mulishly and stare back, she found, when everyone's head is a yard lower than your own. All the angles are wrong for everything you know about stubborn display.

People sat cross-legged or else sprawled on cushions, propping themselves up on one elbow like Romans. Mostly they had arranged themselves around the outside of the horseshoe; there were no cushions on the inside, and the few who sat there had tea towels slung across their shoulders or aprons worn over their other clothes. Cooks and servers, she guessed: doing the job casually, the opposite of silver service. Working inside the horseshoe for the sake of convenience, bringing big pots and bowls and ladles, dropping down to grab a bite themselves, five minutes' rest, a word with a friend over the way.

It was like an arena, that broad open space between the tables. It was hard to see, coming into this high shadowy space from the bright-lit hallway; harder still to see past the flickering lines of candles, the occasional musky glowing globe of an oil lamp; but she thought that was Mother Mary in her white, just where she'd look to find the heads of the family, in the middle of the long row facing her. Most likely that was the promised Leonard sitting beside Mary, a middle-aged man with a grizzled beard, and would she have to walk all that way to face him, so utterly exposed, like a supplicant pleading to be taken in . . .?

Apparently not. Tom took her arm and drew her to one side. She thought he might be laughing at her quietly, behind all that facial fungus. She thought he was most exactly reading her mind.

'Not that,' he said. 'We don't run gauntlets here. Of course people are curious, but they don't get to stare you down, not all at once. This isn't a circus. Here, sit here.' At the end of one of the horseshoe's arms, exactly the opposite of what she'd been anticipating: closest to the door, least easy to look at.

And Tom at her side, tall, overshadowing; reaching out a long arm to hook two bowls closer, working the ladle from a giant tureen. 'If you need to ask what this is, the answer's stew. Best not to ask, I always think. Just let it happen to you.'

She shrugged, which was possibly unkind when he was trying so hard, but right now that was as much as she could manage. Her wrist hurt, in that achy way that wasn't worth making a fuss over; the thought of it was worse, like barbed wire tangled all about her so that every flinch away just dug it deeper in.

It wasn't possible. Her wrist had healed months ago, months. With scars, because the surgeon who sewed it up had made no secret of his contempt and couldn't be bothered to do a delicate careful job – she almost thought he almost wished she'd got it right and was lying cold on a slab for dissection, rather than pale and red-eyed and flinching from his needle – but he couldn't have done so poor a job that they would be tearing open again, could he?

Under the weight of an unaccustomed suitcase, carried for an unaccustomed way? Perhaps he could. Perhaps that long haul had strained ill-married flesh too far.

It was that or she was mad after all, believing that the strike of a bell could slice raw living flesh apart. If that was true, what need butchers? Monks would do. Vicars could take carcases to pieces with their great church bells. Buddhists could bone out quail with little tinkling finger-cymbals. No one need ever cut themselves again with crude and cruel razors . . .

She had stew. She had a spoon, because he passed it to her. She had another hand. She cradled the bad one in her lap and spooned stew listlessly. From hand to mouth, and—

'Oh!'

He was grinning – no, *smirking* at her. Delighted with himself, for making it happen that way. Discovery, untouched by warning or anticipation or any kind of hope.

'Told you.'

Stew, was it? She supposed it was, if soup meant a liquid with solid things in it, if stew meant solid things bound about with gravy. If you could distinguish between them.

Just the gravy was dark and rich and remarkable, a tingling dense eruption on her tongue, like licking the essence of savoury. There was salt in there and spice and somehow meatiness, although she was willing to believe no meat; and she wanted more, immediately and imperatively.

And this time there was a piece of vegetable on her spoon, and never mind, she took that too for the sake of the liquid that cloaked it; and she couldn't have named it but the vegetable was all crunch and flavour and freshness, a delight against the settled maturity of the stock, and she wanted more of that too.

She spooned and chewed and swallowed. At some point, Tom thrust a piece of bread into her other hand, her bad hand; and it wasn't bad enough – as Mother Mary had foreseen – to stop her using it for this, holding bread and lifting it to her mouth for biting.

Tom didn't say anything about the bread. He'd been

purposefully dismissive of the stew, just because he knew how good it was, how rare; the bread he put into her hand, *take it or leave it*, no comment.

She did take a bite, but it was brown and fibrous, chewy, rough, too serious for her. She was a frivolous girl, when she could manage still to be a girl at all. Just across the table was another girl, long hair conscientiously plaited, skirt to her ankles, bare feet tucked under; she was eating bread with conviction, where any woman Georgie knew would be plucking at it, rolling little pellets, leaving the solid crusts on her side plate.

Every woman *Grace* knew would be ignoring it altogether.

Here there was no side plate, nothing so decorous. No tablecloth, either. She had known, had eaten in houses where the polite thing was to use the tablecloth for your bread. The upper crust was strange. They couldn't just afford plates, they had plates by the dozen, by the many dozen, all matching, all frighteningly valuable. That might have been why they didn't use them, except that all the other courses came on that same crockery: just not the bread. Someone had told her once that it was because in olden times there weren't any plates, your bread served as the plate and went straight on the table, and this was a modern version of that – but she hadn't really believed him, then or since. People did like to wind a girl up so, when she didn't understand a thing.

She didn't like the bread much, didn't want it, but didn't want to put it down. She was fairly sure that these people would frown on waste. She chewed her way through a few more bites, but really, the stew was all she wanted. Stew and more stew.

Bless him, Tom had noticed. He served her another ladleful before even her bowl was empty; and a little after that, he reached across to snare that hunk of disregarded bread from her poor sore hand and eat it heedlessly himself.

'Sorry,' he mumbled around the crust, 'it's a little earnest, the bread we make. A bit on the worthy side.'

It was. They made it, he said, in a wood-burning brick oven they'd built themselves in the stable yard. She thought they could have used their loaves for bricks, to build another. And didn't quite like to say so, but the thought made her giggle regardless. He quirked an enquiring eyebrow at her; she shook her head, dropped her gaze, went back to eating stew.

After a while, she remembered that she was here on a mission. She was supposed to be spying, not really in retreat. There was no point actually living out her cover story, shy girl on the run, hiding from her own life. Tony might not pay for that, he might not feel obliged; money might suddenly become an object after all.

Between spoonfuls, then, she looked around as best she could, peeping from below her fringe. Shifting her weight, shifting her legs from one side to the other, taking any opportunity to face another way, snatch another view. She was like a buttonhole camera, secretly bold.

If she caught someone's eye, well. Even a shy girl would peek about, wouldn't she? Once she'd come this far? And then dart her eyes back to her bowl again, then peek again.

She wasn't sure if she'd ever been honestly shy, but she did seem to have Georgie in her bones. She understood that girl, from the inside out. Even if she'd never been her, or anything like her.

There were a lot of people here, a lot of faces to peek at. No point trying to learn them in this difficult light, at distance, in snatched glances through her hair. Any more than there was any point trying to pick out individual voices in the general buzz of conversation. Just impressions, then. It was as much as anyone could ask of her, the first night here. As much as she would ever ask of herself.

There were as many women as men here, she thought, more or less. It was hard to be sure when they all sat together, when so many wore their hair long and loose, when they were bent over bowls or turned towards one another with their heads close, when their clothes had little to say about what sex they were. While they were sitting down, at least. She might reasonably hope not to see boys in skirts, though she expected plenty of girls in trousers.

She was wearing a minidress herself, to keep in character. One more swivel from one hip to the other, one more tug at the hem of it where it rode up high on her thigh; Tom said,

'You're really not used to sitting on the floor, are you? Poor Georgie.'

Actually, she preferred it, though not quite like this. Give her a soft shagpile carpet, room to stretch her legs and a man in a chair behind to lean against, something slow on the record player and his hand on her cheek. With everything that that implied, before and after. Really, she was no good on her own.

She was on her own here, and needed to be good. She said, 'I'm not wearing the right clothes, that's all.' Another tug, another shift, like a girl dressed for fashion but uncomfortable with showing so much leg. Like a little idiot who had run to the country, to a commune, without giving a moment's thought to what that meant. Like a girl whose suitcase was full of city dresses, yes. If anyone was looking, if anyone cared enough to look.

There's something going on there, Tony had said. *Go in like an innocent, and if you get caught – well, be guilty of something else. Of being yourself. Why not?*

He was a clever lad, Tony. She almost felt safe, almost.

'Not to worry,' Tom said. 'We'll sort you out something to wear, something you'll be comfy in. This evening, after you've talked to Leonard.'

Sitting this way, at this angle to the long room, she could see Leonard and Mary quite easily, no need even to move her head. Not that it did her much good at this distance, in this light; they were too far away to read expressions, let alone lips. Not that she knew how to read lips anyway. A proper spy, she thought, would be better trained and better prepared.

If this was a movie, she'd be doing everything right. Being herself in the city, bright lights and cocktails; recruited at a party, briefed in glamorous Soho; going undercover far from home, disappearing into a sinister commune under another name, living secretly among strange and dangerous people who harboured ambitions that she didn't understand.

But then, if this was a movie, she'd be James Bond. Jane Bond. Cool and lethal, enigmatic, desirable.

A lot of men desired Grace Harley, but that was different. That was . . . quite horrible, actually, when she thought about it now. She'd become collectable, something to be bragged

about in that cold, dismissive manner that expensive men liked
to cultivate. 'The Harley girl? Lord, yes. I've had her. Who
hasn't? Grace and Favour, they call her: she'll do anyone a
favour, if you only have the grace to pay her.'

It was almost true, that was almost the worst of it. It
wasn't what she wanted; it wasn't anywhere near or anything
like what she wanted; but she couldn't have what she wanted,
so why not?

This wasn't a career move, just a diversion. She wasn't
really a spy, or a reporter. Whatever happened here, soon
enough she'd find herself back in London and doing what
she did again, being who she was. Grace Harley wasn't a
job, she was a life sentence. The judge had understood that,
she thought. He'd even been sympathetic, a little. *You've been
punished enough.* What that really meant was: *Go out and
be who you are, learn to live with yourself. It's never going
to get any better.*

If she did well here, Tony might hire her to work for his
paper properly. She could write about fashion, maybe. Or be
a gossip columnist. They didn't even use their own names;
that could be a whole other kind of going undercover, being
herself at parties and then writing them up, having the whole
world of London wonder who she was, this Bella Donna who
went everywhere and knew everyone and was so scathing
about them all in print . . .

But she'd still have to go to the parties and be Grace Harley.
From here, already, it looked unbearable. She couldn't imagine
how she had survived it all these months. *Brazen* they called
her, but it wasn't true. Brazen meant brassy, she'd looked that
up; and brassy meant hard. Stubborn under all that surface
polish, the immaculate shine. Not crying yourself to sleep any
night you found yourself alone; not stubbornly setting out to
make sure you never were alone if you could help it. They
thought she didn't care. What they never saw was how hard
she had to work to keep herself from caring.

From where she was sitting, the way she sat, it was easy to
tell when the meal was over. There was no formality to it:
only that Leonard and Mary stood up, bowed a little to this

side of the room and to that, and turned away from the table. Turning inwardly, towards each other, like lovers do. Military men all went the same way, she'd noticed, as though they were drilled to do it, while two businessmen would turn independently, away from each other. If Leonard and Mary shared a word or a touch she couldn't see it, but their bodies declared an intimacy that she ought to be aware of. Whether or not it was passionate or physical. The elderly could still get it on, she knew – too well, she knew it! – but they had ways of mattering to each other without needing to sleep together. She knew that too and envied it, almost. Looked forward to it, almost.

There was another set of double doors behind where they had sat. They went through those alone, with no fuss at all, and let the door swing closed again behind them.

That was when she realized that all the room's talking had died when they rose, that everyone must have been keeping a quiet eye on them just as she had. As the door closed at their backs, there was a single soft sigh, as though the room itself had let out a breath of disappointment. Really, it was half a hundred mouths in unison, acknowledging a loss, the departure of the guru.

It was odd, slightly. He didn't look like a guru: a shortish man, slightly bandy-legged, with a neat aggressive little beard and a weathered face. Commonplace clothes, jacket and trousers: Mother Mary might dress in robes, but not he.

Well. He must have something. She'd find out, one way or another. *I'll do my best for you, Tony love. Even if there's really no mystery, if this is just an excuse to be nice, to get me out of town . . .* It was a suspicion that had crossed her mind more than once, that this was really a charade all aimed at her, for her benefit, to find her another way to live. She liked to dream sometimes that Tony really was that kind underneath and really did care that much, that he'd disguise charity as a job of work. Not even fantasy Tony could seriously imagine that she'd settle to life in a commune at the arse end of the world, but yes: to get her out of London for a while, off the front page of the papers? Even his own paper? Fantasy Tony would do that. Actual Tony not, of course not.

Actual Tony would look for his own and the *Messenger*'s advantage, and do something nice for her if it suited. Which meant that no, this wasn't a hoax and she wasn't being double-crossed; which meant . . .

Never mind. Someone else was standing now, but not turning away. A man, his long hair bound back with a leather thong. He held his hands up against the rising murmur and smiled broadly as it died back again.

'Thanks, people.' His voice was mellow but carrying; he was in his thirties, maybe, as near as she could tell; and, oh yes, he had something. Even at this distance, at the wrong end of a crowded room. A while ago – years now, but she still remembered it – she'd been at the back of a crowd when her host uncorked some fabulous bottle of wine at the front. She remembered how the smell of it had come to her, all that far away, at the back of all those other people; how it had perfumed the air, how it had silenced them all.

This was like that. Whatever it was about him, his gift, his gift of presence: it washed through all that long room like a swell of clean fresh water. People sat back on their heels, put down their bread, would have strained to hear him except that they didn't need to, he came through loud and clear and easy.

'Just a few announcements, to keep everyone up to speed. We're running short of wood again, so anyone who's walking in the valley, do your share and drag back a branch or two. Fallen branches only, of course. Give the trees a chance.

'And Cookie says the power's off in the west wing for a reason, he's very suspicious about a box or a relay or some-thing and he's waiting for parts, so don't fuss at him about it. We don't need electricity out there anyway; it's just an inconvenience. If anybody's sleeping over that side, they only have to get out of bed to switch it off. Candles are easier, so long as you're careful.

'Talking of being careful, there's a leak in the painted bathroom. Just cold water, so don't be alarmed, but you'll get wet feet paddling about in it. Cookie says he'll get to it in the morning . . .'

It was like parish announcements at church when she was little, when her mother still made her go. She should have drifted off, let her thoughts wander and her eyes too. And yet, and yet. He was like the most charismatic vicar ever. Or that really cool teacher that no school ever actually had, the one that all the girls would dreamily fancy while the boys vied for his attention because he came in on a motorbike and hung out with some deep band at weekends and would take half a dozen favourites off in the holidays for an adventure.

There'd been a succession of men at her school who had tried to be that guy. Probably every school had those: the ones who grew their hair and didn't shave, wore coloured shirts and pendants, talked hip and always, always disappointed. She'd been like any of the girls, falling for it, willing to believe. Before they let her down, she would sit in class or assembly trying frantically to catch their eye, to be the one they noticed: to matter, somehow, more than her friends to left and right. It was what she'd always done, to chase after an elusive celebrity. And then catch it, and find it after all not worth the effort, not deserving of the dream.

She wasn't even trying to catch this man's eye, not pushing herself forward, not in the race any more.

And yet he was looking right at her now, his bright gaze snaring her through the shadows as he said, 'As usual, Mary and the captain ask us to leave them alone this hour, to let them have some quiet time together. It's not so much to ask, people, is it?'

It didn't seem like anything at all. Who would worry about letting the old ones go off to bed, while this golden man remained to them?

But Tom touched her hand and said, 'Don't worry, Leonard will see you,' even while a murmur of agreement was still rolling along the tables:

No, not so much, we'll let them be, of course we will, don't we always?

She just shrugged at him heedlessly, her eyes still fixed on that man as he made his way between two tables into the open arena of the floor, as he walked unhurriedly in her direction, as he came directly and indisputably to her.

Training held good; she knew how to stand up gracefully, even from the floor with nothing to hold on to. She was on her feet before his offered hand could be any use to her. On her stockinged feet, because she'd slipped her shoes off when she sat down; her head barely reached to his shoulder, though his own feet were bare. Tall as well as golden, then. And very much a man – nothing of the boy about him, nothing to prove. Not likely to be a disappointment, this one. It was probably just as well that she didn't want anything from him.

He took her hand anyway, although she was up already and didn't need the help: not to shake, apparently, just to hold it as he smiled down at her. Warmth and strength in his silky fingers, warmth and strength in his honey voice as he said, 'I'm Webb. They tell me you're called Georgie?'

She nodded, slightly unhappy at even that fractional lie. She'd never been a natural liar. She'd had to learn the art of it in bed, even, to boost the frail egos of the men who took her there. They only liked to be laughed at with their clothes on. In court she'd told the pure simple truths of all she'd done and everything she'd taken, the men and the money, the advantage and the risks. To the papers, too: nothing but the truth. It had done her little good. If honesty was the best policy, she had yet to be shown any good reason for it. It was just easier, that was all.

She was sorry suddenly to be entering this house on a lie, even such a small one. People changed their names for all sorts of reasons, all the time: for politics, for safety, for escape, for sex, for fun. What kind of name was Webb, anyway? Not the kind you found on a birth certificate, unless it was a surname, and he wasn't the kind of man in the kind of place to be going by his surname. No. He'd just chosen what he wanted people to call him, and so had she, and—

And she was still sorry to be telling him a lie, even if it didn't really matter. Even if he knew it and didn't care. Perhaps it was only her guilty conscience, but she had a feeling that he could see right through her.

He said, 'Well, if you're ready now, Georgie –' *if you've got your story all prepared* was what she heard, though the tilt of his head towards the table seemed to say *if you've finished your supper* – 'why don't you come on through and meet the captain?'

'I, um, thought you said he wouldn't want to be disturbed . . . ?'

'He's not generally available after dinner. If he was, he'd never have a moment to himself, or for Mary. He does always like to meet newcomers, though, as soon as may be. This is the best time, when you can sit and talk and not be interrupted a dozen times an hour.'

'Wouldn't Mary rather . . .?'

'I expect she would, yes – but she won't say so. She learned long since that there's no point arguing with Leonard, for his good or your own, when the good running of the house is an issue. That's why we had to learn to keep away in the evenings, to stop him wearing himself ragged; it's our own decision, not his. I'm not sure he even knows. Come on, now. An invitation to the captain's cabin is a privilege, and no one here disdains it.'

'Oh, I wasn't—!'

But he was teasing her. She realized it too slow, smiled to acknowledge it too late. By then he was already walking, still keeping that loose grip on her hand so that she had to stumble after him or look absurd, tug herself free like a child not willing to be led.

She was willing enough, more than willing. He was playing faithful lieutenant and no more, bringing her to meet his commander – and she was still scurrying to catch up with him, still leaving her shoes as abandoned as poor Tom at the end of the table there, not a backward or regretful glance.

He took her across that open space, through the heart of the room, under everyone's gaze. In her short shift and sheer tights, and never mind that she'd known these clothes were wrong, that she'd planned and worn them deliberately. She still felt like a cow brought to market, exposed to comment and ridicule – except that she glanced from one side to the other and didn't think that anyone was commenting much, let alone laughing. She couldn't see that anyone was actually looking at her, much. A curious glance here or there, but that was only the inevitable curiosity of a settled group finding a newcomer in its midst. Nothing judgemental.

She wasn't sure that she could be so kind towards a stranger – or so unconcerned, it wasn't even kindness – being led by the hand to the heart of things, where everyone else had been so bluntly excluded.

But then, she wasn't a hippy. She wasn't signed up for community living. Grace had hated school and left as soon as she could, left home at the same time, dumped flatmates as soon as she thought she could afford to. Georgie's story wasn't so different, except for being the one who was dumped and dumped again.

She was suddenly practising that story in the back of her mind quite urgently as they squeezed between tables and came to those high closed double doors beyond. It wasn't Webb that she needed to convince here.

He pulled one door open and handed her through. She felt almost like an actress being brought to the front of the stage for her curtain call, except that this was a beginning and, however it ended, nobody was going to applaud. Nobody was going to applaud her, at least.

Webb's fingers slipped away from hers at last, too soon. These next steps she had to take alone, and she was more than sorry about that. She could hear him right behind her, pulling that door closed again; there was small reassurance in that. A man had disappeared here. Maybe. At least one, maybe; maybe more. Something surely had been going on before that, before Tony had sent his man in, or why would he? He hadn't told her much about it: only that there were rumours, worried parents, disapproving locals. The usual. Good fare for a Sunday morning.

If it was true, *if* this wasn't an elaborate ploy to see her out of London for a while, make her feel differently about herself, better if she could.

Either way, she needed to stop thinking like Grace for a while. Think like Georgie. Be Georgie, as much as she could manage. That would be nicer, anyway. She was a nice girl, Georgie. A bit of an idiot, but that was all right. Nice girls are allowed to do foolish things, and feel sad after.

Nice girls are expected to be a little bashful, coming in to face an older man in a position of authority. Father, headmaster, priest, employer. Judge. It was all the same, always. They all judged you. Grace would be defiant, but not Georgie. She didn't have it in her.

Georgie would creep forward, uncomfortably alone: eyes on her fingers as they twiddled with each other, as her right hand fussed at the bandage on her left.

She'd find herself walking over carpets, for the first time in this house: fine Persian carpets, that Grace would have recognized from all those country houses in the days when she was welcomed there, that Georgie would know from the nice homes of her parents' wealthy friends. There was always a story, if you looked for it.

Walking into smoke, into the smells of various smokes. Joss, of course, there had to be joss; and a stale background smell of tobacco mixed with something rougher and sweeter, cannabis, *of course* someone had been smoking joints in here; and more immediately, prominent and demanding, a richer darker tobacco that brought her head up regardless, and there he was.

Leonard, the captain, master of this house and of her fate, at least for this little moment: sitting on an old worn cat-scratched settee, the kind of furniture that was endlessly familiar to Grace – all those rooms in all those country houses: people with houses like that hold on to everything, and pass it down as it decays through generations of guest-rooms and family rooms and servants' rooms and dogs' – and not so much to Georgie, leaning into one corner-cushion while Mother Mary occupied the other.

He was smoking an Indian cheroot, black and thin and lethal. He gestured with it, that hand that was not stretched out along the sofa-back towards Mary, and tapped ash into a bright jade pot on a trefoil table beside him, and said, 'I'm sorry about this,' though he patently wasn't, it was as much a part of him as the beard on his chin. 'Old sea-dog habit that I can't break now – I'd break myself if I tried it. Filthy things, but people put up with me regardless.'

Of course they did. She understood it now. Webb's impact was long-distance, the teacher addressing the hall; it didn't get stronger close to. The captain's was immediate, here and now, you and me, not for sharing.

His beard bristled with iron vigour. His blue eyes were faded, salt-soaked, ironic; his skin had weathered sun and wind, ten thousand days, a thousand thousand miles. His voice still held a Navy crispness, under a roughening of tobacco and hard use. And of course he'd been in the war, so had every man his age, every man worth anything – not half the men she knew in London, those who had fucked her and spurned her and judged her and fucked her anyway – but there was more than that. Something of her own father in him: the last thing she'd have looked for, the last thing she'd have hoped to see, but there it was, clear and authoritative and revelatory.

She said, 'Merchant Marine?' Her father called it the Merchant Navy, with a kind of stubborn pride; when he talked about the king, as often as not he meant George V, who'd given it that title after the first war. The way her father spoke, you'd think he'd been in the service at the time, that the sea was in his blood. In truth he'd signed up in 1939 to avoid conscription, got out as early as he could, and used his wartime contacts shamelessly ever since. She really didn't want to see a similarity here. And yet, there it was: something about distance, experience, another kind of life. In her father it had touched him, marked him, tattooed his skin perhaps. If you wanted to be clever, if you wanted not to remember that he would be the last man ever to have himself tattooed. In this man it was sunk bone-deep, ocean-deep. She might be willing to bet that he did have tattoos, but only the way a ship had flags: superficial, for the benefit of others. Himself, he didn't need telling who or what he was, or where he'd been. Or what his service had been worth. The old sailors she'd met, the real sailors, still called it the Merchant Marine.

He grunted. 'Clever girl. Sit yourself down.' Patting the cushion of the settee beside him.

There was, she supposed, just room enough for three, if she didn't mind being pinned between him and – what, his partner, his co-host? His first mate in the naval sense? Or in the biological sense, his wife?

Grace would have sat somewhere else, deliberately at a distance. By nature she didn't do obedience, or joining. In the war she'd have waited for her call-up and then been the most difficult draftee she could, all lipstick on parade and cigarettes with the quartermaster's men behind the stores. In a commune – well. It was hard to imagine Grace in a commune, willingly or otherwise.

Georgie, though: Georgie only wanted to make other people happy, in a way that she couldn't make herself. She'd sit where she was told to, with never a mulish lip.

Went to do that, then – and swallowed down her huff of relief as Mother Mary rose up at her approach, shared a private women-only smile with her, said, 'Sit here, dear,' in her own place, the far end of the sofa.

She could do that. Georgie would do that; yes, and curl her legs up and half turn her back to the man at the other end, look at him half over her shoulder, self-protective, harmed.

'Don't get him going, mind, on his time at sea,' Mother Mary went on. Standing over her, protective herself. Even Georgie might uncurl, a little, in her shadow. 'He'll bore you half to death. And poison you the other half, with those cheroots. Would you like a cup of tea?'

There was a little spirit-stove in the corner, a kettle already steaming. Adding its fug to the twining smoke of the joss sticks in a brass holder, set on the window sill above. She smiled a nervous thank you, and never mind if she looked a little bewildered; she was a little bewildered. She really didn't understand this place. Nor Mother Mary. The captain was easier, at least in her imagination. She could piece together a story for him. Not for this woman, busy with pot and kettle and water, with caddy and spoon and leaves. She had been a nurse, she said; she ought to be a matron now, ruling patients and probationers alike with a rod of iron, brisk and brutal and beloved. Instead – well, people here called her Mother, though she didn't want them to. Presumably she did the same thing: tyrannized and treated hurts, kept good order, walked about in the captain's shadow and let him take the glory.

Whatever glory there was, guiding a group of long-haired hippies from one day to the next, in chase of something unknown. Perhaps she didn't understand him either. Grace would challenge him about that, ask him straight out: *what are you here for?*

Georgie wouldn't. She'd be too afraid of having the question bounced straight back at her.

She said, 'I'd love to hear about your travels, uh, Captain . . .?'

'You call me Leonard,' he said. 'To my face, at least. I know everyone calls me the captain behind my back, but I don't have to hear it. I had forty years at sea, from deck boy to master, and no one using my own name all that time. It's enough. I'm ashore now, and not even the Royal Navy would call this house a ship. We'll have no titles here.'

'Hear, hear,' came devoutly from the corner. From Mary that would be, then, not Mother Mary. She would try to remember. People should be allowed to choose what people called them.

That was a very Georgie thought. She was almost proud of herself. Of both her selves.

Webb was laughing at them all. Settling on the floor, not far away, where a long-armed stretch would let him drop his ash into the same pot that Leonard used; lighting a long neat joint that he'd had ready, just to be sure that he had some ash to drop. Another candidate for first mate, was he? That was how it looked to jaundiced Grace.

Someone else who took the name he wanted. Fair enough. She wouldn't challenge that, but she did say, 'What's funny?' – and that was all Grace, and she was almost ashamed of herself. Of just the one self, Grace, because of course Georgie wouldn't stand up to her for a moment and couldn't be expected to.

He said, 'You'll learn. But truly, Leonard, you can't go laying down the law and then complain when people salute you for it. Any more than Mary can embrace four dozen folk at once, remember all their birthdays, and still resent it when they call her Mother. Some titles just . . . accrue. You can't choose not to be what you are.'

'Of course you can,' Mary said. 'You can choose to be Webb, plain and simple.'

Which confirmed a lot of her suspicions and underlined, she thought, what everyone was saying here, and even more what they were thinking. But Webb said, 'Oh, that, of course – but I can't choose not to *be* me. I can only choose what you *call* me. A Webb by any other name would smell as sweet. And if you will stalk around insisting that everything be ship-shape, you can't complain when people call you captain, because you are; and if you will insist on mothering everyone, Mary dear – including slapping us down when we're naughty – then, you know . . .'

'Oh, be quiet and smoke your nasty thing. Why you insist on that grim resin when we have perfectly good home-grown weed I cannot imagine, but—'

'You see?' Webb pulled a whimsical face and shrugged extravagantly. 'Even when we're arguing about it, she can't help doing what she does. Give it up, Mother. Some fights are lost before they even begin.'

Some fights are fought over and over again as demonstrations, for other people's benefit. She understood that. She'd seen it happen in the grandest houses in the land, between the highest ranks of people; and all for her own benefit, or at least to impress young Grace Harley, born of Billericay. That wouldn't happen now, but she didn't want it. She never had.

She didn't want it here either, even if it was done with better humour. She said, 'So it's not a ship. That's good, I didn't think that I was coming to a ship – but I'm sorry, I'm still all at sea here. Actually, what is this? What are you all doing here?'

'Waiting,' Webb said, with another snort of private laughter.

'Growing,' Mary said, bringing her a mug of tea.

The mug was roughly thrown and coarsely glazed, and she didn't think it would be very steady if she had a table to set it on; she wrapped both hands around it, in lieu of steadiness, and waited to be enlightened.

'Being ready. Getting ready,' Leonard said – which seemed to be the same things in the same order, but . . .

'Isn't that the wrong way round?' she said, because the only other thing to say would have been *ready for what?*, and she wasn't ready for that. 'Don't you have to get ready before you are?'

'No. You need to be in a state of readiness first, before you can begin to prepare.' His cheroot had gone out. He frowned at it distractedly, fussed a little with matches and flame, puffed

out thin clouds of evil-smelling smoke until it was drawing
again to his satisfaction. Ready then, he went on – or else he
started again, or else changed the subject entirely. Or, possibly,
answered her original question.

He said, 'When I was a young man, I was all over the show.
All at sea, yes. Hong Kong to Honolulu, Surabaya to San
Francisco to St John's. Then the war . . . happened. I was on
the Arctic convoys, Archangel, Murmansk. I saw . . . No, never
mind what I saw. Things I wouldn't tell a lady. I survived,
though half my crew mates didn't. I swore I would never go
into the cold again. I went back to the tropics, worked tramp
steamers around the Philippines for a while, then found my
way to India.

'Where I stayed. For a while. I left the sea. Yes, it was a
surprise to me too – but I wanted something I couldn't find
on shipboard. I wanted horizons beyond a metal hull and the
companionship of a dozen men just like me, war-scarred and
closed in, locked down. Every ship I served on was like a can
of damage, brewing in the heat. It might be the first smart
move I ever made, getting out while I could.

'And then – well, there was India. Before the rush, before
the hippy trail brought us half the youth of Europe and the
States too. Hell, I practically built the hippy trail. All too
literally, some stretches: the road from Hussainiwala down
into the Punjab, I worked my way across that land. It was
unheard-of, a white man labouring alongside the natives, but
they were very good for the most part. They allowed it. I had
no caste, do you see? So people could be outraged, but no
one was offended.

'And I learned. I visited ashrams in the Deccan and monast-
eries in the hills; I talked to holy men on the road. I think I
met Kim, though he was an old man who'd almost forgotten
that he'd ever been white. I found my way up into the Himalaya,
inevitably, and over the border to Tibet. The people there were
careful of me, so that I didn't run into trouble with the authorities. I was there a while – they are a remarkable people – but
I couldn't stay. My simple presence put my hosts in danger.
They went to extraordinary lengths to keep me safe, but I
couldn't do the same for them.

'With their help, I came down over the mountains into Nepal. Even that time was a revelation to me: long nights under the stars, talking and walking and being silent. I had finally turned around and was starting to head home, and I hadn't realized till then quite what I was taking with me. In Kathmandu, I met my first Western longhairs. It was too soon to call them hippies, for we didn't have the word yet. I called them beatniks, I think, though that was really the culture they'd come away from, looking for something else.

'It had taken me years to go as far as I did; it took me years longer to come back. By then they were everywhere. I watched them and envied them – they were young, for the most part, they hadn't had the war as I had – and I seemed to spend half my time helping them out of trouble. They were . . . spectacularly naive. And irresistibly attractive, despite that or else because of it. Those that I helped mostly headed home after, determined to echo the kind of life they'd glimpsed or dreamed of, somewhere they had better hopes of making it happen and getting it right. It's always easier to rebuild Eden in your own backyard, when the original is full of other people who are not at all like you.

'You could say that having taken a hand in building the hippie trail, now I was doing the same for the commune movement, sending kids back to the land, back in their own land. At least this time I knew more or less what I was doing. I'd watched these kids trying to live together in ashrams or villages or improvised communities, I'd listened to them building dreams of how they could live together back home; I already had my own ideas how well that would work, and how I could make it better. Which was the first inkling I had, that I wanted to make it better: which would mean coming home, and then finding a space, and then . . . well, this.'

A gesture of his hands in the soft light and the smoke, to encompass the house and the woods around and everyone who dwelt there.

And her, apparently, presumptively.

She said, 'What makes this better?'

'Discipline.' That didn't come from Leonard, it came from

Webb: puffing at his joint, still laughing. Not stoned, she thought, not yet. Just amused.

'Rules,' Leonard said. 'Oh, don't worry: this isn't shipboard, and I'm really not captain. We don't run everything to the clock. But we do have rules. Everyone eats together, and everyone sleeps together. Not in the orgy sense, unless you really want to, but communally. Nobody sleeps alone. There are rooms for those who want to couple up and those who want to play, for a night or a week or a lifetime; otherwise, we all doss down in dormitories. Walls between us cause more problems than they solve. I won't have them.'

There had been, presumably, hammocks swinging below decks, all swinging together, snores harmonized in rhythm. Something to hold on to. And then, presumably, a captain's cabin, isolation, extremity. Something to let go. The loneliness of command, the man on the summit of the mountain: achievement, and what else? A power that he didn't want, that he'd walked away from. A career and a lifetime left behind. Five oceans left behind. He was a long way here from the sea.

He had been further. Literally in the mountains, sleeping in temples and longhouses with warm bodies clustered all around him. She could see how that would influence a man, how he might try to bring something of it back with him. Even so: 'If you don't want people being private,' she said, 'if you don't want them going off by themselves, why come here?' This house was too big. She hadn't seen halfway around one wing of it yet, and even so. She could take everybody from the ballroom at her back and isolate them, one in each room that she came to, and there would still be rooms left over. A lot of rooms.

'So that we can be ready,' he said. 'As we are. When they come, we'll always have space for them.'

'When who comes?'

'Everybody.' Just for a moment then he was mad, or else he was a messiah, both. His smile, his gesture encompassed the world. This was a church, then, after all.

She just looked at him.

He chuckled and drew his hands back together. *Here's a*

church, here's a steeple – except that the steeple was a chimney, smoking.

He said, 'You came. So have all these others. So will others yet, as the word reaches out. Here's a community that *works*, in every sense. That's the other rule, the one we haven't told you yet. Everybody works. What you work at, that's up to you. Inner peace or world peace, waving joss or weaving jute, we don't care. It's not "do what thou wilt", that's discredited, though it comes from Augustine of Hippo, with love attached. Our rule is "be who you are". One way or another, that tends to keep people busy.'

And then he looked at her, and puffed on his foul cheroot, and said, 'So who are you, Georgie Hale?'

This was it, her moment. Tell her story, explain herself. Little bits of truth, like slates nailed on to a frame of solid lies; they might make a roof, to keep the rain off. For a while.

Be who you are. She opened her mouth to break that first commandment, to be someone utterly other than herself – and back in that corner again, by the shuttered window, Mary lit new joss and rang a little bell.

Just a little brass trill – it was nothing, a mention to the gods, not worth mentioning. But it made the hangings billow all along the wall there, where there must be other windows closed behind them; and there was a shape that formed behind that shifting fabric, small and dire. It might have been a boy just standing there, being there, waiting, ready.

And there was a *drip, drip* between her feet, and that wasn't her cup of tea, no, spilling from her heedless hand. That was her hand, where unheeded blood was dribbling from beneath the bandage and running down her fingers and *drip, drip* dully on to the rug where really she shouldn't have heard it at all because really she should have been screaming.

FIVE

Instead she was crying, just a little: tears *drip, drip* down her face as she stood up, as she stumbled forward, as she went to where that hidden horror waited.

Of course there was nothing there. That was the point. She would pull that vivid cloth aside and there would be a terrible absence waiting for her, the emptiness where her baby grew. It used to lurk inside her, like a hollow in her heart. Now it was here, expressing itself. Taking itself literally. Coming to take her away.

She was terrified, entirely. She could barely bring herself to move. It couldn't call, it had no mouth except the bells' mouths where their clappers swung like knives to cut at her; but it sucked at her, and she tottered towards it because she had no choice. It would swallow her down like a whirlpool, manifest and appalling, and she was doomed and almost glad of it, and—

And there was suddenly a strong stout arm to block her, tangling with her own; and a voice that said, 'Whoa there, Georgie, where are you going?'

She was lifting her arm, either to point or to appeal – *come and get me, reach out, you can do it, you're a big boy now* – but it was the wrong arm, the one that bled, because Mary was gripping the other.

'Hullo, have those cuts opened up again? That's nastier than I thought. I'd better put some stitches in there. Come on back to the bathroom, dear, I'll clean it up for you and have a better look . . .'

Almost, she wanted to protest. But when she looked again, the fabric hung down like a curtain over wood and glass and nothing, no movement in it now, no figure hiding, waiting, reaching. She shuddered, and let herself be blindly led away.

*   *   *

'Why did you, why do you—?' *You. I don't understand you.*

She might have been talking to herself: standing in the bright-lit bathroom under a naked bulb, staring at her own reflection for the first time in hours, seeing neither immaculate distant Grace nor vulnerable Georgie but some pale washed-out clumsy imitation. Hair askew, huge eyes, lips gone to nothing. She never looked like this; she'd never let herself. She had no way to fix it now: one hand, no handbag, and her case was gone from where she'd left it, just over there.

Her other hand was pinioned, laid out on marble, fit for dissection and no more. That was how it felt, at least: quite dead. Mary had numbed it with a needleful of novocaine and now was plying needle and thread, where those cuts were gaping open.

She might have been talking to herself, but she wasn't. The half-formed question, the expression of bafflement was meant for Mary, even if it was only to stop her asking questions of her own, about why healed cuts should suddenly start to bleed again.

'Why do I what, dear?'

'You were a nurse, you said. And now you're here, being mother to a commune. Burning incense, ringing bells. Are you . . . are you married to Leonard?'

'Married to him? No. Not that. Persuaded by him, perhaps. He brought me here, at least. I suppose I came for him. For what he's doing here. I came to help.' Her hands were brisk and impersonal, ideal; she might have been sewing a mattress cover. Her voice was meditative, as though she were thinking this through for the first time, which surely couldn't be true. 'He didn't convert me, if that's what you're thinking. He didn't bring back much in the way of religion. I'm further down that path than he is. I was a believer already; I'm a cradle Catholic, and when he sent me to India I didn't lapse so much as accumulate. Hence the smells and bells. I grew up with them. I'm quite used to making a little noise to ask for God's attention, puffing a little smoke his way. This is just a different flavour. I used to need priests to do this work for me; now I can do it for myself.'

'Isn't it a different god?'

'Oh, I'm not sure it's any god at all any more. Any god in particular, I mean. In my father's house are many mansions, and I do try not to discriminate. I don't suppose they squabble over us in heaven.'

She did apparently still fervently believe in heaven: only that it was more populous now than the imperial palace of her childhood, which had been staffed with angels and blessed souls all in service to a solitary dictator-god and his immediate family. She was happy to make room up there for the Hindu gods and the Muslims' god and whatever gods the Buddhists might believe in, they were both a little confused about that – and if that meant that her notion of heaven was really just a mirror of what she was trying to achieve down here on earth, a big house full of space and ready for anyone, neither of them could see any great harm in it.

'There, now. I think you'll do – but you're not to use the hand, mind. Not for a few days. And if it bleeds again I'm taking you to the doctor, for it'll be beyond me. It's beyond me now, what made it open up like that. Nothing you did, I'm sure, so don't go taking it to yourself.'

She rigged a quick simple sling with a spare length of bandage. 'More as a reminder than anything else; you don't really need to keep it up, but this should help you remember to be careful, not to go knocking it. You won't harm my stitches, but you might give yourself an uncomfortable hour if you bang it about.'

It was uncomfortable already, a dead weight at the end of her arm. She knew too well how it would feel in an hour, as the feeling came back; she thought anaesthetics were like a dam that held back troubled waters, rather than an oil that soothed them. Sooner or later, she was going to feel it all. Sooner, if anybody rang another of those bloody bells. They'd cut right through the chemicals, as they cut right through her skin . . .

Did she really want to believe that? Well, no: no more than Mary really wanted to believe in every god that she encountered. Neither of them would have chosen this, but you couldn't argue with your own faith, any more than you could with other people's. The world worked the way you knew it worked.

For Mary that included the afterworld. Not for her. Death was death and that was that: which was why her son was nothing now, a sucking nothing, a cold and brutal fact lurking in the corners of her life. And bells were blades that used to cut her inside, only now those wounds rose right to the surface.

It was almost no surprise at all: as if she'd only been waiting to see it happen, or to find the space that let it be. *Be who you are.* Very well, then. She might carry on lying, but she'd carry on bleeding too. Sooner or later they'd figure it out.

She didn't think they'd stop ringing their damn bells. She'd be the one who bled, that was all. For as long as she stayed. Every church needs its martyrs.

It was almost an effort already to remember that she wasn't Georgie, and she hadn't come here looking for a place to hide. Or that she was Grace, and she still wasn't looking for salvation. Not here, not from these. Not from anyone. Grace was unsaveable.

Unsalvageable, maybe. Nothing in her worth the trouble.

Nothing at all, any more. She was a hollow vessel, full of blood and nothing. Which the bells did keep letting out.

She muttered her thanks, and almost asked which way to her room; she'd have liked to close a door and cry a little, even before the pain came marching up her arm like sharp little soldiers, bayonets fixed to cut her from the inside. Just in time she remembered, no private rooms here. No separation, no doors to close. And no drugs in her case, wherever that was: she was travelling as Georgie, too nice to dull herself with chemicals.

There were drugs here, drugs in plenty. But Webb hadn't offered to share, and again Georgie was too nice to ask, she'd have to be inveigled.

She might just rather go to bed.

But Mary was taking her good arm suddenly, matron no more. If she was motherly yet, she was more like a mother trying to be one of the girls, eager and conspiratorial. 'Come along now. It's time.'

'Is it? Time for what?' Seeing Mary snatch a glimpse of her hidden fob-watch reminded her that her own wristwatch had been sternly removed and put aside, when her bleeding arm was dressed the first time. She'd forgotten to reclaim it, and it wasn't here now. Like the rest of her things. She didn't think they'd been stolen, only taken away, but it was almost the same thing. She felt like a girl newly arrived at boarding school, all her personal property confiscated.

'You'll see. Everything changes when the sun goes down. Despite Leonard, I think that's when we discover who we really are. If you spend all day working at it, you forget that you don't need to be so earnest. There are walls inside too, which you have to let down sooner or later. Knock down, in some cases. But firelight and starlight and music will at least open a few doors, show you where the walls are.'

Firelight, starlight – she glanced down at her feet, in their endangered tights. 'Should I fetch my shoes?'

'Oh, I shouldn't think so. Take those nasty things off, I would, and go barefoot. Remember when you were a child and it was the most natural thing in the world? I've never understood why girls want to wrap themselves up in clingy nylons anyway; it's all so sweaty and artificial. Peel them off and throw them away and let your skin breathe for a while – you'll never go back. I expect everything you brought with you is the same, is it? You modern girls, you do like your man-made fibres, but they're really no good for you. There's a reason we were blessed with wool and cotton and silk, you know.'

'Some of my undies are cotton . . .' That was Georgie, of course, being a nice girl, trying to please her. Some of Grace's undies were silk, gifts from old admirers, but she didn't wear them. They lived under layers of tissue paper, in boxes, at the back of a drawer. Really she ought to throw them out, if she couldn't sell them.

'Are they? Well, good. Come the morning, we'll find you some nice things to go with them. Or to replace them. We're not so hot on binding underthings around here. A girl should be glad of her figure, not confine it to some rigid conformist shape. I mean, you can wear what you like, of course you can, and no one will point a finger or say a word. Still, we have rooms full of clothes to play with, and fabrics too, and most of us are handy with a needle and thread, so why not try something different? We can't dress you in the height of London fashion, perhaps, but we can make you pretty and comfortable, in clothes you can wear and wash and wear again. That's the point, surely?'

Grace knew girls in Chelsea who would choke and die at the very idea. Time was when she'd have done the same herself, loudly, dramatically; when her flat was full of clothes that she'd wear once and then send to the dry cleaners, or else back to the shop. Georgie – well, Georgie dropped her eyes and murmured her agreement and said she'd be grateful, and swore privately never to mention here what Grace had more recently learned: how wonderfully convenient nylon was, dripping dry over the bath overnight and never needing an iron in the morning.

Mary was perhaps not fooled. She'd take what she could get, perhaps, one day at a time. For a moment she was brisk again, impatiently motherly; she said, 'Off with those, then. You'll only end up with tatters around your ankles anyway. Can you manage one-handed?'

Oh, she could manage, if the alternative was to be mothered. She was at least still limber. A minute later, she had one leg free and the other up on the edge of the basin; she was just rolling the tights – and yes, of course they'd laddered, and no, of course it didn't matter now – down to her ankle when the bathroom door opened and a man walked in.

No one she knew, no one she even recognized. Presumably he'd been there at dinner, somewhere in the shadows, in the vast swallowing spaces of that room.

He took the pipe out of his mouth and nodded a greeting which was casual enough, though she thought his eyes lingered a little on the exposed smooth length of her leg; it was hard to be sure behind the bushy extravagance of his beard, but she did rather think that he was smirking.

Then he went into a cubicle, and did at least have the courtesy to close the door. After a moment she heard the rattle of a matchbox and the hissing flare of a light, sounds of puffing.

Her own eyes may have been bugging out on stalks. Mary patted her shoulder reassuringly and didn't try to talk. A jerk

of the head and a more determined nudge impelled her out
into the corridor, where: 'I'm sorry, dear, I would have introduced you, but I had the impression you might just shriek or
make garbled grunting noises. Did no one think to warn you?'

'Warn me? Warn me of what, that men just wander into the
ladies' at random? No. No, they didn't.'

'Not the ladies', Georgie. Just the bathroom. We share and
share alike here. No modesty, and no shame; those are just as
artificial as your nylons and almost as modern an invention.
Don't tell me you're body-shy, a modern girl like you?'

'Well, no. No, of course not.' Not Grace, at least: Grace
had skinny-dipped with dukes, while an older generation sipped
champagne and hooted from the side of the pool. Georgie was
another matter, afflicted with her parents' morals and the
standards of her private school. And would deny it fervently,
of course. 'I just . . . I don't think I've ever – well. Not in the
toilet!'

'No, probably not. We are quite absurd about lavatories;
there's no reason in the world not to use the same facilities,
if you think about it. Elsewhere in the world, everyone does;
and here, too. And the baths too, you'll find. If you really
can't stand the idea, club up with some other girls and snag
one of the bathrooms when it's empty. If you all wash together,
there'll just be no room for the men. Though that won't stop
them popping in to see. Truly, though, after a week or two
you won't care any more. It'll all seem ridiculous, so much
fuss over a few body parts. Now, that's enough lectures for
today; you're making me sound altogether too much like
Mother Mary. Come on down to the water. Chances are you'll
see a few body parts tonight too – it's warm enough – but no
swimming, mind. Not in *that* water, and not with that hand.
No baths either, come to think of it, until I say you may; which
will mean when that dressing comes off, and not a minute
before . . .'

If she really didn't want to be known as Mother Mary, she
really shouldn't lay down the law so insistently, halfway
between encouragement and scolding, with that natural
assumption of authority. She offered no quid pro quo: no hint
of a carrot, no sight of a stick. Grace had small experience of

it, but even so this was her utter definition of maternal: how she would have been herself, how she had been in her head, as unlike her own mother as she could manage.

Today, here, now, she didn't mind being mothered. She didn't mind being led by the hand, even. Grace would have kicked up a fuss, almost certainly, just because. Grace made a fuss about everything, only to be sure that everyone was looking. Not Georgie. Meek and mild, Georgie was. Bashful. Shy. Always looking for someone else to take charge.

Funny, it was almost comfortable. She went hand in hand with Mary, through the house to that high front door, where the master staircase swept down in two divided curves. She would never have dared to open that door herself, after Tom's telling her they never used it; but Mary never hesitated, turning the heavy iron ring and dragging one great leaf wide.

'We don't usually come this way,' she said, quite needlessly, 'but everyone should experience this once, at least. It's rather special.'

It was. Overhead, the clear sky was wild with stars, the Milky Way hurled across the valley from wall to high fell wall. They never saw stars like that in London.

It was an effort, almost, to drag her gaze downward: to where firelight flickered and blazed, where it reflected itself in still water. She had seen that lake earlier, when Tom walked her by its margin as they came out of the wood. From up here it was long and dark and striking, a bottom to the valley and a mirror to the sky, sewn almost into the landscape like mirrors embroidered into fabric, like Indian cotton . . .

She might have looked more at the lake and the steps that led down to it, the way the gardens were terraced on either side of the steps; but it was dark and the gardens had been let run mad, and they were not what she was here for, by any measure.

That firelight: that, she thought, was why Mary had brought her this way.

Fire draws the eye. Even when it's not designed that way, set like a jewel in black velvet against mirror-glass.

She was fairly sure that something here was deliberate. Even if not exactly designed for her benefit – who was she, after all, a stray girl sucked in at random, not even interrogated yet? – but on general principles, for impressive purposes, they couldn't have done this better.

From the light spilling out behind her, she could see her shadow hand in hand with Mary's, stretching out across a broad flat terrace. Beyond that, beyond the boundary of the balustrade were rising sparks, distant, firework night come too soon, an allotment bonfire, memories of Grace's grandfather and spilling peas from the pod, her clumsy little fingers too eager for the sweet green freshness in her mouth.

Hand in hand, responding to the enticement of Mary's tug, they walked across the terrace. Sharp gravel underfoot, almost painful on her soft soles, only there was moss enough to soften the bite of it, and yes, there was a pleasure in that cool sensual touch, even the touch of teeth in it.

Over to the balustrade, and now she could look down over ranks of overgrown terraces, dry fountains, dead hedging: really it was all shadow, grades of shadow, all the way down to that flat reflective lake-water at the foot and the sparking fire beyond. She'd been to enough movies that she could read that monochrome landscape, even while her eyes were drawn beyond it, to the bright guttering leap of the flames.

They'd built their bonfire on the further side of the lake, where there was a broad grassy bank between the wood and the water. Figures moved in silhouette, between the flames and her; music drifted up, as promised. She heard flute, and thought of Tom.

Then there were the steps down, taken slowly as though they were in procession, as though all this rout were for their benefit after all, a masque for them. Between wild shrubberies and beds of roses desperate for deadheading, alien in starlight; past those dry fountains, dead at the head; down and down, to the level of the water.

Sparks flew, rising, falling in reflection. There were voices now, among the music; voices singing, and voices calling, and voices simply talking the way people do around a fire. Indistinguishable at this distance, comforting at any distance: even for Grace, whose childhood had been absolutely not distinguished by Girl Guides and school camps and songs in smoky rounds. Even she knew how this worked, though her own early bonfires had been scrappy affairs, urchins burning scrap and rags in bomb-site rubble, putting off the hour of going home.

Georgie would know this better. Georgie could lift her chin, like a needle finding north; Georgie could lead the way suddenly, shyness burned away by the promise of flames in darkness, which would never show the flame of a blush on rosy English skin.

Georgie could tell secrets under the hiss and crackle of a camp fire that would be so much harder in the pale revelatory light of morning.

Besides, no one here was going to be ringing any bells.

Around the squared-off corners of the lake, then, and here already were scatters of people, sitting on the grass in couples and threesomes and larger groups, keeping back from the fire's heat. That was good sense, the evening was warm enough already; but nothing on this journey made any sense, and she wasn't about to start being sensible now.

She left Mary behind, then, hearing her name called and called again:

'Mother Mary! Come and sit with us!'

'No, here! Sit here, see, plenty of room . . .'

She went on alone, picking her way between one half-circle and another, closed to strangers but open to the fire's light. That was how it seemed, at least, coming from behind, a stranger, all those backs. Not that they were turned against her, she understood that; but it could seem that way. It did seem that way.

It didn't matter. She wasn't about to join any half-formed circle anyway – not where that would mean sitting with her own back turned to the fire. That wasn't what people did; it wasn't what she was here for.

Be who you are.

She was Georgie Hale, and she followed rules except *in extremis*, when things went very wrong. The rules of the house and the rules of her kind, no different. So she came to the circle of firelight and found a spot where she could sit alone – there was room enough, because the heat and the glare this close were really too much on a summer's evening, but never mind – and she settled down with her legs hitched to one side and her back nicely straight, feeling the fire on her skin, losing herself in the smoke and the noise and the music. *Be who you are*, which was lost and alone and here.

She could do that, all of that, oh yes.

The fire was . . . immense. Not really like the massive civic structures of Bonfire Night celebrations, but that was the closest she could think of: when she and her pack of friends had watched for days in the park while men built up a pyramid of old furniture and doors and boughs from fallen trees. When she and her friends and all the local children else had sneaked up after dark, despite dire warnings, and left their own contributions buried as deep as they could reach into the stacked timbers, or as deep as they dared burrow: broken toys, dolls with missing limbs, long-loved teddy bears given up in a spirit of loud bravado and breathless secret heartache.

Here they didn't build their fire so high, anywhere near; they didn't let off bangers and rockets and Catherine wheels. The fire itself was the point: a summoning and a gathering place, and perhaps an offering too. For Mary, it would surely be an offering. Somewhere in her pantheon must be a god who yearned for flame. Perhaps she too hid little sacrifices among the piled wood before the fire was lit, invisible and potent.

What was there to be seen was achingly nostalgic, as fires ought to be: fallen branches dragged from the woods, broken furniture fetched from the house, all manner of worked timber that might have been anything before it was sawn and split and chopped into handy lengths. Some had been built into the fire before they lit it; more was stacked up beyond the fall of random sparks, to be tossed on when wanted or else saved for another night.

She sat and watched the play of flame and shadow, feeling the skin of her face tighten in the heat, not caring. Not really listening to the breathy flute, only aware of it as one more element in the night; not joining in when people sang. This wasn't the kind of music Grace knew, nor Georgie either.

She barely noticed when the music stopped. A minute later, though, she was immediately, intimately aware when another body dropped to the ground beside her. Not in her light, not close enough to touch except with purpose, but even so. In her space, deliberately so.

She turned to look, and of course it was Tom. *Be who you are*: he couldn't see her alone and not come to change that.

He laid his flute at his feet and said, 'How was the captain?'

'Fine. He let me in.'

'Of course he let you in. What, did you think he'd turn you away? That's not how we do things here. Everybody's welcome.'

I thought he'd see straight through me. Aloud, she said, 'He didn't even ask why I wanted to come.'

'Did you? Want to, I mean?'

'I – no. No, actually. Not to say want.'

'No. People mostly don't. We come because we have to, or because we need to; because we haven't anywhere else to go, or because there isn't anywhere else that offers whatever it is we're looking for. There are communes all over, of course, in England and everywhere; or you can go to India or Thailand or Japan, find something more authentic. Find somewhere warmer. California.'

'It's warm enough,' she said, almost a protest, almost defensive already.

'Tonight it is. You wait till winter. We had three feet of snow in January, and there's nowhere in the house to build a fire like this.'

Of course not. The house had fireplaces and hearths and chimneys, but this wasn't the kind of fire you could contain or channel or control. Fire wants to be free.

Even without music, someone was still dancing to the hidden rhythms in the flame. A girl, all long skirts and long hair, dreamily swaying and spinning, making shadows almost solid in the night. She had a lit joint in her hand, but she wasn't smoking it: waving it, rather, like a sparkler, writing letters in light, weaving patterns of smoke and movement that existed only for the little moment of their making.

Like the fire, she was something to watch, to save them looking at each other.

'Oh, I'm not sure I'll stay till winter.' *I hope not.* 'I hadn't thought . . .'

'Don't. Don't think. Just be here, let it happen. Stay a day, stay a week. Stay a month, a year, a lifetime. I think Cookie's been here a lifetime, since before the house was anything like this. Since it was a house, I think. Stay until you have a reason to move on. That's what it's for. How it works.'

'Yes.' That ought to be true. Really, she hoped it was. Then there'd be nothing to discover, nothing to report back to Tony. No story. His missing journalist would just be one of these men, hiding behind the flares and paisley and the facial hair, sending no news to London because there were more important things to be doing: a life to be lived, true discovery, rules to follow. Being who he was.

'So why did you come, Georgie? If you didn't really want to?'

I really didn't want to. That isn't quite the same. Aloud, she said, 'I didn't, I couldn't . . . I couldn't stay. Where I was. Not at home. Not after . . .'

It was funny, she'd practised this: out loud before she left, and then endlessly in her head on the long journey here, again and again, around and around like a stuck record playing the same line over and over. She'd practised it until it was second nature, pure Georgie . . . and even so. The words caught like barbs in her throat. Every one of them wanted to make her bleed.

'What happened, Georgie?'

'My baby died.' Vaguely, she was aware of someone else sitting down the other side of her. She didn't think that was a coincidence, just bad timing. It didn't matter. She didn't even turn her head. Something collapsed deep in the heart of the fire, and there was a whoosh of sparks lifting high into the air; she watched that happen, and went on talking. 'I had a baby, and he died. Inside me. He was born dead, and they took him away. They wouldn't let me see him, it was . . . He was mine, and I wasn't let have him.' Not by the world or her parents or the hospital or God. There would have been an adoption, if there hadn't been a death.

It was all true, and none of it was anything close to the truth: not for Georgie, not for Grace.

Still, it ought to be enough. 'I couldn't stay,' she said. 'I needed . . . not to be there any more. Or anywhere like there, anywhere I knew. Anywhere people knew me. So . . .'

'So you came here.' A match flared, a fresh tiny point of fire, enough to drag her eyes around.

That was Webb, sitting on her other side, firing up another joint.

'Yes.'

'Why so? Don't get me wrong, you're very welcome – and besides, there isn't a test; we don't turn anyone away, I'm just curious – but as Tom says, there are communes all over, and I don't think you're local, are you? I think you've come a long way, to come to us.'

She thought he knew full well how far she'd come. It was far indeed, in more than miles, and she thought he knew that too.

There might not be a test, but she thought there was an interview. She thought this was it. She thought there was a process: Leonard told the newcomer about the house, about his dream, what they had come to; and Webb interrogated them to find out why they'd come. Or got someone else to start his interrogating for him, while he listened in and chimed in when he chose to. Like a bell.

She said, 'I'm from London.' *Never tell a lie, where the truth will do it for you* – a lesson Georgie could learn from Grace and be grateful. 'Someone was talking about this place at a party –' still true! – 'and, I don't know. You're never quite so much a stranger, are you, when you come on a recommendation?'

She might have been quoting Georgie's mother. She could imagine having a mother who would say such things, often enough to be quotable.

'There aren't any strangers here, sweetheart.' That was Tom. 'Only friends we haven't met yet.'

He really did sound like he was quoting someone, but he really didn't need to. It might as well have been his own heart speaking, simple and shallow and bright as a stream in sunlight.

'Can you remember who gave you the recommendation?' That was Webb again, coming back to what mattered. What mattered to him, apparently. He was neither simple nor shallow, and she thought he might be dangerous. To her, maybe.

She said, 'No, of course not. It was a party. I didn't know them then, when I was tiddly; I wouldn't know them sober. I hardly remembered what they'd said. Only that there was this place, and it was cool, it was somewhere a person could come; and it was a long way away and that was good, that was better than good. That was what I wanted.' *Too far to go home*, she wanted that to sound like. *You can't get there from here. Bridges on fire, all the way.*

'Well,' Webb said. 'You're very welcome.' Which didn't at all sound like it did when Tom said it. From Webb it sounded like a visa, a stamp in a passport, *officially approved.*

She thought she'd rather settle for Tom's welcome, even if it didn't carry the same authority. It was less complicated, more heartfelt. More honest.

The opposite of her, so many ways.

'Thank you,' she said, but her heart wasn't in it. Her wrist was aching suddenly, quite sharply, in its sling: not the dull ache of torn flesh mending, as it should be.

She almost didn't want it to, but her other hand reached to touch. The bandage felt damp beneath her fingers. When she looked, there was a stain against the white.

Despite herself, she listened out for bells.

And heard a soft and constant jingling under the voices and the fire's sounds, like a belled cat at run across a lawn, its every movement a betrayal to the birds, *tin-tin-tin.*

No, like a dozen belled cats, a herd of them all moving together, with purpose. Just one would be lost here, however carefully she listened. One hair-fine cut on her wrist she wouldn't even feel, but this was like razors, light and slender and relentless.

She'd pulled her arm out of the sling without even thinking about it; she cradled her aching wrist in her palm, and rocked a little against the pain, and tried to understand.

No one was herding cats. There were no bells on collars. Maybe the jingling was all in her head. In her wrist. Maybe her wrist was just bleeding a little because that's what cuts do, and she was hearing bells because she was listening for them, because of what lay buried in her poor broken head, her poor broken baby in his churchyard bed.

But her eyes watched the girl as she danced around the fire, danced to no music – and the *tin-tin-tin* that she heard seemed to dance itself in time with the girl as she turned and twisted, all slim and sinuous within the swaying reaching shadows of her hair and skirt.

There was something woven into her hair, lengths of it among the loose dark flying mass: something that flashed fire every now and then when it caught the light, here and here and here again.

She watched and puzzled over that, distracted, bleeding. Trying to distract herself.

Oh – that Indian fabric, with the tiny mirrors embroidered on. The girl must have ribbons of it plaited into narrow braids – and, oh. Yes. Something at the end of each braid, a little weight, shimmering silver. A little bell.

Her skirt flashed too, that same mirrored cotton; and a fringe around the hem that was not enough to muffle the bells sewn there too, which jingled as she swayed.

It wasn't fair. Grace wasn't much inclined to feel sorry for herself, but Georgie could. Georgie could hug her poor sore wrist and huddle up and want to stick her fingers in her ears like a child, to shut out that cursed jingling, as if that would make anything better.

Tom was saying something to her, or trying to. She wasn't listening. She couldn't hear anything, except *tin-tin-tin*.

She couldn't see anything except the girl dancing out her destruction, cutting deeper with every step. Stamp stamp, jingle jingle, and the deep throbbing in her wrist like a backbeat, in time with her heart, pumping blood to the rhythm of the dancing girl.

Until she went too close to the fire, the girl did, swirling and swaying with her eyes shut, not to see the damage she was doing.

She went too close, leaning into that wall of heat as if it would hold her up; and a hand, two hands, reached out from the fierce heart of it, as if to push her away.

Hands of flame, and not pushing, no.

Clawing at her.

People weren't looking, until it was too late; but Georgie was looking, staring numbly. Georgie saw.

She saw those hands, their fingers hooking, snatching.

She saw them catch at the skirt and nothing else. If the dancing girl was lucky, she was lucky then: that they missed the legs beneath the skirt, that they couldn't catch her flesh.

Nothing to grip, then, to drag her into the flames. Only that sudden flaring fabric, burning through; and the girl could scream and stumble back and the hands had nothing to cling to, only cloth that turned to ash as they did the same, as they fell apart in disillusion.

And maybe it was only an illusion to begin with, but the girl was really burning, all her skirt aflame and the ends of her hair catching now, fire running up those braids; and Grace was on her feet already, the only one moving, running into the light and the vicious reaching heat of it.

SIX

B are feet, bare legs. It didn't matter.
No hands came clutching out of the flames for her.
Of course they didn't. She hadn't even thought.

She didn't need to think. There was a girl on fire, screaming and helpless, batting her hands at the fury of her skirt and doing nothing but spread the flame to her cheesecloth sleeves, making everything worse in a moment.

Girl on fire, and a lakeful of water just three paces off. What was there to think about?

She had no idea how deep the water was. That didn't matter either. If there was only one thing Grace did well, with a natural confidence and the virtue she was named for, swimming would be that thing. Water became her.

She didn't need to think.

She hurtled into the burning girl, full on, face to face. Flame to – well, lucky she was only wearing a sleeveless minidress, there wasn't so much to catch fire. Nylon all through it, though, which would melt to a sticky horror on her skin – except that she wouldn't let it; it wouldn't have the time.

Someone had told her once she had a rugby player's shoulders. It wasn't true – they were trying deliberately to be unkind, and not making a very good job of it – and she did watch her weight with care, but she wasn't ever one of those wispy girls who need a man to open an envelope for them.

She slammed into the screaming, skipping, burning girl, scooped both arms around her and just kept going. Feeling heat and not worrying, keeping going. Momentum and determination and the thrust of her legs – *thunder thighs*, that same unfriend had called her, loudly at a party – carried both of them over the grass and over the stone rim of the lake and into the air and down, into the water.

She'd grabbed air on the way because that was what she did, it didn't need thinking about; and if it was hot, the air, if there was a mouthful of flame in there it wasn't burning her.

She was ready, when they hit. Ready for the impact, ready for the plunge. Ready for the water closing over her head, and for her unready companion's struggles. She'd done life-saver training at the pool in Billericay, her sixteenth summer, when there'd been a man to train her. She could handle this.

She wasn't ready for the cold of it or the depth of it, the falling-away beneath her, falling and falling; that sudden crushing squeeze that made her air feel ridiculous and shook her confidence to the marrow.

It couldn't be that deep, this deep.

Could it?

And the girl couldn't still be burning, she only thought she was. And was flailing, frantic, still trying to beat out flames with burned palms, didn't seem to notice that they were under-water now and sinking still.

Until she tried to catch her breath for screaming, and—

Well. That was a hard time. From trying to burn, the girl was trying suddenly to drown: doing her very best, doing everything wrong, fighting Grace and fighting to breathe and dreadful in her panic, dreadfully dangerous.

In all the watery stories Grace had ever read, a rugby-playing man would administer a swift clip to the jaw and thrust the fainting female to the surface before she could drown of her own wilfulness.

Still lacking the shoulders, she did what she could: kicked like mad and hung on grimly, tried to keep below and push the girl upward, not to let her cling like weed and drag them both down beyond saving.

No swimming, mind. Not in that *water*, Mary had said. It must have meant something. Maybe it meant this: the depth and the shocking chill of it, an icy clutch at her confidence. *Not even you*, it whispered deep in the bone of her. *You're out of your depth here . . .*

Well, but she always had been. Out of her depth all her life, and fighting all the way: grabbing for air, for a handhold, for a helping hand, for anything. Learning to swim the hard way, by learning to stay alive.

She held her breath in the sour murky water, kicked against the bitter sucking grip of it below, pushed hard at the flailing girl above.

Brought them both abruptly to the surface, gasping and choking, to find too many people crowded at the lake's margin, trying to be helpful: too many hands reaching down to them, too many voices calling, all those bodies shutting out the firelight and only making it harder.

Still. She heaved the girl into those willing hands and felt her drawn away on to solid ground. The same hands clutched for her, but she kicked off from the stone-faced bank and backed water a little way, out of their reach. The cold was vicious but not killing, not yet; if all she had to do was float, she could manage that. And there was a comfort in it, this brief space between her and them like the walls they disapproved of, an absolute line. No one was jumping in to join her. *Not in* that *water.*

She could understand that. She could relish it, almost. She'd be glad enough to get out herself, but not until they cleared away from the bank. She didn't want all their hands hauling at her, touching her, dragging her away. She didn't want to be one of them, this suddenly easily; she didn't want to be their hero of the hour. *I'm a spy, not a sister.*

A good spy would take any advantage, she supposed, whatever they might offer her: congratulations, gratitude, towels.

Perhaps she didn't want to be a good spy either. Even to please Tony.

She raised an arm to wave them away, all those hopeful helpful people – but that was her left arm, her bad hand, and it was aching fiercely now that the cold had got into it. *Not in* that *water, not with that hand.* Maybe she was due a scolding, rather than congratulations. It didn't matter, but in this darkness a wave might look like an appeal for help, a drowning girl going under again. She let her arm drop and snatched a breath to yell at them instead. *Clear back out of the way, let me get myself out* – the last thing she wanted was anyone pulling on that bad hand, ripping open the stitches again. Mother Mary would understand, she'd corral their eagerness, it only needed a yell . . .

But the air was thin and foul out here over the water; it didn't seem to be enough. She gasped and gasped again and couldn't raise her voice. For a moment she thought something dark and sinuous and massive moved in the water beside her.

Oh, that was nonsense. There weren't monsters in the water. Nor hands in the fire, nor—

Nor a bell, no, tolling deep beneath her, deep deep down. Great thudding strokes that seized hold of her, that crushed her, flesh and bone together; that doubled her up in the water there, no swimmer now. Just a mortal suffering body, breathless and racked with pain and sinking, slipping down into the dark and the cruel cold, and . . .

And something brushed against her body as she fell, and she hadn't ever been the screaming sort but honestly then she might have screamed if there had been air in her lungs, if she had been in air and not this gripping suffocating water.

The touch startled her eyes open, when she hadn't really realized she'd closed them. Not that eyes were any use in this dark, this double-dark, dense clouded lake-water in the night; but she'd rather go down fighting. Even if she couldn't see what it was she fought against, even not believing in monsters even as they swallowed her.

A touch again, fumbling first to find her and then seizing hold. She did try to fight, but that grip had pinned one arm against her side so she only had the other one to fight with, and of course that was her bad arm, which felt almost too heavy to lift now as it burned with cold, as it ached deep in the bone. And she had no air, and there was no strength left in her, and no hope; and she might as well just hang here, seized and helpless, and let whatever had her drag her down . . .

Except that she was rising, all unexpectedly; and that wasn't a monster after all. Of course it wasn't; she didn't believe in monsters. Just a man, she could feel the familiar shape of his body against hers as he kicked powerfully, kicked them both up to the surface.

And she was still in the grip of the tolling bell, still helpless, and that didn't matter any more. He was strong enough for both of them. All she had to do was breathe, finally, at last: great sodden shuddering breaths as he towed her to the side, as she floated slackly in his arms, as far too many hands grabbed hold and hauled her out.

Then she could lie on the grass and cough and shudder uncontrollably, heedless of all those people all around her; until at last here was Mother Mary pushing through, taking charge, what they had needed all along.

'Stop crowding them, stop standing there like goons, how do you think you're helping? Someone run up to the house, put a kettle on, fetch towels and dry clothes for them both. Yes, all of you go if you want to, you're no use to me here. What they need is the fire's heat, and you lot are just in the way and I don't have time for you. Go on, vamoose . . .'

Of course, not everyone went. There's always someone who thinks general instructions don't apply to them. And perhaps they were right this time; she was glad enough now to have help to bring her closer to the blaze, where she could sit and shiver and wish that she could dive right through into the fire's heart. If there were hands in the fire, where were they now? Not reaching out for her, no, to embrace her and draw her in where it was warm. She thought she would have gone. No fighting now, no fight left in her. This numbing cold had frozen out her heart and her will together, every stubborn grain of spirit that she had. She thought she might be crying, perhaps.

'Hey.'

She turned her head slowly, effortfully to find him. He was sitting cross-legged in the fire's bask, which was more than she could manage. He was long and lean and angular, his limbs jutting in all directions, and the way he sat, slumped forward – and no blame to him for that! – his long dripping draggled hair hung down over his face, and for that little moment she wasn't sure.

Then he lifted a hand, tucked most of his hair back behind his ear, and she saw a shaven chin and a predatory gleam, almost a possessiveness, as he gazed at her, as though he had saved her life and so could claim it now.

Not Tom, no. She hadn't been able to tell in the water, and she had wondered – but no, of course it was Webb. Strong and dominant, taking charge, seizing control. Seizing her, while he had the chance.

He would think so, at least. The water had first claim on her, though, and a tighter grip. She was still coughing, still wheezing through a constricted throat, as though all the passages of her body had clenched up. The fire's heat wasn't coming close. Her clothes were starting to steam, and even so: she still felt bitter, shaking cold, inside and out.

He could see that, she thought. He hitched himself over and put an arm around her shoulders, drew her in close against him. She had no resistance. She felt once again close to tears, unsure that they weren't actually already leaking down her ice-wet cheeks.

At least that was easy to hide. She turned her face into his shoulder, which was wet enough already. For a minute, she let him cradle her; she thought he was probably enjoying it, despite everything.

He didn't get it for free, though. Not for long. After that little minute, she made an effort and peeled herself away, face and body both; and scowled up at him and said, 'It isn't fair.'

'What's that, love?'

'Why aren't you shivering?' He didn't even feel cold, on the inside. Under that skin of wet clothes, she could sense the heat of him, pulsing through. 'Look at me, I can't stop . . .'

Even her teeth were chattering. She'd always thought that was a myth, but she tried to talk and they clattered together like dentures coming loose.

'So come back here and borrow a bit of what I've got.' He was imperturbable, pleased with himself, irresistible apparently. When he tugged, she went. 'You were in longer than I was; I expect that's it. You saved my poor Kathie twice over: once from the fire, and then again from the water. It's no wonder if you're feeling a bit spent.'

'It's more than that, you idiot. Sit her up and let me look at that arm again.' Mary, of course, back from wherever she'd been: tending Kathie, presumably, seeing how bad her burns were. At least they'd had the cold water to suck all the heat out of them.

'Yes, of course. Here, Georgie, you just lean back on me,

that's the way, and let Mary get at you . . . What's she done to herself, Mother, anyway?'

· 'Never you mind.' Of course he'd want to know; information is power. He'd want to know everything. And of course Mary wouldn't tell him, even the sum of her guesses. 'She's in a bad way, that's all. Hold this arm still, if you want to make yourself useful. I don't think you can do it yourself, can you, Georgie pet? Where are those towels, anyway? How long does it take to run to the linen cupboard and back? I can't be expected to do everything . . . Oh, at last. Thank you, Tom. That's right, just put it round her shoulders, and you go at her hair with another one. Webb can look after himself – or more likely Kathie – but not for a minute, please. Keep holding Georgie, just as you are; you won't die of pneumonia, any of you, for one more minute . . . Yes. That's what I was afraid of: all the stitches gone again, and no telling how much blood she's lost, but I don't like the look of her at all. Honestly, Georgie. What did I tell you . . .?'

Not in that *water, and not with that hand.* But it wasn't really a question, and she certainly didn't expect an answer: which was just as well, because she certainly wasn't actually going to get one. Not from Georgie, who was hardly even there; and Grace was lost in the tolling of a bell, impossibly deep and impossibly cold, the sound of it felt rather than heard. She thought it was still sounding, thrumming through the ground she sat on. Unpicking her mind as easily as it unpicked stitches, slicing the threads of her thoughts apart, opening her up to bleed and bleed.

She was glad enough just to lean shiveringly into Webb's lean strength, sorry when someone – was that Tom, of all people? – bullied her into leaning forward so that he could get at her hair, violently, with a towel. It'd dry all wild, but oddly even Grace didn't seem to care. She couldn't manage it, somehow. Even her arm wasn't hurting now; it was just numb. If Mary wanted to sew it up again, she wouldn't need to bother with any novocaine.

Oh. Apparently, she was sewing it up already. Grace hadn't noticed, and neither had Georgie – well, no reason why she should: it was Grace's arm, wasn't it? Grace had done the cutting first, before those damn bells started – but she heard, 'Pass me my scissors. Or no, better, just cut. Cut there, and wait. I'm putting another one in. I'm putting in a whole lot more, actually. I'm going to hem these cuts, to stop her tearing them open again. I'd do them cross-stitch if I could. Lord knows what she found down there in the water, to cut them through so cleanly. Something that had rusted to an edge, I suppose . . .'

But the light had changed, and they weren't huddled by the fire any more. When had that happened? She blinked around, and here they were: herself, and Mary, and Tom. No Webb. Tom was holding her with one arm, helping Mary with the other; and they were back in the familiar bathroom again, bright lights and clean water and Mary's medical bag opened up on the marble side there.

She didn't quite understand what had happened, but she was glad enough to have the lake water washed out of her. And she wasn't shuddering now, and she couldn't hear the bell, and all of that was good. And Mary said, 'She'll do now. I've put in double the number of stitches this time round. You get her to bed. Up with Kathie, please. They'll be company for each other and I won't have to disturb anyone else when I check on them. Oh, I'm sure half the house will be sitting up all night anyway, but not on that corridor. You and Webb can take turn and turn about, if you insist . . .'

And then she must have drifted off again, by herself or perhaps with help if Mary gave her something: because now she was in bed, in a bedroom, or at least in a room set aside for sleeping. The bed was only a pallet on the floor, but she was a little surprised to find that she didn't mind that. For Georgie it would probably be like camping with the Guides, a girlhood pleasure rediscovered, nights of whispering in the dark with friends when they should have been sleeping. Grace was more practical. She was warm and cosy and weary to the bone, and she never wanted to move again and had no reason to. Half the aristocratic beds she'd slept in had been more lumpy and less comfortable than this.

There was another pallet in the room, the other side of the little window where a night light burned. That was just enough to show her a muffled shape asleep, and that must be Kathie the burned drowned girl, not burning now, not drowning. That was good, that must be good enough.

Between the two of them sat a third figure on the bare board floor. A shadow, long straight hair lit by the window's candle. A sharp red glow as he inhaled; a slow breathing-out, and the smell of acrid leaves.

She murmured a soft, 'Webb?'

'Tom,' he said, half apologetic. 'Webb's sleeping the sleep of the justly famous. So are you supposed to be. I said I'd keep watch over your snoring forms.'

'I don't snore!'

'Yeah, you do. Little feminine snorts, it's quite cute. Maybe it's just because you're full of lake. Or drugged up.'

'You can talk.' He could, but his voice was slurred a little, slow and dreamy; that was surely not his first joint of the night.

'Hey. Got to do something to pass the time. You wouldn't like it if I made a noise.'

She might, actually, if he made it with his flute. She could see herself lying here in the dark and letting soft breathy music carry her away. Like a child floating on a lullaby. It wouldn't take much; her body was half asleep already.

'I'm not drugged up, anyway,' she said, just because it was needful, not because it was true. 'I don't.' Grace did, of course, she was a party girl, she took anything she was offered if anyone was looking; but Georgie did not. Of course not. Georgie had never even had a cigarette. She was trying gamely to be cool about it all, but the waters had closed over her head long since.

'You do now. Mother Mary stuck you full of things. Don't ask me what. They were supposed to make you sleep, though. Like poor Kathie.'

'How is she?'

'Better than she would've been without you. She's got burns, of course, but they're all superficial. Mother Mary says she'll be sore for a few days, but nothing worse than that.'

'Well, that's good news. So why do we need you to watch over us?' *Just let us sleep.* Kathie was comatose, and she herself was wrapped in a lovely lethargic feeling, safe under blankets, nothing to do but lie here and let the world turn beneath her . . .

'Just in case. Mary's confident, but she could be wrong. She's not a doctor. What if Kathie comes round and she's really hurting? Webb said someone should be here through the night. And he was falling asleep where he sat but still in a state over Kathie and trying to hide it, the way he does, so I said I'd spell him for a while. And just as well, see? Here you are, awake.'

'I might not be, if you weren't sitting there smoking at me.' In truth, though, she didn't mind a bit. There had been times when all she wanted was unconsciousness, if she couldn't actually be dead – but not now, apparently. Not right this minute. She was oddly happy, half afloat inside her body, bickering lightly with this boy. She felt like a night light herself: barely awake, barely troubled.

Even her wrist didn't hurt right now. Well, there were no bells cutting at it. She thought about that, about houses like this, how she had lain awake on other nights with other men beside her and listened to their snores interspersed with a community of chimes, a carriage clock in the room and a grandfather clock down the hall and the big clock over the stable all out of time with each other and picking fights about it, loudly, all through the night.

The thought became a question: 'Why aren't there any clocks here?'

'Oh, there are plenty of clocks. All in one room, put away. Nobody winds 'em. The captain won't have 'em around the house.'

'No, but why not?' He wanted discipline and order, didn't he? Everything shipshape and Bristol fashion – and ships ran to time, she was sure of that. She'd known sailors enough, and seen all the movies too. Everything was governed by the ship's bell, which in olden times was governed by the captain's watch. These days they'd do it the other way around, she supposed: run the bell off a clock and let that govern everybody's watch. Here they used the bell to announce a stranger, and no one ran a clock at all. Except Mary, with her secret fob.

'He says that clocks are tyrannical, and that tyranny is the enemy of order. He says that time and clockwork are anti-thetical, that the universe is consensual and not mechanistic. God is not a horologist, he says.'

'Says a lot, doesn't he? Uses big words, too.'

'He does. Also, he says when it's time for lunch and dinner. Well, lunch is noon, that's easy enough. We ring the bell anyway, but we can pretty much all tell that. Dinner is when his stomach says it's dinner time: which is sunset around the equinox, which makes sense, but this far north the sun's no guide at all. We hardly see it in the winter, and it hardly goes away midsummer, so we rely on Leonard.'

'Leonard and a bell,' she said, with an edge she hoped he wouldn't hear, because he couldn't understand.

'That's right. He says, "Make it lunch," or, "Make it supper time," and someone runs down to the kitchens to tip them off, and someone else runs up to Frank in the wood. Frank rings the bell to tell us all.'

Frank. She was here to look for a Francis Gardiner, as well as to learn what she could about the set-up here. Francis might well come down to Frank. If she was going to bleed twice a day, though – if he was going to make her bleed – then she couldn't stay. *Sorry, Tony,* but she'd be like a vampire's victim, ever more pale and ever more frail, mysteriously weaker every morning. Mary would summon doctors, or send her to the cottage hospital more likely. She'd be away from here, anyway, safe and useless.

Bells didn't make her bleed in London, except in her heart. Something here took her literally. She ought to be more scared than she was, maybe. Except that she really wasn't scared of dying any more. Well, you couldn't be, after you'd cut your own wrists open; it wouldn't make sense, would it?

Just to be clear, she said, 'Not for breakfast, then? The captain's tummy, I mean, telling you when it's time, and that big bell to wake everybody up?'

Tom laughed softly in the darkness. 'Not for breakfast, no. The captain doesn't eat breakfast. Except at sea, he says. Dawn watch, sandwiches and cocoa. Here he has a cup of tea and leaves the rest of us to look after ourselves. Or each other.

Somebody usually makes up a cauldronful of porridge and leaves it keeping warm. But some people are early up, and some sleep late; you really couldn't make us all eat at the same time in the morning. Not without sacrificing what this place is really about.'

'What's that, then?'

'Us,' Tom said. 'Each of us individually, and the group of us together. We're like a hedge: lots of separate different plants growing all together, growing tough and strong and intertwined, marking out a boundary, making a shelter. It's the new way, the coming thing. Have you ever seen a hedge being laid?'

No, of course she hadn't. She'd seen a bishop being laid, but she decided not to say so. Georgie wouldn't dream of such a thing. She said, 'No, I haven't. Is that what you call it? I thought you just planted hedge plants, and they grew . . .'

'No, it's a real craft. And at the start, it's all about discipline: chopping back what's there, cutting and bending the green wood and weaving it into a sort of frame, so that the new shoots will bind together the way you want. Then you can encourage all the growth and variety you like, shape it if you want to or just leave it alone, let it run rampant. That's what the captain's after, you see? Something enduring, where every individual adds to the strength of the whole, and everyone can flourish. It's why he needs the big house; it's a big ship he has in mind. And this is just the start. We'll be a beacon, and a seed pod. People will go out from here, spread the word, set up daughter-houses all over. We can change the world. Everyone will want to live like this, once they've seen how it works.'

'What, smoking pot and dancing round the fire? I know a lot of people who absolutely wouldn't.' She knew a lot of people – in houses like this, mostly – who'd come stomping down the hill with shotguns, if people tried to do it on their land.

'Not that, no. Even now, even here, not everyone wants to get high. Some of us do, sure – but that's not what it's about. The captain doesn't, and he's our guiding light. Give us ten years, time to settle in. Time to make a mark. Already we're doing what we can in the neighbourhood –' ladders on a roof rack, screaming at passers-by: she wasn't impressed – 'but we'll be a power in the land, once we're settled. People will see, people will listen. And they'll want this, and eventually they'll realize they can have it, just for the asking.'

She couldn't say so, but she didn't think she wanted it herself. She would never have come here, if not for Tony; having seen it, she wouldn't stay, if not for Tony. What did this house have to offer her? She wasn't some older generation that could safely be outlived, so that the young and hopeful could inherit the world. She was Tom's own kind in every way that mattered, or ought to matter, except this one. Which was, of course, the only one that mattered. She was a city girl, he was a hippy freak. Back-to-the-land meant nothing to her, and what else did he have in his gift?

She said, 'This isn't paradise, you know.' That was OK; she could say that. Cynical Grace would have said it already, but even vulnerable Georgie would work her way up to it at last.

'Of course not, but we can make it a garden of Eden. A guiding light. Word will spread, people will come. You came, all the way from London.'

'Yes. Yes, I did.' *I wouldn't have. Don't call me as a witness. I'm being paid for this.* She'd almost forgotten the money. She shouldn't do that; it was the only reason she was here. Georgie didn't care about money, she'd never needed to. Grace, though, oh yes. And it was Grace she'd go back to, when she went.

Poor Grace. Even this little distance gave her perspective, to show just how mean and cramped and bitter Grace's life had become. A good-time girl who was just not having a good time: how sad was that?

But it was still the life she had, the life that waited. She couldn't afford to get too judgemental about that, nor too sentimental about this. It was an effort just to roll on to her side, to look at Tom more clearly. She made that effort, grunted as her body settled again into a delicious languor, and said, 'Yes, I did. I don't suppose I was the first, either.' *Tell me about Frank* – except that she didn't give him the chance. It was like opening a door and walking on by, not even glancing in, never mind waiting to see what came out. 'But I've only been here a night, Tom, and look at me. Look at Kathie.'

What they could see of her was insensible under the covers, and just as well. Even if her burns were superficial she'd be horribly sore when she woke up. No comfortable way to lie. Grace might envy her unconsciousness; Georgie was happy just as she was, and couldn't imagine ever wanting to move again.

Well, Georgie could stay here when Grace moved on. Shrugged off and left behind, she could be, like an old coat no longer wanted. Right now, all Grace wanted to do was move Tom just a fraction, shake him out of his complacency. He was a true believer, and they were dangerous: to themselves, and to everyone around them.

He said, 'Accidents happen, in any community. What matters is the way we meet them.'

'No,' she said. 'What matters is the way they happen. What makes them happen. There's no such thing as accidents.' She did, perhaps, believe that. Certainly she believed it here. Maybe she was a true believer too; maybe this place made them so. She took a breath, took the plunge; said, 'How come you think I keep bleeding? I'm not cutting my own arm open, just to be dramatic. There's something here that cuts me, every time you ring your bloody bells. You know that, you were there the first time. You wanted to think it was brambles, remember?'

He was quiet, smoking, listening.

She pressed on. 'And Kathie, she didn't trail her skirt in the fire, to have it catch like that. She wasn't that stoned. You couldn't get that close, anyway; it was way too hot. Something reached out for her. I saw it. It was hands, fiery hands . . .'

Now he was laughing at her. Softly, not unkindly, but still laughing.

He said, 'Never mind how stoned Kathie was – how about you? What had you been smoking?'

'Nothing. I don't.' Well, Grace did, if some man passed her something. Georgie, not. Something to be grateful for, that she needn't pretend to want it.

'Well, you must have caught a backblow from someone; there's enough dope in the air here to send anyone high.' Indeed, he added to it deliberately, blowing out a thick cloud into the small room. 'Or you've taken too much acid in your time, and you were having a flashback. There's nothing in the food, I know that. We don't spike people. But straight up, Georgie love, come on – hands reaching out from the fire? Something collapsed in there, that's all, an old cupboard or whatever; everything else fell in on top of it and blew out a shower of sparks. We ought to be more careful. So should you. How did you cut yourself anyway, the first time?'

'With a razor,' she said nastily.

He sat over that for a while, smoking, thinking. Then he said, 'Why?'

'Because . . . Because I was in trouble, and I couldn't stand it any longer.' Let him sit over that. He'd think she meant *I was pregnant* when she said *I was in trouble*, and he already knew about the baby. Let him do her lying for her. Lying for herself was far too much effort, with this warm lethargy laid over her like an extra blanket. It wasn't really lying anyway, if she just allowed him to misunderstand.

'I'm sorry, love. Poor Georgie.'

She thought he might let it go at that. He was a nice boy; he might be too nice to bother her further. Maybe she could just drift off again; she only felt half awake anyway. Mary's drugs, or his: she was breathing a lot of that smoke. If this kept up, she really could find herself high on the backdraught.

Perhaps she already was. She had to be, didn't she? He did have to be right. Fire and bells . . .

As if reading her mind, he said, 'Bells, though, Georgie? What do you mean about the bells?'

'Just the sound of them cuts right through me. I hate bells.' And then, because that wasn't enough – his silence said so, and her own creeping honesty, masks slipping one by one until she was almost dizzy with confession – she went on, 'They let me out for my baby's funeral, and the bell, the bloody bell . . .'

They'd tolled a single bell that morning, on and on. Three strokes three times, to say they were burying a man, though he was just barely begun, not properly born even; and then a hundred and one strokes more, because the parish custom was to ring the number of years the dead had lived, but stillbirths counted none-at-all so they did the other thing, they rang their bell for ever. And she'd stood there for every stroke in her foul black coat and veil, and they'd pounded through her like body blows while the camera shutters clicked and journalists yelled questions across the wall of the graveyard – 'How do you feel, Grace? And how are they treating you? And have you got anything more to say, any secrets to share while we're waiting? And how do you *feel* . . .?' – and she bled and bled on the inside while her face showed nothing at all.

And no, she'd not been punished enough.

Still not.

Really, it had been no punishment at all, nothing but relief when they took her back to jail to wait for her trial; and it was no release at all when the judge then let her go. He was so pleased with himself, with his own generosity, lecturing her pompously from the bench and then throwing her back like a tiddler, too small to be worth keeping; and the baying pack outside the Old Bailey, so much worse than anything or anyone in Holloway; and they followed her home and bayed all night outside her flat, and followed her all the next day, and some of them just kept on following.

'What do you mean,' he said slowly, carefully, 'they let you out? Out of where?'

Oh. Damn. 'Out of hospital,' she said: which was true, sort of, almost. 'They didn't usually have a proper funeral for a stillbirth – I think they just went into the furnace with all the, you know, waste. But I couldn't stand that. I'm afraid I made a fuss, and then they made an exception.' Or really it was her lawyer on the outside who made the fuss, scenting advantage in it, scenting release: which would work in his favour, at least, if not hers. She really didn't believe he'd thought at all about her. 'So I did have a funeral,' she said, 'and I really wish I hadn't, now.'

'Still,' he said, coming back to where this had started, 'it's not the bells that make you bleed, Georgie. Really, it's not. That's just in your head.'

Of course it was in her head, she knew that. Her head was a dangerous place. She thought about things, she worked things out, and then there they were: in her head and in the world, doing damage. Hurting her and hurting others.

In her belly, going bad. Hurting her, from now on in.

All her own fault, but Tom didn't need to know that.

She didn't say anything, only lay there watching him while he puffed his joint down until he was sucking on the roach and burned his tongue and yelped like a little boy and stubbed it out crossly against his jeans; and she might have laughed but really she was too sad and too sleepy, and she closed her eyes and listened to his breathing until he went away, or she did.

When she woke again, it was still dark, darker. No smoking-glow, no smoking boy. The night light was still burning, but all that did was define the edges of every shadow, to show her where was darkest.

Between her and the slumped form of Kathie – *lucky Kathie*, she was starting to name that girl privately: lucky to be alive, perhaps, and lucky to be as little hurt as she was, perhaps, and lucky for sure to be sleeping so soundly, hurt as she was – at the foot of their beds was the darkest point in the room, just where it ought to have been brightest. Where there was no furniture – nothing to block the fall of moon and starlight from the window with the night light's glow to back them – darkness had gathered itself together. Shape and substance, all of a piece, physical dark: she could have touched it if she sat up, if she reached out, if she dared.

It wasn't the lethargy now that held her motionless. She felt frozen, bitter cold where she had been so warm before; and frightened, where she had felt protected.

Tom, where did you go? Weren't you supposed to be watching?

But no one ever watched over Grace, not in a good way, not to keep her safe. They gathered by the pool to see her swimming, naked and tipsy and *look at me!*; they watched her in prison, on remand, every hour of every day; they watched her flat for sight of her; they watched her at parties and on the street and in the papers; they watched her for opportunities and for pay.

When she really wanted watching, there was no one there.

Tom had saved her once, in the woods, by chance perhaps and all unknowing. He wouldn't come again.

There were no feral pigs in the house here, snorting among the leaves, shoving though undergrowth, coming.

This was that sucking solid emptiness she'd seen between the trees, come for her again.

Waiting for her, perhaps, only that she couldn't move.

That was odd, maybe: to be saved by her own terror, if anything could save her. It didn't seem to be coming any closer. Settling, maybe, like a little boy sitting in the dark to watch his mother while she slept. If she lay here long enough, still enough, perhaps it would go away, like a little boy disappointed.

She held her breath, not like a mother at all: like a little girl, trying desperately not to be noticed. It was like being underwater again, sinking, helpless. Her wrist ached fiercely, her muscles cramped with the effort of not moving, and she found herself listening for the sound of bells—

—and almost thought she caught it, that deep-sunk distant tolling, rising from the lake. Her hand spasmed beneath the blankets, and the shadow perhaps drifted closer.

She didn't think she'd ever really been bad at heart, not to say evil. Only out of her depth all her life and struggling, snatching for something to hold on to, perhaps not caring too much who she hurt in the process, or how badly. Perhaps not caring enough.

She might have liked a little boy, she thought. Something to hold on to. She might have made a terrible mother, but she would have liked the chance to try.

Too late now. You never, ever got the chance to go back and try again.

What she had was what she'd given herself, what she'd made: a terrible hollow at the heart, absence made flesh, brought here, set now between two beds.

She probably deserved it. She'd surely never deserved better. What had she ever done that was worthwhile? Maybe she should be sitting up right now, holding her arms out, drawing this close. Making an end of it. Going with grace.

Poor Georgie. Maybe they'd bury her here and never know, no one would ever know what happened to Grace Harley . . .

Tony would know. She'd make him one more story, gift him another front page. He'd like that.

She only needed to sit up. Let it happen. What did she have to lose?

Only a life she hated every time she stopped to look at it, every time she dared. A life not worth living. It took so much and gave her back so little; it was dreary habit that kept her going. Habit and fear, perhaps. She was deathly afraid of this thing, this nothing at the foot of the bed. Fear was like a weight on her chest, holding her down, keeping her from that one swift move of welcome, of surrender, of . . .

It wasn't her who sat up, in the end. It was Kathie.

There was a moan from the other bed, and then that sudden movement, the girl sitting bolt upright all in a rush. And it wasn't fair – to either of them, perhaps: she might not have deserved it, but Grace did think she'd earned it, and she'd almost argued Georgie into reaching out for it – but this had happened all her life, that other people paid the price on her account.

Swiftly now, too swift for interception, that woven, textured shadow went to Kathie.

Then, safely too late, Georgie sat up and screamed.

SEVEN

I thought she was the lucky one.

People did come, at last, too late, as ever. By then Georgie was on her feet: standing in the doorway, holding on to the open door, bellowing for help.

She was holding on because standing up was actually quite hard; she was urgent for help to come because – well, because there was nothing she could do herself.

Grace never had been any good at anything actually useful. Except the swimming, perhaps – and what use had that been, now that she'd actually used it?

Right now, here and now, the girl she'd saved was doing worse than before, and she could do nothing for her. She had no gifts of healing, no training, no power to save. Here and now, all she had was a voice.

Even that was weaker than she liked. She who had screamed delight across terraces, through whole sleeping country houses to be sure that every man in hearing would at least know that Grace was at it again, doing what she was known for, what she was invited for: she barely had the wind to rouse a corridor tonight. And even now she wasn't sure; she harboured some treacherous little Tom-voice that whispered *you're dreaming, you're delirious, you're weak from loss of blood. Lake water and shock have poisoned your mind. You see monsters in the fire, remember? You hear bells underwater and think they cut your wrists. And what, you think you should wake the house because you think some horror vampire creature you spun from the dead baby you couldn't bear is sucking the life out of this other girl instead of you . . .?*

Put like that – well, she didn't have to put it like that, or like anything. She didn't have to make sense, only noise.

She screamed, she bellowed, and people came. Mary came, and the captain and Webb came together; and behind them more people, people she couldn't name, she hadn't met them yet.

Something at least was obviously wrong, beyond this new girl shrieking blue murder in the corridor. Kathie was lying sprawled half across her pallet and half on the bare floor. Someone knocked the light on and she looked appalling, pale and gone, worse than she had in the ruddy firelight below when she was half burned and the other half drowned.

Georgie hadn't been wrong, then, to rouse people. Any more than Mary had been wrong to set a watch; any more than Tom had been right to abandon it. He was here too, running in, squeezing through: too late, and desperately guilty.

It was what happened. Other people suffered, for her fault.

Mary and the captain bent over Kathie, lifted her back into bed, tried to rouse her. Webb was awkward, uncertain, trying to help and only getting in the way: which was unfamiliar ground for him, emphasizing his uncertainty, making things worse. Eventually, Mary snapped at him; the captain spoke more solicitously.

Webb grunted and came away. Came to her instead: blocking her view into the room, turning her around with irresistible hands on her shoulders, drawing her down the corridor.

'Come on, you come with me. Poor Georgie, you are having a bad time of it, aren't you, since you came to us . . .?'

I was having a bad time before this. She didn't say it. There wasn't any need; he knew already. Why would she have come here, else? And the last thing she wanted was to start, even to *start* to explain how everything bad that happened here was all her own fault, it had to be, everything stemmed from her.

She believed it, because it was true, but even so.

Webb took her through a door she'd never have found by herself, hidden in the panelling; down a narrow stair to another floor, and along to another room.

This was his room. She knew it the moment she walked in. Indeed, she knew it beforehand, just from the way he opened the door for her. There had been a hundred men or more – well, boys, a lot of them, but still – and a hundred rooms, and every one of them was different, a new occasion, but even so . . . They might be shy or anxious or embarrassed about showing her their room, they might be proud or excited, they might be utterly offhand; it didn't matter. There was still that sense of a passport issued and a boundary crossed. It might be by invitation rather than invasion, she might be utterly and thrillingly welcome there, and even so. She was a female entering male territory, his. It was always an occasion.

Even here, even in the middle of the night, in crisis. He opened the door for her; the light was already burning. She stepped inside.

And stood looking for a moment, as she always did, just to see what she could learn. What his room had to say about him. It was often more revealing than what a man would say about himself.

She used to use that information for herself, what little benefit – less and less, these days – she could scrape up. Mostly that used to mean money. It still did, she supposed, even here. *Money's not an issue*, but of course it was for her, and she was doing a job of work for Tony. This was what she'd be paid for if she got it right. It was quite hard to remember that in all the dizzy strangeness of the place; she felt more like a supplicant than a spy, when she didn't feel like a victim or a heroine, both.

And when she thought about making Tony happy, it wasn't about the money, much.

Right now she wasn't thinking about Tony much at all. Webb's room, and Webb himself standing right behind her, above her, as he drew the door closed at their backs; and there was his bed under the window, a mattress on the floor like her own, with the covers thrown back as he must have scrambled out of it, some of yesterday's clothes still scattered where he hadn't scrambled into them. He was wearing jeans and nothing, bare-chested and barefoot with his hair caught back in a ponytail for the night, and she said, 'I thought you weren't supposed to sleep alone?'

He looked down at her and laughed and said, 'You know, most girls would blush when they said that. Or a second later, more likely, when they realized what they'd said.'

'I . . . don't blush much.' But that was Grace, not Georgie talking. It was wrong; of course Georgie was a blusher. Nice English girl in trouble, of course she was. But she couldn't fake that, and she couldn't make it true: only hang her head and hope he'd hear it as a lie and take the blush itself for granted.

She wasn't sure that Webb took much for granted. He was too careful.

Still: he laid a hand flat against her shoulder and steered her towards the bed, while she felt curiously grateful for the worn cotton grandad shirt she seemed to be wearing for a nightie, which was certainly not her own and she couldn't quite remember putting on. Mostly, she didn't bother with nightwear. She liked to be a little shocking, and she didn't really see the point of clothes in bed. They only got in the way. She liked to feel a man's bare skin against her own; it told her things, the same way that his room did. Different things from what he said himself.

'It's true,' Webb said, 'we're really not supposed to have our private spaces – but this is where I work, it's not a bedroom. Sometimes the work gets on top of me, though, there's so much to do I can barely take a break; and then it makes sense to have a bed in here that I can crash on for a few hours. Leonard doesn't mind, so long as I don't treat it like a privilege. It's a tool, is all. This is how I contribute best to the family.'

And, what, you don't ever share it with anybody else, this tool, this room with a bed and a door and a key in the lock?

Not that he'd need to, of course. If they wanted to shag, he and Kathie, there were rooms for that. But this was inescapably his own room. Everything here said so: his things on the floor; his papers on the desk; his maps and plans and pictures on the wall.

She wanted to look at those more closely, but she'd rather he wasn't watching while she snooped.

'I'm sorry,' she said, 'I thought you were taking me somewhere I could sleep . . .?'

'I am,' he said. 'I have. You can. Oh, not with me, don't look so wide-eyed awkward.' He was laughing down at her from only inches, almost an open invitation whatever his words were saying. 'I'm not about to seduce a girl on a night like this, when she's been through so much already. Besides, Kathie's my girl. Didn't you know? But if you're not too fussy about the sheets, you can use my bed for the rest of the night.

I won't be needing it any more.' Whatever had happened to Kathie, he meant to be right there at her side.

I'm sorry my nightmare came and ate her instead of me. I'm sorry . . .

She should let him go, then, pronto. Then she'd be free to nose among his things. Only she started shaking, a little, when she only thought about that scene upstairs: the girl fallen back into unconsciousness, fallen half out of bed and utterly into the dark. Her own personal dark, the emptiness of Grace. She really didn't want to be left alone with that guilt, but she had no way to say so; only, 'Wouldn't you be better here, just for a bit? If this is where you work? It'd settle you down, at least . . .' *Sit at the desk there, do whatever it is you do, I'd find that comforting. I could sleep, I think, maybe, if there was just another presence in the room.* No doors, no walls between them. She had more sympathy with Leonard than she knew; she almost asked to go up to a dormitory, to sleep in with everyone else, as everyone else was doing.

She didn't want to be picked out, set apart. That was the last thing.

She couldn't ever have what she actually wanted. That was the first thing, the rule of her life.

He said, 'My work is everywhere, love. Wherever I am, there's work for me. This is where I come when everything else will let me, it's my refuge; but I'll watch over Kathie the rest of this night. You can sleep easy, undisturbed. That's why I want to put you here, because no one's going to come in looking for either one of us. There aren't many safe spaces in the house; this is one of the few. When that door's shut, people steer clear. So go on, get your head down. I'm going to sit right here –' turning the desk chair around to face her and doing just that, emphatically, just the thing she wanted – 'and watch until you're asleep, the way I should have been watching over you upstairs. Whatever's happened, I ought to have been there, and I'm sorry I wasn't. I don't know what happened to Tom; he said he'd sit in for me but obviously he didn't.' A distracted frown promised trouble for Tom.

She was curious herself, what had taken him away, but she

didn't want to see him disciplined. Whatever they had in
the way of discipline, these people . . .

She said, 'He was there, I remember, I spoke to him – only
I fell asleep, and then he wasn't . . .' It wasn't much of a defence,
but defence never worked anyway. The prosecution always won;
that was how the system worked. How it looked after itself.

He said, 'Well. I'll ask. I'd like to know. But it doesn't
matter now. I don't suppose he could have done anything
anyway, except fetch help and save you having to scream your
head off. Bed now, you. You look dreadful, all eyes. Like
piss-holes in the snow.'

'Oh, thanks . . .' That was automatic; so was the face she
made, little-girl rudeness, sticking her tongue out at him. It
was the kind of thing her old men enjoyed, Kensington suits
puffing cigars and dressing her up in baby-doll outfits,
expecting her to behave to suit. She was too tired and shaken
to be right tonight, to be Georgie.

She didn't think he'd noticed. He just smiled, a little, and
sat waiting, the epitome of patience. After a minute, she slithered obediently into his bed.

Her body seemed to fit naturally into the dent he'd left. It
was still warm, and it smelled pleasantly of male occupation.
She pulled his blankets in under her chin and blinked up at him.

'Close your eyes,' he said.

She might have been mulish and refused. She might have
been foolish, little-girl stubborn, demanding stories; she might
have been all Grace, trying to lure him in with her: 'Just for
a while, just for company.' But she seemed to have rediscovered Georgie; or else she was just glad to give over control
for a while, to do as she was told for once; or else she was
just too tired to do anything else.

She closed her eyes and didn't hear it when he left the room.
Her body had remembered just how much it favoured lying
still and warm and silent; her conscious mind had left the
room already.

True to Webb's word, no one came to wake her before the
sun did, striking down through a gap between closed shutters,
sliding over her face like a hot slow feather.

She opened her eyes on a sneeze, closed them indignantly, couldn't recapture either the dream or the sleep that she had lost both together. Accepted reluctantly that she was awake, then, and took a moment to work out where.

Only a moment: too much had happened, too quickly. She felt already as though she'd been here too long. A sensible girl would be packing already, heading out. Heading home.

But Tony would be unhappy, and none of her questions would be answered let alone his, and – well, Grace had never been a sensible girl. It was a point of honour, almost.

And she was alone, in what might or might not be Webb's bedroom but was most certainly his office; and sooner or later he was going to come and check on her, so her best chance for snooping was right now.

Out of bed, then, and straight over to that desk. Webb had a scarily organized mind; she could tell that just by looking. Box files, folders, a Rolodex – a hippy with a Rolodex! – and ledgers. Accounting ledgers, and a daily diary, and what seemed to be copies of every letter he sent out in response to the letters he'd received, and . . .

Really, it was easier to look at the wall. And more interesting, unless that only meant less scary. She could look at the wall and not have to think, not have to play detective: though it was still clearly important and probably did still need thinking about. Here was a map of the world, and here all around it and overlying the edges of it were postcards pinned up, and a thread of one colour or another ran from each postcard to a point on the map, where it was twined around a drawing pin. Presumably the pins marked the place the card had come from. It was all very sweet and a little bit obsessive and very male, she thought, boy all through. Only, it seemed too young for Webb, the sort of decoration she'd expect in her twelve-year-old cousin's bedroom, if he had pen pals across the world. It wasn't unlikely; the last she heard, he was collecting stamps. But that had been a while ago. Maybe he would have moved on; maybe he was collecting rock and roll albums by now, with girls on the side. Maybe he wasn't even twelve any more, he might be older. She hadn't really been paying attention, this last year or two. But then, she'd had no cause to. His mother had made it perfectly clear, *publicly* clear that Grace was not to see her precious boy again, not corrupt him with gifts, not taint his pure innocence with words or kisses from her sullied mouth.

It hurt, but she could live with it. Everything hurt, and here she was, still alive. Despite her best efforts.

Maybe the house would help out there. Webb had saved her, last night, maybe; but Webb wouldn't always be around.

Perhaps he wouldn't always be willing. If he ever understood what she was here for, who had sent her, who she really was – perhaps next time he'd leave her to sink.

She might be grateful. Kick a bit, struggle a bit, sink in the end.

She didn't really understand what she was here for herself, why Tony would really have sent someone so obviously unready for the task. Untrained, untalented. Here she was, making her first clumsy attempt at spying for him, trying to work Webb out; and here she was, getting caught already.

Hearing the door open behind her, when she was leaning over the desk trying to make sense of it all; and Webb was the only one who ever came in here when the door was closed. He'd said that as if it was a guarantee and not a trap. This would be him, then: and apparently she could blush after all as she straightened abruptly, as she turned around to face him, as—

Oh.

Not Webb.

'Hullo, Tom.'

'Hi.' He almost sidled into the room; she couldn't tell behind his hair and beard, but she thought he might be blushing as fiercely as herself. He couldn't be embarrassed, could he, catching her with her legs bare, obviously nothing on under the hem of the shirt? Surely not: it was decent enough, as long on her as her dress of yesterday. And this was a commune, for crying out loud. They shared bathrooms and bedrooms without a second thought. He must be used to nudity; he should be utterly casual about it. So not that, then. But something was making him awkward, coming between them, keeping his eyes from meeting hers . . .

Oh. Yes.

'Are you in trouble,' she asked bluntly – anything to distract him from what she'd been doing, how he'd caught her spying – 'over leaving us last night?'

'Webb had a word with me, yes.' He sounded like a schoolboy, after an unpleasant encounter with a prefect. Those were always worse than teachers. So Grace had been told, at least, time and again, by rich old men nostalgic for their days at public school. At least only a couple of them had been nostalgic for the cane that apparently came part and parcel with such encounters.

Georgie would know all about prefects, from her own experience rather than billiard-room reminiscences and bedroom favours. She smiled sympathetically. 'Poor Tom.'

He shivered, crossed his arms over his chest and rubbed his hands up and down his shoulders. 'Poor Tom's a-cold.'

He was being deliberately theatrical, his turn to offer her distraction. She did at least know that much. Georgie would know what he actually meant, most likely. Grace not, but she bluffed it anyway: changing her smile to a laugh of recognition and then allowing him a change of subject as he clearly didn't want to linger on that one. She turned boldly back to Webb's desk and the wall behind it, and said, 'What is all this?'

If Webb had been as nasty as she guessed, Tom shouldn't mind betraying a few of his secrets. Maybe she was cut out to be a spy after all; maybe she had a natural gift for it, turning one man against another . . .

'That's Webb's web,' he said, coming to stand beside her. 'He says it helps him keep track of all the connections in his head, if he has it spread out on the wall like that. Me, I reckon he just thinks maps are cool.'

'I'm sure you're right. And I expect he is, too. Both ways. But what *is* it? What does that mean, Webb's web?'

'He has this network, places like us all across the world. Well, not like us, exactly. People who think like us – except not that, either. People like the captain, who'll play host to people like us. It's how we're going to change the world.'

'Is it? How's that, then?'

He pulled a face. 'It's really hard to explain to people outside the web. Which is the point, really. You have to be able to think like us, before you can think like us; you have to learn how. And then you can't think any other way, and then it doesn't need explaining.'

'Try anyway. Because, you know. I don't think like you.' *And I don't think you think like Webb either, but if you want to tell me different, go ahead.*

'Right. Webb does this better, because . . . Well, because it's his idea. And because he's Webb, y'know? But he says that if you only think rationally, then war is impossible. Not just wrong, it's *impossible*. You're not a pacifist if you *can't* fight, you're something else, something higher . . . you've evolved. That's what Webb is all about: helping us to think rationally. Which means writing a new language to think in and teaching us how to use it.'

'What, you mean like *1984*?' Grace couldn't often bring books to the conversation, but here she could: memories of school time, where hers must overlap for once with Georgie's, because everybody did Orwell. Days and days of sitting in the back of the class and being bored, but still something seemed to have sunk in. 'Doublethink, and "Peace is War" only the other way around, and stuff like that?'

'No, not like that. Almost exactly not like that.' He shrugged helplessly, then apparently decided that was feeble and tried again. 'In Orwell's book, everything is a lie. Big Brother is lying to the people, and the people are lying to each other, they're lying to themselves. Newspeak is an instrument of lies: that's what it's for, that's all it's capable of. Webb's universal language will be an instrument of truth. It won't be possible to lie. That's the point. If you can't even think a lie, if you can't express it, then how can you conceivably go to war to defend it?'

'What, are all wars started over a lie? Is that what you think?'

'It's what Webb thinks.'

He spoke with all the passion of the convert. Grace had met young men fresh from a Billy Graham crusade, high on Jesus; they had that kind of fervour. It was like a fever; she didn't trust it.

She thought she was starting to get the measure of this place, maybe. It wasn't the captain who'd be the guru here, that wasn't what he was after. He just did what he said: he kept the place ready. Waiting. For Webb, or people like him. Leonard and Mary were the housekeepers, not the guiding lights. They laid the fire and stood back, waited for someone else to set the blaze.

She wondered if Webb was what they wanted, what they thought they'd been waiting for.

'Webb's language,' she said slowly. 'You said it will be this, it will be that. Isn't it finished yet?'

'I don't think it'll ever be finished. As we evolve, so will the language. It'll have to. But at the moment – no, it's not ready. In a way it's barely even begun. He's still putting his teams together. All across the world, see?' He took her back to the map, to all those strings and pins and postcards. 'He's got teams building vocabulary in ashrams in India, grammar in lamaseries in Tibet. Teams in communities in Australia and California and upstate New York. He went all the way around the world, talked to everyone who'd listen, gave them the same basic grounding, all the work he'd done already. Then he left them to it. It's about trust, as much as anything. But if the seeds are right – and they are – there's only one way it can grow. And that's upright, beautiful, incontrovertible . . .

'Somewhere along the way, he met the captain. Leonard wasn't interested in the language, not to get involved – he says he's too old to learn a new trick, and he's been through war already, he knows what he thinks about that, and sometimes it's necessary. I think he's right, he's too old to reshape his mind to fit a new reality.'

'Or he just doesn't want to. Maybe he's happy the way he is.' She thought Leonard seemed pretty sussed already, content with himself and what he was doing here. What he was making happen.

'Maybe. He doesn't know what he's missing. But I suppose no one ever does, do they? Unless they've had it and lost it, I mean. If you haven't tried, you can't know. Like sex, or getting high, or . . . Georgie? Are you OK?'

'Yes. Yes, sure. I'm fine. I'm sorry, I just . . .'

'Oh – you had your baby, and you lost it. Him. And I reminded you. It's for me to be sorry; my words run away with me sometimes. I love this thing so much, I forget to think who I'm talking to. That won't be possible either, in the language.' He tried a smile, weakly, hopefully; she gave him one back, a little wetly. Each of them trying as hard as the other. He was nice, and so was Georgie. And he was unexpectedly sensitive, for a young man; he cottoned on quick, to see what had upset her.

That was useful, maybe. She could use it. Professionally. She sniffed and rubbed her cheeks on her sleeve like a little girl – and then cursed herself silently and looked around for a mirror and couldn't see one, and glanced surreptitiously at her sleeve and no, it was fine, no make-up: that was long gone, what little she'd been wearing yesterday – and dragged them both back determinedly to what mattered. 'So they met in India or wherever, Webb and the captain, and . . .?'

'Yeah. And they kept in touch, and when he was back in this country, Webb came up here to see what Leonard was doing. It was a promise, you see, that there'd be a space for him. A place to work, where he could pull his own group together, and then send them out to spread the word. Words. Spread the words. That's what we like to say, do you see . . . ?'

She did see. She gave him the distracted smile that he was working for, to reassure him that she really was past the tears now; then she peered more closely at the postcards on the wall. If they had pictures, they were pinned up the wrong way round, with the message side facing out into the room; that was what had seemed strange when she'd looked before. That, and perhaps she'd subconsciously recognized from a distance that she didn't recognize the letters they were written in. A close, dense script, angular and regular, exact, nothing like the vague and friendly loops of scribbled English.

'This is headquarters now,' Tom said quietly behind her. 'As soon as Webb was settled, he wrote to all his groups. One by one, they've been replying. In the language, in the bare-bones version that we all have. The postcards are just for fun, really. They're a sort of: "Are you receiving me? Report signal, over," not much more than that. But there are sheafs and sheafs

of paper too, going back and forth. Webb pulls it all together.
He's brilliant, you know. He's a genius.' It was said very
plainly, in that way that hero-worship can be between men. A
girl would have been starry-eyed and romantic, not trying to
hide it. Tom struggled to be matter-of-fact, and gave himself
away completely. 'And then he teaches us. You should come
to class, Georgie.'

'Me? Don't be daft. I can hardly speak English, and I never
got the hang of French. You'll never teach me another
language.'

'Webb could. And the language is . . . natural. Inevitable.
It practically teaches itself.'

He was really eager, but she wasn't here to sit in classes
all day. Grace had left school behind her, just as soon as she
could. Not Georgie, of course, but even so . . .

'I don't think so, Tom. I'd rather be making myself
useful to Leonard and Mary.' And Tony. Using any chance
she had to nose around. Ask questions. In a language she
understood.

One thing Grace had always had going for her, she understood people too. Better than she did English, sometimes. The
silent language of the body: gesture and expression and
the way they held themselves. She read Tom's disappointment,
and Georgie wanted to be kind to him; she said, 'Perhaps you
can show me the shapes of the letters later, and explain how
they work. It looks like code to me. Or maths, or music.'
Anything she couldn't read. Signs to tell her future. She didn't
have a clue where she was going or what she would do next.
Sometimes that terrified her, more than anywhere she'd been
already, or the worst thing she had done. Or the way it followed
her, sat in her head, curled up beside her in the dark.

'It is,' he said. 'It's all those things. You can write music
as easily as words; I'll show you that. When you write your
name, it'll be like you're writing the song of you.' And he
whistled that little trill of notes again, which she'd thought
he had made up just for her. Apparently, it really did say
Georgie. 'Or formulas. You could do engineering in the
language, and know that your buildings were safe and your
machinery would keep working.'

And your milk won't turn sour, and your dogs and your
children will all behave with strangers, and your babies won't
die whatever you do, and . . .

She didn't believe in a perfect society. She didn't believe
that she'd found one. Ruthlessly, she said, 'How's Kathie, do
you know?'

'Oh. I'm not sure that anybody knows. She's . . . not really
awake. Her eyes are open, but she's not there. Not responding.
Acid flashback, maybe? Or she's just got lost, somewhere
inside herself. We tried to call her out, but . . .' A helpless
shrug finished the sentence.

I guess she doesn't speak your language well enough. Or
you don't. That was Grace, being nasty. Seeing true, though:
he was thinking, for sure, that if the language had been perfect
and both of them fluent, he could call and she would come to
him, from wherever her poor mind was wandering.

'She needs a doctor,' Georgie said, anxious and guilty.
Thinking that what Kathie most needed was for last night not
to have happened: not to have danced too close to the fire,
not to have plunged too deep in the water, not above all to
have spent the night with her. Not to have been betrayed,
blindly and absolutely: *her, take her, don't take me . . .*

Was that really what had happened? She wasn't sure, she
couldn't think – but it might as well have been. Deliberately
or otherwise, it came down to the same thing in the end. Kathie
suffered for Grace's fault.

'She's getting one. Mary knows, if Leonard doesn't – she
knows when something's beyond her. We've a doctor in
London; he's something to do with the house. Always has
been, I think. He dates back before the captain found it, at
any rate. Like Cookie, he came with the lease. Webb's gone
to phone him.'

Of course there was no phone in the house. It was one of
her great expectations, that the essentials of life would be
taken from her. But: 'Wouldn't it be quicker just to take Kathie
into town?' It took a day to come up from London, even if
their doctor was prepared to drop everything and come right
now.

'To the cottage hospital? Sweetheart, there's nobody there

who could help. To them she'd just be a drugged-up hippie chick taking up a valuable bed. They'd be horrible to her and horrible to us. And they'd take her anyway, take her away from us and not do her any good, and we can't have that. She's better here. We'll keep her comfortable until the doctor comes. Meanwhile, for my penance, Webb says I have to show you everything you didn't see last night.'

He didn't seem too distressed about it. Georgie thought his real penance had happened already, in that interview with Webb; Grace wanted to think he hadn't been punished enough. She wanted to blame him. *If you'd done what Webb said, if you'd been there in the room, the . . . thing might not have come, wouldn't have come because I wouldn't have been all alone and afraid in the dark like that, I'd have been talking to you; and if it had come anyway you could've protected Kathie from it. From me . . .*

She wanted to, but even she couldn't really make it his fault. She knew what she'd done. Perhaps it was only that she'd been too slow, but even that was a choice. She was quick enough, when a thing was to her benefit. Grace couldn't hide in Georgie.

Even so, she said, 'So where were you last night? Where did you go?'

'Out to see Frank.' He had a mulish cast to his mouth, apologetic but defensive; he still thought it was a reasonable thing to have done, despite the consequences. *Not my fault*, he wanted to say. *I wasn't to know.*

He probably had said exactly that, and it had done him exactly no good whatsoever.

'In the middle of the night?' And *out where?* and *who is Frank, is he Francis, is he the man I'm looking for?* But one of those questions was unaskable and the other could wait.

'Yes. He doesn't sleep much, and he doesn't like to be alone all night.'

'I thought nobody was ever alone here?'

'Nobody should be. But Frank won't come into the house. We usually go out to him, one of us or some of us, at some point, just to scare his spooks away; and I wanted to ask him not to ring the bell, if it upsets you.'

'Oh, what? But – no, you can't upset the whole house, just for me . . .'

'Of course we can. We could, if we had to. This is a community; we take care of our people. But it won't upset anything, not to use the bell. It won't upset Frank. I'll take you to him, you'll see.'

'Can you take me to a bathroom first?' Even dressed as she was, even knowing there might be men in there, that was suddenly rather urgent. 'And find me something to wear?'

Webb says I have to show you everything, but actually that only seemed to mean the things that Tom found interesting, which mostly meant things outside the house. There were dormitories in the attics that she hadn't seen yet, there was a whole wing she hadn't even looked in; these people fitted this house about as well as these clothes fitted her. A woollen shirt and a long plain skirt: rough to look at, and rough on her skin. She didn't quite understand why she couldn't have pretty Indian cottons, though she was grateful not to have bells on the hem. Shifting her shoulders uncomfortably within the coarse fabric, clenching her toes to keep simple handmade sandals on her feet, she felt as though she'd been swallowed by some over-earnest primitive religion.

When she asked about the other wing, Tom shrugged. 'Just rooms we don't use yet, mostly. We'll need them when the language spreads, when people want to come here from all over. Leonard thinks they'll come for other reasons too, but it'll be the language more than anything. Come on, I want to show you the gardens.'

'It needs a better name,' she said.

'What?'

'The language. What's it actually called? What do you call it?'

'The rational language, the universal language . . .' He seemed at a loss. 'It doesn't have a name. Why would it need a name?'

'Because it's new, because you need to sell it. You're excited, I can see that, but it doesn't sound exciting.'

He was shaking his head, bewildered. 'You're not getting

it; it's not like that. It's not a commodity that we have to sell. Once people understand, it'll sell itself.'

'You're the one who doesn't get it. You need to sell it to people who *don't* understand, who haven't learned about it, who don't dig languages or hippies or communes or peace or politics. It needs to have a name.'

'Oh, I don't know. Talk to Webb.'

She didn't want to talk to Webb. Nor did Tom want her to, she thought. He was happy enough to talk about Webb, but not to hand her over; he wanted to have her to himself. It was quite sweet, and obligingly obvious.

In perfect accord, then, they came out of the house and crossed the yard behind. Here was the arch through to the stable yard, below the stopped clock; she suppressed a shudder and tried not to cradle her wrist. No bells rang out, nothing happened, she didn't start to bleed.

'Welcome to the Museum of Failed Endeavour,' Tom said as they came out into enclosed sunshine on cobbles.

'I'm sorry?' She was being idiotic herself, she knew, looking about for curious horses and a dungheap. She'd stayed in too many great houses, swept through too many stable yards in too many sports cars; expensive motors and expensive beasts were still what she expected, even while her head knew perfectly well that there were no horses here, and no sports cars either.

Even so: she was being idiotic, but he was incomprehensible.

He grinned. 'That's what Webb calls it.' So naturally it was what he called it too. 'Well, he uses our own word; that's a translation, but it's close enough. We're all interested in self-sufficiency here. A place this large, it has to feed itself and more, better. It needs to contribute to the wider community. We need to earn our place. We do voluntary work in the neighbourhood, and we make things for sale or to give away. Simple, wholesome things. Craft things. At least, we try. People have ideas, and this is where they come to try them out. Oftentimes, this is where they stay . . .'

Proper stable doors led to workrooms, rather than proper stable stalls. No straw on the floor, no tack hung on nails on the walls. Instead, old reclaimed machinery stood on bare and dusty stone. She stood looking at a giant wooden corkscrew, and knew that it couldn't possibly actually be a giant wooden corkscrew, and said, 'What is it?'

He was almost laughing now, but not at her. At his friends, his housemates, his community: almost at himself. 'It's a cider press.'

'Is it?' She thought about that for a moment, and found an obvious other question. 'Where do you get the apples from?' As far as she knew, apple country was the other end of England. She'd walked in orchards with lordlings and generals' sons and eager politicians, she'd watched young men gather wind-falls and seen urchins scrumping in the trees and scrambling over walls to get away; but those had been all in Devon and Somerset and Dorset.

Now he was laughing aloud. 'Quick, aren't you? Yeah, we had to buy the apples in. Even if we could grow them here, if we planted an orchard, it'd be years before we had fruit. Decades, maybe. And I don't think the ones we bought were the right sort. Anyway, the cider tasted foul. If you want to try it, there are bottles and bottles in the old still-room, back in the house. We can't throw it away, but we sure can't sell it. We keep trying to hide it in the dinner. If there's a nasty aftertaste one night, that's because another bottle's gone into the stew.'

The next door down stood wide, and the space inside was occupied. She didn't go in, only peered from the doorway: shifting lights and busy shadows; an old tin bath raised up on bricks over a trough of flame. The smell of paraffin, and – 'Oh! Candles!'

Long dipped tapers hung in pairs, in colourful tangles on the walls.

'It's almost our only successful industry,' Tom said. 'One of these days they'll burn down the stable block, but in the meantime we have light for ourselves and more that we can sell at market. It pays for itself, at least. I don't think it actually makes a profit, but it keeps the electricity bill down.'

And they enjoyed it, clearly, those people in there: felt

themselves useful, doing their bit. She remembered what Leonard had said about that, and she still thought they were like children, playing with wax and string and fire. They wanted her to come in; they wanted to show her what they did; they wanted her to join them. She backed away from their welcome, *not what I'm looking for, no.*

The next stable held woodturning tools, lathes and chisels and mallets in racks. No people.

'I think they've given up,' Tom said. 'Rick and Paulie thought they could make plates and goblets and candlesticks, but apparently it's quite hard.' Indeed, the work gathering dust on the bench bore witness: split and misshapen pieces, bowls and cups that looked more like they'd been hacked with blunt edges from twisted trees. 'I think it needs a decade of practice, and they didn't give it a month. They're off in the woods now, gathering dead timber for Frank.'

'Why does Frank . . .?' *And who is he, and is he who I'm looking for? And will he want to be found?*

'Charcoal,' Tom said. 'It's his thing; he makes charcoal. It's all right, Cookie keeps an eye on him. He won't let anyone burn down the woods.'

She had no idea how charcoal was made, or really what it was for. They used to draw with it at school, but she didn't think he meant those long neat sticks that would snap in a moment in careless childish fingers. People burned it, she did know that, but she wasn't quite sure why.

This wasn't the time to ask. Here was another workshop, where they did basket-weaving and made willow hurdles and wanted to learn how to thatch. She wasn't sure there was any thatch up here in the north, but that wasn't going to stop them. An intense man with a pale wispy beard and vivid eyes told her it was the finest way to roof, the only honest way to roof, a tradition that dated back to earliest times. The passion for slate had ruined the countryside, he said, and ruined the villages of England too. The cities could look after themselves, apparently; they were beyond hope and deserved whatever they did to themselves – self-scarring, he called them – but the villages should have been protected and were not, but could still be recovered. If people would only learn to live under thatch . . .

Tom rescued her, quite bluntly. 'Sorry about that. People get passionate here. Cob's safe to be passionate about thatch; nobody's ever going to let him rip their good weatherproof roof off and sleep under reeds instead.'

'Does he sleep under reeds himself?'

'No, of course not. He sleeps in the dorms with the rest of us. Come on now. I really do want you to see the garden.'

The garden was his passion. Along with Webb and the logical language, of course: but this was something Tom could show off, legitimately his own. He led her down an unexpected passage in the far corner of the stable yard, and here at the end was a dungheap and a narrow wooden gate in a wall beyond; lift the latch and step through and it was almost like Narnia, almost another world.

It was a walled kitchen garden, as four-square as the stable yard, but everything there had been messy, dirty, decaying almost as she watched. Here was order, neatness, regularity, success. Cabbages and cauliflowers and leeks marched in regimented rows, vigorous and thriving; the dark soil between was free of weeds, freshly watered, freshly turned. It reminded her of her father's allotment, her ritual Sunday visits – except that small patch of council land had always been a trial to him, a duty, sheer effort. This was vast in comparison, and a labour of love.

Tom took her up and down the rows and introduced her to his peas and beans in their pyramids of hazel, his raspberry-canes and strawberry beds, his solid swedes and turnips and his potatoes in their mounds. More and more, celery and salsify and: 'This will be asparagus, it will, you'll see. Three years, we'll have our own asparagus.'

Three years, she wouldn't be here. She hoped to God she wouldn't be here. She didn't say so.

After the vegetables came the herb beds, and the same in squads of pots: cuttings of lavender and rosemary and thyme and tarragon, dozens and dozens of them, rank after rank. 'We sell these too, at the weekly market. They're really popular.' And he was really proud.

Lastly his joy, all along the north wall, where it would catch all the sun that England gave it: 'We call it the orangery, but it's not really, it's a peach house. Frank found the account books somewhere, so we know. There aren't any peaches yet, I just use it for a greenhouse and a potting shed, but all the pipework's still here for the steam heat, and Cookie's checked the boiler out; he says the system's sound. The stove's in that hut in the corner there, where I keep my tools. Next year, I'll plant peach trees . . .'

This year, he'd spent every moment he could spare in replacing broken panes and repainting the framework, so that the peach house was a gleaming white monument that ran all the length of the wall. It was hot in there under the sun's hammer, and she wasn't sure she liked it. She praised it for his sake, but was glad to leave.

Still glad when he took her at last out of his wonderland, through a gate of open ironwork on to a path that led up into the woods. Now she was working for Tony, going to find Frank.

A stream ran across the path, a narrow freshet with bare mud banks, too small to bridge and too steep-sided to allow stepping stones. Tom leaped across, barefoot and casual; then he turned back, held a hand out. 'Can you jump?'

Obviously, jumping was what people did; the mud bore many proofs. If she tried it in these sandals, she'd lose them and probably slip backward down the bank and into the water, flailing for his helpless hand. On another day in other company, Grace would have done that regardless, gone with a shriek and risen up dripping, cackling with laughter like a child, deliberately childish to amuse the man she was with.

Here, today, she slipped off the sandals and hooked the fingers of one hand through the woven straps, tested the mud cautiously beneath her feet, tensed, and leaped.

And landed, cool damp mud absorbing the shock of it, oozing between her toes as they dug for grip. Tom's hand was there but she didn't take it, didn't need it. She found her own balance, lifted her face triumphantly, smiling, happy – and the phrase was there in her head already, *like a child*, and it turned itself unexpectedly into a question.

'Why aren't there any children here, Tom?' There should have been small bare footprints among the adults', rocks and branches in the water from where muddy hands had tried to dam the flow. A rope swing hanging from a tree. There really should be a pack of giggling, chasing children, here and everywhere: all over the house, heedless and hungry and beloved, cared for by everyone indiscriminately. That was her notion of a hippy ideal, and she couldn't believe she was alone in that. Not here, of all places. She was just as glad not to have children about her, but she didn't understand it.

'Cookie won't have them on the property. That's about the only rule he has.'

'*Cookie* won't have them?'

'That's right. He says this would be a bad house for children, and that's that.'

She wanted to ask why the janitor got to make the rules, but there was a smell of smoke in the air, sudden distraction. And the path turned, and here was a clearing, with more than a swirling smoke to surprise her. There was a great turfed mound leaking smoke here and there between the turfs, like a man leaking smoke between his teeth. The smoke rose white and thin, drawing her eyes up to where an old stone tower reached higher than the trees. It looked like a church tower in miniature, plain and strong, only that the church was in ruins now and only its tower was left to point like an accusing finger at an abandoning god.

Among the half-fallen walls and heaped rubble of its ruin, someone had built himself a home. It looked half like yesterday's bonfire before the flame: a shapeless structure of salvaged planks and doors, covered over in places with tarpaulin and in places with more turfs, a green and growing roof.

'Hey, Frank! Are you in?'

'And where else would I be?'

Tom's call produced first a sour response, a voice that seemed almost to rise from the earth itself, and then a figure that did the same. He emerged like something dark and dangerous from an unexpected hole between one door and the next, which startled her almost more than anything: if a man built his house with doors, surely one of them should open?

But these doors were walls, apparently, and this man was as mad as his house, or looked it. Grimy and wild-eyed, he wore a suit that Grace could recognize as Savile Row, though it was caked in mud; his feet beneath it were as bare as theirs, as bare as his chest where the jacket hung open because the buttons were long gone.

The trouser buttons too – the fly was gaping wide. She did try not to look.

'Frank, this is Georgie. She's our new arrival.'

'Oh, aye. The girl who can't hear bells, or else they make her bleed.'

Now she sounded mad, and she hadn't even said anything yet. She glowered at Tom for giving away her secrets, but he didn't get the message; he was most likely pleased with himself for being so thoughtful, bringing the problem to the source.

The source was looking at her almost hungrily; she couldn't meet his eyes. Instead, her gaze slid back to that sudden tower, and she said, almost without meaning to, 'Is that where the bell is?'

'That's right, aye. It's not the original, mind; that went when the chapel went, fire and fury. Story says the old bell's at the bottom of the lake.'

Heavy sonorous striking through the water, cutting and cutting. Making her bleed. She believed it immediately, and wanted to know the story without actually wanting to hear it, for fear that simple talk of bells might open up her hurts again.

Tom said, 'Well, you're the man for stories, Frank. That's why I brought Georgie to meet you, so that you could tell her about the house.'

He thought it was a kindness, to both of them. She thought it a cruelty, each to each.

Frank said, 'The house? I don't like to talk about the house. I won't go in there now, and nor should you. Nor should anyone. There are spirits abroad in that house. I have them bring my meals to me here. You should go home, young lady.'

'I don't have a home to go to.' Grace tried to say that as a lie, as part of Georgie's story: only that it felt suddenly and immediately true. She had a flat to go to, nothing like a home.

Into the silence that followed, she added, 'I want to stay here,' which was a lie pure and simple, just to remind her of her purpose.

Tom brightened abruptly, and she could have cursed herself, but apparently she didn't need to. Frank said, 'That house is cursed,' and he might sound as mad as he looked but she thought he was right none the less. Except that he thought he could take shelter in the woods, and she remembered last night when she arrived and something – nothing – had been coming for her through the trees, and she thought he wasn't at all safe out here, on his own in his troglodyte life.

She said, 'Cursed how?' and he shook his head.

It was Tom who had to answer her, saying, 'Frank knows more than any of us about the house. More than Cookie, even. He vanished into the library as soon as he arrived, pretty much, and researched all its history. If there are ghosts anywhere, Frank knows where to find them.'

'There are ghosts everywhere,' Frank said. 'The house gives them shelter, but they don't belong there. People fetch them in.'

The sucking shape that was her own unborn child, dead before he came into the world, growing in the shadows, getting bigger, getting worse. He was right, she was sure.

A breeze stirred the smoke, wrapped a thin sheet of it around them, made her cough.

Frank stretched his nostrils and inhaled contentedly. 'Aye,' he said. 'That's a good burn.'

'Is that . . . how you make charcoal?'

'In a clamp, aye. Build the logs around a chimney, high and tidy; turf it over and drop lighted coals down the chimney to make a fire at the bottom, low and slow. Then the collier's task is to watch it, five days and nights. If the coat cracks, if air gets in, it'll burn up and all your work is wasted.' Even as he spoke he was stalking around the mound, slapping fresh damp earth from a bucket wherever he thought too much smoke was oozing out.

'Five days and nights – and just you to watch it?'

'Aye. It's a lonely life.' But he relished that, had set himself deliberately apart here. And people came out to talk to him, Tom had said so; he wasn't really that solitary.

But: 'What about sleep, how do you manage?' No clocks, so he couldn't have an alarm to wake him up.

'Oh, I don't. I daren't. Not during a burn. If a log shifts and tears the turf, it could all be gone in a flare. I'm always here, always watchful.'

'We come out to keep you company, Frank.' Tom sounded almost indignant. 'You know you could sleep while we watched . . .'

'You kids? I'll not trust you. You'll get high, or get heavy with each other, and not notice when the whole clamp collapses and sets the wood ablaze. No, I've learned, it has to be me. You're welcome to sit with me, help me stay awake, I'm grateful for that – but I'll watch my own fires every time.'

Five days, five nights without sleep. Time and time again. No wonder he looked half mad. No wonder if he *was* half mad. She'd known people do that at weekend house-parties, never go to bed at all between Friday and Monday, but only with the help of pharmaceuticals, and they were mostly incoherent by the end.

She thought he was Tony's missing journalist, he must be; she just wasn't at all sure that he'd remember it.

Tentatively, she said, 'So where are you from, Frank, what did you do before—?'

And wasn't at all surprised to be cut off, before she'd even found an end to her question: 'You don't ask that, lass. Not ever, not of anyone. We're here now. Someone wants to tell you, fine, but you don't ever ask.'

It was like being in prison, then. She'd thought it might be. People might tell you, but you never asked what they'd done to put them there.

With her, of course, no one had ever had to ask. They all read the papers; they all knew already.

Frank was looking at her now with something more than speculation in his eyes. Something knowing. He might not remember his own past, but he might remember hers. Her face, her real name. A Fleet Street journalist, working for a red top – for Tony's red top, above all: what could be more likely? A rational man might tell himself that he was wrong, that there was no possibility of Grace Harley being here, but this man wasn't rational. There was nothing to stop him leaping to insane conclusions that did just happen to be true.

Hastily, she said, 'What's that you were saying about the
old chapel here burning down? And the bell in the lake?' It
was the last story she wanted to hear, but the first thing she
thought of, sitting high in her memory, right there, just as
she sat here on the chapel's old stones right in the shadow of
its tower, under the mouth of its dreadful bell.

He said, 'Back in the day, in the seventeenth century, the
master of the house had his private chapel out here, with a
priest's house by. Why he didn't want him in D'Espérance
itself – or why the man wouldn't go, more likely – I'm not
clear. There is no record, though I do have my suspicions. I
think he was a wise man, though he did a foolish thing.
Anyway, here he was, in place and in authority; and the master
of the house was murdered. By his wife, it may have been,
or by his housekeeper; there are different tales told. By a
woman, though. And that was petty treason either way, the
murder of her lawful master by a subordinate, wife or servant
as she was. A man would have been drawn and hanged; for a
woman, she must be burned at the stake. And so she was, at
the priest's order and at the hands of the house servants, by the
waterside here, and her remains flung into the lake. There was
no due process, no trial. The local Justice of the Peace
was outraged. He sent his constables to arrest the priest, but
the man was tipped off; he was long gone before they came
for him. His house and the chapel burned that night, though
it's not known who set the fire. As I said, the story has it that
the chapel bell went into the water in chase of its mistress,
and no priest has served here since.'

Her head was full of pictures, then and now: fire here, fire
by the lakeside. A woman in the flames. A woman in flames.
A hand reaching out of flame, to set another girl alight . . .

A bell in the water, endlessly tolling a death that had not
quite happened yet. Endlessly sounding a warning, perhaps,
like church bells in the war: *beware, beware! Fear! Fire! Foes!*
Trying to tell a world that would not listen how she was not
dead yet, how her spirit still lingered somewhere between the
fire and the water, how she could still snatch out at the
heedless.

Doing that good work, a word to the wise, to any who could

hear – and still finding time to punish Grace, that relentless bell, to slash her stitches and cut her wrist to the bone. It should warn the world, maybe. Have her burned too. She didn't quite know what petty treason was, but killing your own baby had to count, surely? And dying in a fire, horrible, maybe that would finally be punishment enough.

Maybe she should have thrown herself into the flames last night, instead of the water. Tried to find the lady. If she'd known she was in a three-card monte – the woman in the flames, the bell beneath the water, her baby dead and everywhere and coming – she might have done just that. She knew she couldn't win.

Here came an interruption: a boy in corduroy, jacket and jeans, running easily up the path. She shouldn't call him a boy, perhaps, he was maybe her own age, but oh, he looked so young in his tangled hair and his tangled innocence. He nodded to her dispassionately, said something to Tom that she couldn't understand, couldn't even disentangle the complex sounds of it enough to write them out in her head; when he said the same thing to Frank, he won himself no more than a scowl and a curse.

'Speak English, damn you, if you don't have the Gaelic! I've none of your heathen tongue and do not want it.'

'Oh, come on, Frank. You've learned that much. The captain says it's time for lunch.' And he repeated the phrase, slowly and clearly, still unintelligibly.

Frank snorted and turned towards the bell tower, towards the bell rope, towards the bell: and then remembered, and glanced at her, and snorted, and ducked back inside his subterranean home.

And came out with a long straight coach-horn, set it to his lips and blew a blast – to the north, she thought – and then another to each of the other points of the compass.

Tom looked smug as echoes rang back down the valley. His idea, to save her the cutting bell – or at least to save her imagining, as he thought, that the bell was cutting at her.

She could be grateful, even if he thought it was all her imagination. The horn couldn't scratch her. All it did was make her feel hungry, thinking about last night's stew and the long night since, all that had happened, the shock and horror of it and the skipped suggestion of breakfast.

They made a little party, then, leaving Frank and going back down to the house: she and Tom and this new boy – Leaf, he called himself – and he only wanted to talk to Tom and only in that language, which left her feeling deliberately cut out of the conversation. That was nothing new. Half the men she'd known for half her life had done that as a matter of course, treating her as furniture or wallpaper or pudding. It was more or less what she expected, but not here. Oddly, here it made her furious.

As they bypassed the walled garden and came back through the stable yard, she let the two young men drift ahead of her: a step or two, and then a yard or two, then further. Heads down, intent on what they were doing – walking, yes, and talking too, and in their private code which needed concentration and paid it back with delight: *how clever we are, and how different!* – neither one of them noticed they were leaving her behind. They walked out under the shadow of the archway into the further sunlight of the courtyard, and neither one of them noticed that she wasn't even following them any longer.

She stood still and watched them go, just in case; then she turned and walked quickly out of sight. Sooner or later, one of them was going to notice she was gone. Tom, she thought, she hoped. He'd come back to look for her. She thought, she hoped. But she wanted him to find her doing something, something else, not waiting for him to remember her.

She was being adolescent, she knew – it was the kind of behaviour that got her into trouble at school, often and often, *we don't like attention-seeking here, missy* – but even so. She did it anyway. Being honest with herself – Grace, perhaps, being honest with Georgie, because why not? – she did absolutely want Tom's attention. And expected it, had come to expect it, because he'd given her so much of it already. And would probably have expected it in any case, because he was a young man and that was what they did, they paid attention to her. Because she was a woman, or because she was Grace Harley, or because she was available or famous or any reason else. There always was a reason.

In the meantime, though, she did also want to make Tony happy. That was what she did, because she was Grace Harley, because he was Tony. It was very simple, really.

She thought she had found his missing journo, and that was good. She thought Frank was at least halfway mad, and something in this house had made him that way. That was not so good, at least for Frank. For Tony, it might make a story; that was good. If she could find it. *Journo Goes Mad* was not a story. *Commune Drives our Undercover Reporter Crazy* might be, but she'd need more than that. She'd need to find out why and how.

And not be driven crazy herself in the meantime. And not just bleed and bleed and be a stranger.

She didn't want to walk into the house right behind the boys, because Tom might or might not remember about the bell waiting just inside the door there, he might or might not think about her, but Leaf knew nothing. He'd reach out and strike it, twice and twice; and every stroke would cut her, and she'd bleed and bleed.

Instead she cut herself away like this, and Tom would come to find her. By himself. They'd be alone again, because everybody at work in the yard here had gone to lunch; and she'd snare him in the shadows, half tremulous Georgie and half impetuous Grace. Nothing reckless, nothing to scare him away: just her arms around his neck and a nervous kiss like a nice girl, her not-very-girlish body warm and suggestive against his, cooperative under his hands if he dared to reach to touch. Whatever more came later, that would be fine. Right now she wanted him wanting her, thinking about her, not focused on his precious language. Not at all. If she was a spy, he was her double agent, and she wanted to turn him. Here and now.

Actually, she thought he was half turned already, only he hadn't realized it yet. She just needed to make things clear.

Boys could be very dim. Give her a man, every time – except this time. She wouldn't try to turn Webb. She might let him seduce her while Kathie lay adrift, but that would be a different thing, another kind of spying.

Another world, and at least his pillow talk wouldn't be in his secret language.

Where to let Tom find her, now? There was the cider press, but that was a failure. The same for the woodturning workshop. Those were all the wrong associations.

The Museum of Failed Endeavour, did Webb call this place? Well, she wasn't going to fail in her endeavours. Not this time. *Tony love, I've got your story for you. And, look, it's not about me this time, except in a good way . . .*

There was the bread oven, a cube of brick with a heap of wood beside – but she'd been rude about the bread and hadn't eaten it. Again, the wrong story.

The candle-making workshop, though: candles were good. Useful to the house, and profitable too. *I wanted to help, Tom, so I came in here to volunteer: only there's no one around. I'll come back another time. After lunch. Only – well, I don't want to go into lunch with everyone else, they'll all be ringing that damn bell as they come, so I thought I'd hang back. Thanks for coming to find me. You're really sweet, you know that . . .? Oh, come here.*

That would do it. She supposed there must be boys who could resist her, but Tom wouldn't prove to be the first of them. Let her once get her fingers in his hair, he'd be hers for the taking. Any way she wanted.

Her wish, his command. *Help me understand this place, Tom love. Tell me everything.* He'd do that, and more. All unwitting, he'd spy for her, be her decoy and her translator, her bodyguard at need. And a friend in need, that too. A friendly body in her bed, a guard against the horrors of the night. There'd be no more running off and leaving her, she'd see to that. It wouldn't be hard.

She stepped inside the workshop, leaving both halves of the stable door wide so that he could find her easily when he came looking, but in the unlit gloom where he wouldn't be so shy, in privacy so he wouldn't be looking over her shoulder to see who else was looking.

She could be smart sometimes, in some things. *Sly*, some people called it. Her.

Gloomy it was in there, but enough light spilled in at her back. Enough to give her a shadow, even, throwing it across the tin bath elevated on its bed of bricks. No fire beneath that now, though the whole space still reeked of paraffin. The bath was about half full of molten wax; on a rack above it, a hundred wicks hung warmly dripping. The candle-makers must only just have left, at the summons of the horn. It was odd to think of the whole house, the whole wide estate this way: people trooping through places just abandoned by other people just ahead. *Mark my footsteps, good my page.* Ghosts and followers – only, she was unsure slightly who the ghosts were. Those who went before, or those who came after?

Or those who never came at all. It wasn't fair, suddenly to find herself thinking of her baby again: but that was life, unfair all down the line. You can never be punished enough.

Not even when still wax stirs all by itself, when ripples run of their own accord.

When flame erupts beneath, from a pool of paraffin that had been out and dead.

When shapes form in that shifting wax, hands that shape themselves and rise and reach for you with long deadly fingers.

When you don't, can't make the effort to pull away out of their reach. When it isn't worth the trouble.

When you almost bend forward, indeed, to make it easy for them to close their hot soft lethal grip around your throat, as you're still thinking *oh, my baby . . .*

EIGHT

Not her baby, though.

These hands were full-sized, mature. Adult.

Even if he was growing, her baby-ghost, he was doing it in true time, being true. Barely a boy yet. Not like this.

These were the hands that had reached from the fire for Kathie. Not her baby; not her ghost.

She didn't have to submit to this.

But there was still nothing in her head, no resistance, only that yearning grief for what she had done, her dead baby. She had no fight in her. She felt those deadly fingers melting into each other, drawing yet more tightly about her neck, dragging her down towards the seething mass of molten wax they rose from; and still she lacked any hint of struggle. Grace would have kicked and screamed against anything but this, which might finally be punishment enough. Georgie would never kick or scream at all; she was too submissive.

It wasn't fair, to drag poor Georgie down, but that was life.

Only, Grace was still thinking about her baby, wanting to make amends; and she might almost be glad to go down into the dark, but it ought to be her own ghost that took her there.

In her head she heard that tolling bell, setting a rhythm that she thought she ought to march to, slow and sombre. These hands were in too much hurry.

She still wasn't fighting, exactly – but her hands had clenched on the edge of the bath, and the heat of it helped her focus. It was almost hot enough to burn; she supposed it would burn if she only held on long enough. If she didn't die of strangulation first as the warm waxy grip tightened and tightened on her throat; if she didn't black out and slump head first into the bath and drown there. If you could drown in wax. If it could get as far as your lungs before it filled your throat like a plug. Drown or choke or strangle, she'd be dead which-ever way it went.

She'd almost wanted that, for so long now. Had thought she did want it, enough to cut her wrist that one time, twice; knew that she deserved it, but – no, not like this. Not for this, for someone else's reasons. When she did go, it should be her baby who fetched her. He was all around this place, everywhere she turned, every time she heard a bell ring; she'd wait for him. A little longer here; she could stand that. She couldn't stand this; it felt like cheating. Like cutting her wrist again, trying to dodge what was due.

She still didn't fight against the ruthless grip on her throat, no.

She set her feet, set her stubborn shoulders. Set her hands and heaved.

One monstrous effort, and she tipped that whole tin bath over.

Tipped it off its firebed of bricks, away from her, so that all the molten wax flooded out across the cool stone floor before the inverted bath landed with a sonorous clang that sounded almost like a bell, that made her almost look around for her baby after all.

Just for a moment, the hands seemed still to cling to her neck. Then there was a wrenching tug and that grip was gone. She looked down dizzily, and there was nothing: no disembodied hands of wax lying revealed on the floor, only a spreading liquid pool.

She stood there foolishly, wheezing, gasping, her own hands lightly at her throat now, touching smooth sore skin while spilled wax lapped around her sandals.

When it was over, it felt suddenly as though everything was over. As though she had no strength to move now, and no reason. She might just stand there until Tom came at last to find her, or the candle-makers all came back from lunch, or came back tomorrow, or . . .

She might, she thought – except that a voice spoke suddenly behind her, to say that someone at least had come already.

'Well done.'

Soft, well spoken, male – but not Tom.

She was far, far beyond being startled now. Curiosity turned her head, slowly, cautious only for her sore neck. At first all she could see was a shadow in the doorway, outlined by light. When he stepped inside, she made him out as much by dress and movement as by his face.

'Cookie.' It was what everybody here called him, so a plague on *Mr Cook*. 'Was that you?'

He was applauding, or at least approving – but that could be the manners of a well-bred enemy, obliged to praise an effective counterstroke. His might have been the hands reaching to choke her, though she couldn't imagine why. Or how. She didn't want to try. She only wanted truth, not understanding.

'No, not me. Nothing of mine. You face your own demons, in D'Espérance.'

She knew that, she'd worked that out already; but she shook her head determinedly. 'That . . . was nothing to do with me. That was Kathie's ghost, not mine.' It was insane, this whole conversation – but she'd had two waxen hands around her throat, and he had seen it. Madness had nowhere to go, in such a world.

He was quiet for a moment, mulling things over. Then he reached out a hand, oddly courtly, like a man helping a woman step across a puddle: 'Come out of that, here, before it sets.'

Her turn to stand on the threshold, then, with the sun on her back, watching as he took his turn in the wax. His work-men's boots were less troubled than her sandals, but she still wasn't sure why he was wading into the stuff, until she saw him kick over the piles of bricks that had held the bath above the flame and stamp one or two of the fallen bricks into shards and dust. After that she was utterly bewildered, until he said, 'I've been telling them for months now that this was unstable. The fire degrades the brick; it was bound to fail. No one's going to think it was overturned deliberately – only that they were lucky this happened when the stable was empty. Now come with me –' stepping out of the wax, stepping over to her, taking her hand in the most sexless way imaginable – 'let's get you cleaned up and sorted out.'

He led her like a child, and she went with him like a child: trusting, bewildered, hurting and hopeful.

*   *   *

Out of the yard and up into the woods again, but not anywhere
near Frank and his desolate chapel. Another path – narrow but
well trodden, as if one man used it over and over – took them
away through the trees and deeper into the valley. She quickly
lost any sense of where she was, in the dim light amid the
tangle of trunks and branches and undergrowth; there was only
the path to say that the house and the road and all the world
lay behind them. She wasn't sure she trusted even that. If
hands could reach from fire or wax, if the stroke of a bell
could cut her flesh, if her dead baby could grow in his own
absence, wait for her, come for her, come and come and come
– then surely paths could shift and shape themselves, lead
people who knew where?

She wanted to ask Cookie exactly what he'd seen, if only
to reassure herself that it really had happened, that she wasn't
gone entirely mad; but her voice came as a croak from her
poor sore throat, and he shook his head. 'Don't try to talk,
not yet. I've something at the house to ease you.'

The house was behind them, unless this path was winding
itself all the way around. That wasn't what he meant. There
was something up ahead: a bulk beyond the trees, a sense of
structure, something built among all this wild growth. They
hadn't come far, or she didn't think so, but her legs were
trembling and her head was dizzy with reaction. Really, she
just wanted to sit down and maybe cry a little. A walk in the
woods with this strange man was the last thing she'd
have looked for, the last thing she would ever have agreed to
if he'd said that straight out. And now here she was stumbling
along behind him, while he kept that soft grip on her wrist
and gave her not a chance to rebel. She was all Georgie anyway,
broken and obedient and desperate to please. Grace was somewhere behind her, out of reach.

The path turned one more time, and here was their goal at
last, that building she'd sensed more than seen. If D'Espérance
was a house, she couldn't call this one, though apparently
Cookie did. Overshadowed in her mind by the great building
at their backs, it was overshadowed all too literally by the
trees around, like a fairy-tale refugee: a little low cottage, slate
roof and ivy walls, with a tended garden behind a picket fence.

Even that was utterly unlike what the big house had to offer, the ordered productivity of Tom's vegetable patch. Here was a profusion of colour: lupins and hollyhocks and irises fighting for height and attention in this unexpected glade.

Oh – is this where you live? It's lovely . . . She really didn't need to ask; there was his van, parked behind the cottage, at this vanishing end of the drive. Georgie would have said it anyway, just to please him; but he'd told her not to talk, so she swallowed down the jagged, difficult words and was glad to do it.

Mute and obliging, she followed him up the garden path and into his home. A narrow stone-flagged hallway; a stairway rising; a door into what ought to be a sitting room, but that was closed. He took her to the kitchen at the back.

'Sit yourself down.'

He wasn't a man who looked for visitors; there was only a single chair in any case, but the small table was set into a corner in a way that wouldn't allow two to sit down together.

She sat anyway and was glad to do it. Glad to fold her hands in her lap just to stop them shaking; glad to sit like a good girl and watch while he gathered up what he thought was good for her.

The table was scrubbed clean, bare but for a tobacco-tin lid that he'd clearly been using as an ashtray. He swept that away and replaced it with a bottle and a little sherry-glass. 'Here, sip this while I warm some soup. It'll soothe your throat.'

She really didn't want to swallow anything, let alone his kindness. His apparent kindness. She knew already that he was not as kind as he seemed. She hadn't forgotten being stranded in the coming dark, with her terror coming for her.

Anyone she knew in London would have offered her brandy, or more likely a brandy cocktail, make a joke of it: 'This is good for shock, isn't it? And fizz is good for anything . . .'

This . . . wasn't that. The bottle was green and old, reused; it didn't have a label to say what might be inside it. Apparently, there was a limit even to Georgie's willingness; she only sat and looked at it while he fussed at the small stove in the chimney breast.

When he glanced back to see her still sitting, sitting still,
trembling still, not making a move else, he tutted aloud. And
strode back across the tiled floor, pulled the cork from the
bottle, poured.

A thick golden liquid flecked with green, the scent of
herbs and sweetness. She made some soft noise with the
air in her mouth – nothing that could scratch or stick in her
throat.

He understood that to be a question. 'This is called metheglin. I make it myself, so I know it's good. Honey from my
own bees, herbs from my garden. Sip it slowly, and when
that's all gone, take more. Two glasses, before you try to talk.'

She lifted the glass, looked at it doubtfully, raised it to her
lips under his stern gaze. Took the least possible sip, barely
more than a breath of vapour – and was astonished at the
flavour that flooded her mouth, rich and complex, sweet and
deep and soothing. Took a proper mouthful and found that
swallowing was an effort, a harshness, but not the pain she
had been dreading – or at least only a dull muscle-pain, nothing
worse. And the second swallow was easier, and then somehow
her glass was empty and she was being good, doing what she
was told, reaching for another.

Cookie grunted, repeated what he'd said about sipping slowly,
and then turned back to his stove, apparently satisfied.

She sipped, and savoured, was happy just to do that. She
wasn't too interested in soup, now that she had this astringent
sweetness on her tongue; she had lost all interest in questions:
what did you see? or *what did it mean?* or *how could that
possibly happen . . .?*

Either she was secretly, unknowingly stoned, or it had
happened. Her sore throat said that it had happened; so did
his abrupt and unexpected care of her. She wasn't really in
any doubt.

Nor, apparently, was she in terror, though the experience
had wanted to kill her. Her terror was another thing, and
deserved, and hadn't come.

Mr Cook left a saucepan heating on the stove, rolled himself
a cigarette and came to perch on the edge of the sink, where
he could watch her through his smoke.

She couldn't tell quite what he was looking for, but again he seemed satisfied. He grunted softly and said, 'D'Espérance can be a hard house, if you come here with baggage – and who doesn't have baggage, these days? For the older ones, it's the war; for you kids, it's whatever you've been up to since. I don't want to know.'

'I remember the war,' she said, though it was only barely true. She remembered the end of it, though mostly what she remembered was being too young to understand and needing to have her memories explained later.

She thought Mr Cook was old enough to have been in the first war, maybe. And wondered about his baggage, and decided not to ask. Those few words just now had been sharp in her throat, made her reach again for the medicine, metheglin. Made her pour herself another glass.

He watched, then took the bottle and corked it. Put it away.

'You kids,' he said, as though it was a revelation. 'You're all greedy these days; you all want to snatch. Nothing's ever enough. But – well, D'Espérance is a hard house, but she's not usually this hard on someone newly come. You're having it rough, and I'd like to know why.'

Because I can never be punished enough. She didn't say so. She sipped at her glass and fidgeted with the cuff of her bandage – no fresh blood, despite the effort of upturning a bathful of wax: that was a relief, late but powerful – and said nothing at all.

He said, 'What have you brought here, missy? You've a secret, and I mean to learn it.' He sounded . . . grim. Not so much like a teacher now; more like a soldier, or a policeman. An officer, either way. She had ample experience of both. Soldiers in the bedroom, policemen – well, everywhere. Prison officers, too. In the prison.

They were relentless, his type, but even so . . . She had no secrets – all her privacies had been paraded over and over again – and even so . . . She still wasn't going to tell him anything that mattered. If he wanted to know about her, he could learn it the way everyone did, all the rest of the country, from the pages of their favourite papers.

She shook her head resolutely. 'It's not me. Not mine.

You – you saw them too, right? Those hands . . . you saw the hands?'

'I saw what I saw.' But he wasn't denying the hands.

She said, 'I saw them before. Last night, reaching for Kathie from the fire. They're nothing to do with me.' *I'm a victim here, just another victim, not responsible* – it was such a rare feeling, she could hardly believe herself that it was true.

He just looked at her: not disbelieving, not yet, only utterly judgemental. Talking more was like pulling a strand of barbed wire from her throat, but this was important. It mattered suddenly, enormously, that he should believe her. She said, 'I was talking to Frank, you know, at his place in the wood –' *not like yours* – 'and he was telling me about a woman who was burned to death here, by the lake. I think it's her. Her ghost. Fire by the water, and there was fire under the wax. It must be her.' *Not me,* she was saying again. *Not my boy.*

'No,' Cookie said flatly. 'That's not what happens here. D'Espérance has no ghosts of its own: only what you bring with you.'

She had brought one of her own, enough for her – but he was a good boy: he wouldn't play with fire, and he wouldn't hurt anybody else. Besides, he was only little yet. She shook her head again, stubborn still. 'Not this. I didn't bring this. It's nothing to do with me.'

'It wants something to do with you. It tried to kill you, just.' Perhaps he was coming round to the idea of believing her, though; he went on, 'Kathie too, you say? Mary told me she was an accident, and unlucky, and perhaps underwater too long.'

'No. I saw – well. What you saw. Hands. Hands of flame, for her.' *And then what came for her later, and that was my fault,* but she still wasn't confessing that.

Her own hands seemed to be shaking. What they called shock, she supposed, delayed reaction. She knew what to do about that, but her glass was empty and he had taken the bottle away.

She might have asked, but he was back at his stove now, busy with ladle and bowl. She wanted more drink, but he brought her soup: silent now, and she couldn't tell if he had accepted what she told him or rejected it entirely, if he thought he was feeding a liar.

She really didn't want soup, except that the steam of it was in her mouth like the perfume of the metheglin, potent, overwhelming. She lifted her head just for a moment, looked at him, said, 'Do you do the cooking for the house too?'

He smiled. Just a little, a thin thing, almost meaningless, but still a smile. 'No,' he said. 'I only taught them a few things.'

She would have bet on that, at least. This bowl of soup looked different, smelled different, and even so: just the smell of it was reminding her of last night's stew.

She said, 'What is this?' – stirring it with her spoon just to raise more steam, to give her mouth something to enjoy while she waited for it to cool. It was too hot for her poor throat right now, and she wasn't going to spoon it up and blow on it. Not here, not under his eye.

'Mushrooms, mostly. What I gathered this morning, with some of last year's ketchup for added flavour. They use the ketchup for stock up at the house; that's probably what you're recognizing.'

She hadn't known till now that you could make ketchup out of mushrooms. Ketchup was bright tomato-red, and you ate it with sausages and worried that it might be fattening. She tried to imagine what he meant: something thick and gloopy, creamy white like mushroom caps or brown like the fins underneath, but sweet and tangy like tomato ketchup. She didn't think there was anything like that in the soup. What there was – what she could smell, even before the temptation grew irresistible and she risked burning her mouth on the first spoonful – was that same darkly savoury flavour she'd found last night. Except that last night's stew had been all root vegetables, and this was all mushroom, and they tasted completely different. Except for that undertone, that bass note that lifted them both.

She'd have liked to say something to him, something about that, but she didn't have the words. Georgie might, but not Grace, and she was all Grace now: reduced, stripped down. Frightened.

Instead of talking she ate, spooning down soup gracelessly, greedily. Every swallow hurt, but even so. She didn't want to stop.

He seemed content just to watch her. And then, when she was done, to chivvy her gently out of his cottage and see her on her way back to the main house. Letting her go alone, just as he had before, even though he knew this place was dangerous to her.

If she was going mad, then they both were; and there was something coldly, unkindly sane that underlay everything he said, just as his ketchup underlay everything she'd eaten since she came here. She wasn't at all sure about herself, but she didn't think that he was mad at all.

She didn't want to walk the narrow path he'd brought her by, back to the stable yard. Particularly, she didn't want to walk through the stable yard again.

She could tell herself she didn't want to face irate candle-makers, with their wax all spilled and their bath upturned. She could tell herself that, so long as she recognized the truth, that it wasn't true at all. What she didn't want to face was – well, something else. Something with hands. Not her dead baby, who had nothing and was nothing and would have sucked wax in rather than reaching out with it.

Maybe that was how he grew, how come he was growing: he sucked in stuff and made it into nothingness. It's what he was doing with her, she thought, slowly and surely. She had been something once: not a great thing, maybe not a good thing, but something at least. Already she was only a shell, hollow and pretending, inhabiting the story of who she used to be. Soon enough now, she'd be nothing at all.

Avoiding the stable yard, though, meant walking the other way, down the wide rough lane until it joined the drive from the road. Deeper into the wood, that meant. Some girls she knew would be frightened as a matter of course, going in among the trees on their own. She had better reason for it, a dozen better reasons, everything that had happened to her since she came here; all the strangeness had started when Mr Cook dropped her in the wood.

Except that – she thought – it had started when Frank rang his bell, and it would have happened wherever she was, whenever she heard it. She thought. It wasn't the trees to blame. She was no more afraid here than anywhere – or just as much, which came to the same thing in the end.

Her clothes were splashed with wax, like a vivid confession; her sandals were slimy with the stuff. She wanted to sit and pick her feet, peel wax away like dead skin. She'd like to bathe and change, if she could find something clean to wear. She'd like to hide the evidence, whether or not.

She came on to the drive with nothing else in her head, blessedly free of premonitions or memories in the cool shadows under the trees. Dressed in guilt and wanting only to be free of it, she turned towards the house – and heard a car coming, and stepped back into the leaf litter before she saw it, before she could even think how unexpected that was.

She knew the car as soon as she saw it, perhaps even before she saw it. There was only the one car up at the house, though she supposed they might have had visitors. It might have been a new recruit, brought by a taxi that was now returning. Or it might have been a police raid, against all the drugs in the house; or an old shipmate of the captain's, come to pay a call; or . . .

All sorts of things it might have been, but she didn't believe any of them, and she was right. The car that came bumping into sight around the curve of the drive was that same old Morris Traveller, without the ladders now but still gaudy, still decorated with strange symbols that she might guess to be letters of their new language. Still inhabited by two hairy people who honked cheerfully at her, slowed unexpectedly, stopped right where she stood.

'Hi!' The boy with the Afro leaned out of the passenger window. Squinting past him, she decided that the driver was almost certainly another boy, though it was still hard to be certain, to see through long hair and shadow. Hippy men should be obliged to wear beards, she thought, just to keep the poor girls clear, who was which. 'I'm Charlie,' he went on, 'and this is Fish.'

Which was no help at all; and *why Fish?* was as impossible

to ask as *what sex is Fish?*, so she settled for a neutral, 'Hullo. Where are you going?'

'Into town, if you want to come along. Run a few errands, pick up some stuff. Have a drink, if any pub in town will serve us. Fancy it?'

'Oh!' *Yes*, but . . . 'I don't know. I ought to . . .'

'Ought to what? There isn't any *ought to*, not here. That's why we like it. One reason why. Anywhere else, we ought to be doing something useful too, but we're not. We've decided to skive off for the afternoon, so we are.'

She seemed to be opening the rear door already, as though some decision had already been made. Sitting down on old rubbed leather, she said, 'I thought you were running errands? That sounds useful to me.'

'That too – but we'd decided to skive first, which is what matters.' Apparently that was important, that their choice had been for idleness, whatever came after. Whatever they knew must come after. 'Then people started loading duties on us, "while you're there". That's how it works. It's the old "while you're up" trick.'

If he wanted to sound aggrieved – if he wanted to feel aggrieved – he should probably work harder at it. She was fairly sure that the truth was entirely the other way around: that he had volunteered and was trying to cover for it after the fact. Maybe it didn't do to seem too keen. Like girls at school, where it didn't do to seem too bright. Boys didn't like that. She wasn't clear here who he wanted to impress: the silent Fish, perhaps, who had to do the driving? Or her, perhaps? She had after all been walking quite the other way, but the car had stopped regardless . . .

Anyway. Here she was and doing things his way: seizing the moment on an impulse, accepting his offer with no thought at all, and now thinking how handy it was. She had errands of her own in town – one errand at least, if she could rid herself of company for half an hour.

That shouldn't be hard. In London, she'd only need to ask the way to the nearest chemist's. Grown men would blush and jump to conclusions, point mutely and vanish. With this crew she wasn't so certain that would work. They'd probably try to convert her to sphagnum moss or wild sponge or something equally natural and repulsive.

Still, the day had not yet dawned when a determined woman couldn't shed two young men in a public place. And yes, she was sure now about Fish; his arm might be as slim as a girl's, but the hand on the gearstick was raw and awkward, man-sized, masculine. He didn't speak, but she was still sure. His cheek was smoothed by razor, not by nature.

They parked in the cobbled square. She sat for a moment in the vacated car before she remembered: they weren't in Soho any more. Two young men, and neither one of them would think of opening the door for her.

She did it for herself, then, and slithered out with grace enough to out-Rank the Charm School. And was all set to ditch the pair of them with a delicate murmur about shopping for delicates, when they did it themselves, for themselves, ditched her: 'We're going this way, things to do. See you at the Golden Lion later? It's OK; we're welcome there. Cookie vouches for us.'

She knew that; it was where she'd found him. 'Oh – yes, of course. What time . . .?'

But they were gone already, side by side, so close they could almost be hand in hand; so close she could truly have confused them again and thought them lovers.

Oh . . .

Never mind. She pulled her thoughts back to her own needs, her own desires; headed straight for the Golden Lion and asked the landlord if she might use his telephone.

'There's a public phone on the square, miss.'

'Yes, but someone's in there. Please, it's very urgent. It won't cost you anything. I'll reverse the charges, and I can pay you for using it – only not until next week.' *Money's not an issue*, she had money back at the house, only, stupidly, not in these spattered clothes. She hadn't anticipated a trip to town, a trip anywhere. She wouldn't have had pennies for the call box either, though in honesty she hadn't even looked for it. How long had it been since she'd used a public call-box? She couldn't remember; not since she was a teenager, at any rate.

There were things you just didn't do any more, you shouldn't need to.

He hesitated a bare moment – wax-spotted stranger – before leading her down the passage to the hotel reception-desk and leaving her there alone with the telephone. She wasn't sure whether or not he remembered her from yesterday, but it seemed likely. He might think she'd survived one night at the commune and was yelling for help. He might encourage that.

He might listen in on an extension, but she didn't think so. Mostly, she thought he was doing this for Cookie's sake, as he had with the scone and tea yesterday: some long-standing complicated exchange of favours that she was now tangled up with. She wasn't sure how she felt about that.

She picked up the receiver, rang through to the operator and said, 'I'd like to place a trunk call, please. To London, and reverse the charges.'

At home she could just dial his number directly, any time she felt like it, so of course she never did. Here there was a delay that seemed endless, clicks and hums and a heavy physical silence, like a blanket, stuffy and full of dust. Then she heard his voice, his simple public-school: 'Fledgwood,' as though that would always be enough, and the operator's brisk response:

'Will you accept a reversed-charge call, sir?' Her accent, perhaps, was a giveaway; he was already saying yes before she'd named the exchange. And then, 'You're through, caller,' and the only sound on the line was his breathing, and suddenly she couldn't speak. Which was her own kind of giveaway, and potentially fatal.

He said, 'Grace?'

Which at least gave her the chance to say something: 'No. Georgie.'

Bless him, he didn't laugh. 'Of course. Georgie.' His employee, not his subject matter. 'How's it going, Gee?'

Gee. She liked that. She said, 'I'm not sure. I'm in, but – well, this place is wacky.'

'Of course it's wacky. That's why you're there. Wacky how?'

'Different from what I expected. It's not all long hair and free love. I mean, it is that, but it's more too. More serious.'

And haunted, but she didn't want to say so. Instead she said, 'I found your reporter for you.'

'Francis? Did you? That's quick work.'

'I think I did. He's called Frank here. But – well, he's wacky too. Wacked, I think. I think he's certifiable.'

'Occupational hazard, pet. He was never the straightest pipe-cleaner in the box. What's he been swallowing?'

'I don't know. I haven't seen anything here harder than dope, not yet.'

'Well, it's only been a day.'

'Yes, but . . . I don't think drugs are the thing here, Tony. Not for most people. There's something else; it's bigger than that. More ambitious. They don't just want to get out of their skulls, they want to convert the world.'

'Religious?'

'No, not really.' Or only Mother Mary, and she'd likely call herself spiritual instead. 'They're like . . . like Billy Graham without God. They still think there's a better way to live, and they're going to tell everyone about it. Once they get it sorted out for themselves.'

Tony laughed. 'That could be a long wait. But it sounds . . . harmless. Which is not what I'd heard, and not why I sent Francis in.'

'I wouldn't say that. I wouldn't ever say that. They might be innocent.' But that wasn't always the same thing. The innocent could trail harm behind them like a fire trails smoke, like the Beatles trailed fans. Like she trailed harm herself – *sorry, Kathie* – even though she was far from innocent. The opposite of innocent.

The house knew. It knew her, better than anyone did. Better than Tony. It saw through her, where he only wanted to see her through.

She said, 'I'm sure there's a story here.' The captain and Webb between them: the builder and the evangelist. John the Baptist and Jesus Christ. The fuel and the spark, perhaps. 'But I think maybe you should talk to them, not spy on them. I think you could learn more.'

'What's up, precious? Are you buying into what they offer?'

'What? No! No, I'm not.' Though she could see how it

worked, at least. She could feel their separate allures, Webb's and the captain's. If she only stayed here long enough, who knew? Maybe she would buy into one or the other, believe in the place as somewhere to be, or the man as someone to follow.

Not that she planned to stay that long. She didn't think she could afford to. She didn't think she'd survive it.

Perhaps he heard something of that in her voice as they talked, as she described the house and the way it worked as best she could after so short a time there. She didn't mention her hurts or her fears, but they were hard to step around when the whole time had been a progression from one strange happening to the next, and she bore the scars of every one of them.

At all events, abruptly and out of the blue, he said, 'Sweetie? D'you want to come home?'

'No. Not yet.'

'Sure?'

No. 'Yes,' she said aloud. 'I'm sure. You gave me a job and . . . and I want to do it.'

'You found Frank already, and that's the main thing.'

'Yes, but I want to find out what happened to him. I want to *understand*. And so do you, Tony Fledgwood, that's why you sent me here.'

'Yes . . .' But he sounded uncertain even of that, as though he'd had another better reason underneath. Saving her from herself, one way or another. 'Not if you're going to crack up too, though. It's not worth that.'

'I promise, I'm not going to crack up too.' Unless she was cracked already, seeing ghosts at every turn – but she really, really didn't think so. She thought the ghosts were real. So did Cookie. She could rely on him, she thought, if not so much on herself.

'No,' Tony said, unusually solemn, oddly not laughing at her. 'I don't suppose you are. One thing I can rely on: you've got a rock-solid grip on what matters, deep down. I wouldn't have sent you, else.'

Oh, Tony. If you only knew . . . He was right, of course; she did, rock solid. What mattered was the hollow at the heart, the missing space, the baby. She had that and would never let it go.

It was her turn to laugh at him; he was waiting for it, but she couldn't manage it either. She muttered something disparaging that the phone line must have garbled; it was as much as she could manage not to be crying now.

'You're sure, now? You don't want me to come and get you? I would, you know. I need you to know that.'

'No, you wouldn't. You'd send Robbo. But you don't need to do that anyway. I'm fine. Nothing's going to happen to me here, if it hasn't already.' She could feel quite pleased with that, if it hadn't come out quite so gulpy and sorrowful; it was true twice over, in different directions. *If it hasn't already*, when of course it already had, and now she didn't need to tell him about the bandage on her wrist or the bruises on her throat; and *nothing's going to happen to me*, which was of course exactly true, only that *nothing* was a very great deal indeed, an absence, a vacuum that would happen to her in the worst way imaginable, a reality that would suck her down. Sooner or later, ready or not.

Mostly, she thought she would just try to be ready.

Punished enough. Ready to go.

He called her a good girl, and she promised to call him again and hung up hastily before she could get herself even more tangled up between what she was saying to him and what she was hearing in her head.

And then she'd done what she came for, and she didn't know what else to do. It was far too soon to sit and wait for the boys, and she had no money to buy herself a pot of tea or anything at all; *money's not an issue*, but it is when you neglect to bring it with you.

The landlord had disappeared, so she couldn't even thank him. Instead she spent some time in the lavatory, cleaning wax off her clothes as best she could, and then she walked out on to the square and into the sudden tumbling clamour of a tower of bells.

It wasn't Sunday, and it was only mid-afternoon. Nothing was ever fair, but this was purely cruel. The ringers must just be practising, but that would make no difference to her. Her

hand moved instinctively to her wrist, to cradle it against the
inevitable ache of fresh blood running.

And found the bandage quite dry and the wrist only aching
in that good way that flesh does when it's starting to heal; and
remembered that she wasn't at the house any more. She was
in the world, where bells only cut her on the inside.

That was something. She supposed.

What did people do, in market towns with no money? She
had no idea. She couldn't really remember what she used
to do when she was a teenager with no money. Hung out
with her friends, talked, smoked, listened to music: all those
things that she couldn't do here or now and saw no point
in anyway. None of it led anywhere that mattered; it had
only brought her here. What was there left to say, or to
smoke, or to listen to . . .?

Feeling unutterably depressed, she thought she might just
stay by the car, under the sound of the bells, and wait the
hours till the boys came back. Why not? She had nothing more
useful to do. Nothing to do at all, so she might as well suffer.

Suffer in public. Standing there and looking around, she
was abruptly aware of people looking at her and stiffening,
turning away, hurrying on. It wasn't London, and they weren't
staring or spitting or crying down curses on her head, but even
so . . .

Gradually, she understood. This wasn't London, and they
weren't seeing Grace Harley. They weren't even seeing Georgie
Hale. All they saw was a hippy from the big house, someone
so utterly different from themselves there weren't the words
to describe it.

Rather than linger by the car, then, she did the other thing:
she walked deliberately away. That didn't help. The car was
a giveaway, yes, but so were her clothes. *You are what you
wear* – there had been times when that was a cause for
celebration, times when it was a weapon of war, times when
it was a prison sentence. Right now, apparently, it was a
condemnation.

Brightly dressed, oddly dressed, she drew every eye with
every movement. She moved through this conservative
country town in its tweeds, its greens and browns, like molten

wax in water: vivid and apart, surrounded but not swallowed. She seemed to have a force field around her that
pushed other people aside: except that it was their choice,
every time. They saw her coming and looked away, moved
away. Crossed the road, or changed their minds about
crossing; or simply blatantly waited until she'd passed, to
be sure she didn't infect them or their precious children or
their dogs.

Perhaps it was just as well that she had no money. She
couldn't imagine how they would treat her in any of the tea
shops here. Or rather, she could. She could imagine it all too
well, because it was how they treated Grace in half the
boutiques on the King's Road.

She had thought it might be different for Georgie. Still, at
least she knew how to deal with this. Chin up and eyes front,
her face a mask until she found somewhere to go, somewhere
to be out of the public gaze.

That wasn't going to be easy. If they weren't ringing that
damn bell, she might have risked the church, but—

'There's one of them now.'

It was a male voice, young and rough. Off to the side, a
little group gathered by a fountain. She didn't turn her head,
she didn't scurry on, but something deep inside her held its
breath. Young men were the worst. In the right mood, with
enough beer inside them and their mates watching, they'd go
for confrontation every time.

Here they came. The sun was behind her; their shadows
were all about her, hemming her in. Three of them, she thought.
Maybe four. They wouldn't, surely they wouldn't actually
attack her, in broad daylight, in the middle of town where
everyone must know who they were; but nobody would care
if they gave her a hard time any other way. She was the outsider
here, the natural victim. No one knew who she was, and still
she was the victim.

It was only fair, and still she would have given plenty to
escape whatever it was coming. She always did escape her
just deserts, that was what she counted on; so—

So a door opened abruptly just ahead of her, and the sudden
jangle of its bell brought her to a dead stop just when she

needed to keep moving, but no matter; here was rescue, apparently, though she didn't understand it.

Here was a woman, a stranger, middle-aged and dressed to suit – dressed for town, but even so: one of the enemy here, one of those who made a point of making space, not letting her near for fear of contamination – holding the door open for her, smiling at her, beckoning her inside.

Seeming as though she knew her, had been waiting, was glad to see her now.

Seeming utterly blind to her escort, that pack of lads at her heel.

She didn't need to understand it; she just grabbed, as she had done all her life. How the world works: take what's on offer now, whatever you can reach. Pay for it later.

She ducked straight inside the tea shop, heard the woman close the door behind her, felt almost grateful – almost! – for the dreadful *jing-jang* of the bell. At least it couldn't hurt her here, and it was like another door, a lock, a wall to hide behind. Boys who hung around in the street wouldn't follow her in here, the bell said.

'They won't come in here,' the woman said, uncanny, clear and bell-like. 'Come on, sit with us.' Right in the window there, where she must have seen exactly what was happening outside. 'You're from D'Espérance, aren't you?'

So she'd seen it and understood it, that too. And acted, swiftly and effectively; and *who are you?* was a question bubbling under but not ready yet, not ready to be asked.

Here was her companion, a man maybe ten years older than she was, rising to his feet.

'Edward Dorian,' he said, reaching to shake her hand. She'd almost forgotten already that that was what people did. 'And you've already met my wife, Ruth.'

'Well, not to say met, exactly.' The other woman smiled, her own hand at the ready – and then hesitated, frowned a little, said, 'Haven't we, though? Met? In London, perhaps . . .?'

'Oh! No, I don't think so, I really don't.' She really didn't; it was most likely just that sense of familiarity that people carried away from newspaper photographs, a half-recognition that had brought her half-waves and vague smiles even before she was notorious. After that she thought that everyone knew exactly who she was – but only apparently in London, at the centre of things. Here she was distant enough and changed enough, dressed otherwise and not made-up, her hair flat and dirty and her whole presence just so utterly unlikely, she could get away with it. She hoped. 'I'm Georgie Hale. Thank you, for—'

A gesture through the window-glass covered the rest of that sentence. They were still out there, those boys, baffled by lace curtains and the smell of scones. They wouldn't cross the threshold, and they wouldn't linger long. Grace might not have lingered either, but Georgie felt obliged. She took the chair that Mrs Dorian drew back for her, and said thank you to the tea and refused the cake, and was taken aback when it was the male half of this unknown couple who turned abruptly personal. She called him 'Mr Dorian', and he said:

'That's *Doctor* Dorian, actually – and the doctor in me wants to know, what have you been up to, hmm?'

'What? Oh, um, I cut myself . . .' Fidgeting with the bandage on her wrist as though it were the cuff of a blouse, nothing more significant. Checking that it hadn't started to bleed again. Trying to be angry – who was he, that he should interrogate her? – but not really managing it. He was a doctor; this was what they did.

'That was careless, but that's not what I meant. You look like you've been half-strangled. I know they play games up at the house, but not – I thought – that sort of game.'

'Oh . . .' Unwillingly, almost unwittingly, her hand moved to her throat. And yes, she was sore to the touch; and yes, likely it did look bruised. It must do, or he wouldn't have noticed. She said, 'No, no, nothing like that,' when perhaps she should have said *yes, exactly that, sex games,* just to deflect him.

It might have been too late already. He was looking at her more closely than was comfortable, his examination of her neck moving up to her face now as he said, 'I think my wife's right, though, isn't she? We have met before. At a party, I fancy.'

'Really? I'm sorry, I don't remember.' She was, perhaps,

trying to sound world-weary – *so many parties, so many people* – but that was only a last-ditch gesture, almost a surrender in itself.

'I wouldn't expect you to,' he said, oddly kindly. 'You must have seen so many faces, the way you've been living these last years. I expect they're a kind of blur, aren't they, Grace?'

Well. There it was, then. Sooner than she'd hoped for, perhaps, but inevitable sooner or later, even in a backwater like this. It might not matter – random strangers taking tea, passing through – except that they knew about the house and called it by its old name, so not so much strangers after all. Maybe not so random, either.

Maybe not so bad. Another man would have said it differently, slammed it home – *aren't they? Grace?* – to make his point, not broken it to her so gently that she only just caught it.

She didn't try to deny anything. What was the point? In a way, she'd come here to be discovered. Still, she said, 'I'm Georgie, please, not Grace. While I'm here.' And then, a sudden bright idea that left her thoroughly pleased with herself, she added her own argument from earlier, her prepared defence. 'Webb gets to call himself Webb, and I bet that's not what it says on his birth certificate. If you can't choose your own name, what can you do?'

He smiled; his wife laughed aloud. 'Fair point,' she said. 'You might want to hold that ready, for when he learns who you are. He will learn, you know. You do know that, I hope?'

Oh yes, she knew. And now she knew that these two were far from random strangers. They knew the house and its lieutenant, and presumably its captain too. And they knew her, apparently, from a London party; and he was a doctor. It might have been any party, she really didn't remember, but he couldn't just be any doctor. You needed to know the right people to catch an invite to the kind of party she'd be at. Before or after the trial. Everything had changed, but that was still true. And . . .

'Oh,' she said. 'Are you the doctor we've been waiting for, come up to see Kathie?'

'That's me,' he agreed quietly. 'It's both of us. Ruth nursed pilots in the war; she's had as much experience with burns as anyone in the country.'

'It's not the burns. I'm sorry, not to put you down, uh, Mrs Dorian—'

'Ruth.'

'—but it's not her burns that are killing Kathie. It's my fault.' Because apparently she did still have to confess to someone, and who better? A doctor and a doctor's wife: people with authority but no governance. People who would come, speak their minds, and go again. People who could stand in line with the judges and the journalists and the lords, condemn her utterly and never, never punish her enough.

'Oh? How's that?' He didn't argue with her implicit diagnosis, that Kathie was dying. Well, he hadn't seen her yet. Perhaps he was just ignoring it, paying no attention to a hysterical girl. She could hope, she supposed, that there was still hope. Though it didn't seem likely.

'I . . . I'm the one who took her into the water, after her clothes caught light. And I kept her under too long. I think I did. I must have done.' Because confession was one thing but she wasn't going to tell the whole truth, not to anyone, not for anything. She never had. Not *I killed my baby*, and not *I did for Kathie too. I think I turned my baby's ghost on her to save myself.* 'She couldn't, you know . . . She didn't breathe for ages, and she's never woken up since.'

'Anoxia? Well, perhaps. Perhaps.' He didn't sound convinced. 'It may be in her head, more than a physical cause. She may just have . . . retreated.'

Head doctor, was he? A psychiatrist? That seemed all too likely. She'd met a lot of those. Most of them had wanted to fuck her, one way or another. Maybe not this one.

She felt a hand close over hers, and was startled. It was Ruth, of course, not her husband. She said, 'You mustn't blame yourself. You were trying to save her life.'

Which was true, as far as the woman knew, as far as anyone knew. *Or maybe I just wanted to save mine, because I was too scared, so I gave her over to the ghost* – she wasn't going to say it, but she couldn't escape it either. It was something else to carry, a deep weight that would drag her down in the end. Would have done, if she hadn't been all the way sunk already.

'I take it they don't know, up at the house. About your other name, your past life?' That was the doctor, being practical, clearing the air.

She shook her head mutely.

'Well, they won't learn it from us. You may yet have a period of grace. I'm sorry, of not-Grace,' he added with a wry smile. 'Though I'd like a chat with you while I'm here, to find out why you want it.'

Wasn't it obvious? Being Grace was hell. That ought to be enough. But he'd want to hear her say it, no doubt. They always did.

Well, maybe she'd oblige. If that was the price of his silence, she might. She'd like a few more days at least, before the penny dropped for someone and stage two of Tony's plan kicked in. Feeling like Grace again, even for ten minutes under their scrutiny, was . . . less than comfortable. Not something she wanted.

'Well,' he said, gesturing for the bill, 'we'd better get moving. We only stopped off for a last cup of decent tea, before the barleycup and that dreadful Tibetan stuff, the brick-tea the captain drinks.'

'We could bring proper tea, you know,' his wife said, with a long-suffering tone and almost a wink aside. 'And coffee. Nobody would care.'

'I'd care. You don't do well in a community if you start out by separating yourself. Even from what they eat and drink. Especially, perhaps, from what they eat and drink. Why do you think so many tight and surviving communities have dietary laws? We are what we eat; if we eat together, we are together.'

'But we're outsiders in any case, Ned. We come, we go. We don't stay.'

'All the more reason to share what they have while we're here.'

It was clearly an old argument, well worn, unworrying. It lasted them from the tea shop to the car. She went with them, just for the comfort of their company in the abrupt discomfort of the streets. She had honestly not been angling for it, but she barely hesitated when he turned to her and said, 'May we offer you a lift?'

'Actually, I came in with Charlie and Fish.' But that was not a way to say *no*, more an appeal for help: *tell me how to leave without them.* Grace wouldn't have hesitated for a second, but Georgie didn't want to upset anyone.

'I don't suppose you know where they are?'

'No. They said they had errands . . .'

'Which might mean anything, knowing those two. Not to worry –' it was Mrs Dorian who had unexpectedly taken charge now – 'we'll leave them a note.'

She wrote it out herself and didn't show Georgie what it said; only sent her trotting across the square to leave the folded sheet tucked under the windscreen wiper of the Morris, where nobody could miss it.

Grace would have read it on the way, but Ruth had explicitly given it to Georgie – 'Here, Georgie, you take it,' like an absolute guarantee, *your secret is safe with us* – and of course Georgie wouldn't do any such thing. She just slipped it between blade and glass, left it, hurried back.

He drove a big black Bentley: terribly suitable on the outside, terribly comfortable within. She used to take cars like this, rides like this for granted; now she took them with a kind of tentative pleasure, wondering each time whether this might be her last. Luck was something they could take away from you, she had learned. However hard you worked at it.

She headed automatically for the back, where the girls go and the third wheels too, but Ruth waylaid her: 'You sit in the front, dear. Ned will want to talk to you.'

That sounded ominous. She settled nervously into the passenger seat, fidgeting with her bandage cuff again and almost wishing that she smoked seriously, that she had something to smoke.

He glanced across and smiled, as though he read her mood exactly. She hated that in psychiatrists; she always had. It was presumptuous, she thought. Where was a girl to keep her secrets, if not in her head? And who from, if not these middle-aged men with their outmoded values, who would condemn her as soon as look at her, if they could look that far inside her . . .?

Not that she wanted their approval. Of course not; why would she? There was nothing she could do with that. She had no use for it.

Even so. Something in her did still want to satisfy this quiet, steely man, or at least to avoid his contempt. Her London life – both sides of it, before the court and afterwards – had been all about satisfying older men, but this was different.

Besides, his wife was in the car.

A psychiatrist – himself, maybe? – would probably say she was still looking for a father figure. The papers – Tony's, maybe – would say she was looking for a sugar daddy. She didn't think either of those was actually true, but they'd say it anyway.

Apparently, though, he didn't want to talk about her. That was . . . unusual. And welcome. She was quite determined about that. She didn't want to talk about her either.

'Tell me about Kathie,' he said. 'Everything that happened, last night.'

It really was, it was only last night. That seemed extraordinary. She felt like she'd come so far since then. Down and down, mostly.

'She was dancing,' she said slowly. 'In the firelight, with everything swinging loose: her hair, her sleeves, her skirt.' *Those bloody bells.*

'Was she high?'

'I don't know. Maybe. She was smoking, but what's one joint worth? I don't know if there were others first. I don't know her.' *I didn't know my baby, either. I only do harm to strangers.*

'All right. We do know her, a little; she's not the type to get stoned and fall into a fire. Mostly when I've met her she's been head down over a notebook, working on Webb's language project. She's one of his prime lieutenants, and you need a clear head for that. Webb would say that the words themselves keep you sober; Tom would probably say that the words themselves are enough to make you high. I'm not saying for certain

that Kathie wouldn't get out of her skull, but if she was looking
to wind down, I'd have thought that music and dancing and
firelight would have been enough for her. We'll know more
later, but in the meantime, let's assume that she was clean. So
what happened?'

'She danced, and I guess she went too close to the fire. Tom
says something collapsed in there and blew out a shower of
sparks . . .'

'Never mind what Tom says. What do you say? What did
you *see*?'

He asked the question like it mattered. Not like he knew
the answer already – not like the police, or the lawyers in
court – but like he knew there was an answer to be discovered,
a change in the story, a truth.

She didn't want to say. She'd told it to Tom, and he'd
laughed at her; she didn't want to tell it here.

'I saw . . . I saw her burning. I saw her skirt catch, and
then the fire just spread everywhere, all over her . . .' Which
wasn't an answer to the question he was trying to ask, but it
would do: for her, for now. Whether it would do for him
– well.

She didn't have to find out immediately, at least. From
behind her, Ruth said, 'Ned, why is it always fire?'

'Hmm?'

'This house. It always turns to fire, at the last. But why?'

*I don't think this is the last. I don't think this is the end of
anything.* She didn't say so. This was suddenly interesting.
And a question that she didn't have to answer, let alone dodge.

'It's elemental,' the doctor said. 'Fire, water. They both
speak to human need. Earth and air we can take for granted,
more or less, most of the time. Fire and water we always seek
to control. Our minds turn that way. I'd like to say by nature,
but I'm not sure that's true. It may be we're trained to it, very
early on. Campfires and swimming lessons; not to play with
matches, not to take a bath straight after dinner. The power
of fire, the strength of water. Both of them together, in a
steaming kettle and the iconic sound of a locomotive. Diesel's
not the same. Coal-fuelled power stations: every child gets to
learn that fire and water together make electricity. It's ingrained.

We carry it with us, that sense of what matters most, what's most dangerous and most needful, both at once. Of course the house picks up on that.'

They spoke like Cookie, almost; like Frank, not at all. As if they knew the house intimately, the spirit of it; as though they studied it clinically. And were not mad, and still believed in ghosts.

It was reassuring. If they weren't mad, then likely neither was she.

'It's all fire, though, isn't it?' Ruth repeated. 'The water's incidental.'

'I don't believe so. It was the lake that burned for the colonel; it's the lake maybe that did the damage this time. We haven't seen her yet, but everyone's saying she's not that badly burned. Let's say that she danced too close to the fire, and never mind why for now. Tell us what came next, Georgie.'

He was doing it too, using the one name even though he knew the other. She didn't want to see that as a kindness, she didn't want to be grateful to him, but it was hard not to feel a warmth rising in response.

More urgently, she didn't want to diminish herself in his eyes; she really didn't want to talk about what she had done, after that moment of rescue. Instead, she tried to turn him back, to ground where she suddenly felt unexpectedly more comfortable: 'Frank thinks the house is haunted by the ghost of a woman burned to death at the lakeside. He thinks the ghost reached out from the flames, to catch Kathie.'

'No.' From the back seat, from Ruth, flat and final. And then, 'Frank's mad,' which was her own opinion too, but she hadn't expected to hear it reflected quite so bluntly, or not from there.

'Never mind Frank,' the doctor said, more reasonably. 'What do you think?'

'I think . . . it's what I saw. I think it was. Two hands, snatching.'

'You see?' Ruth said. 'It's always fire. But not some ancient ghost, Georgie, no. Nothing lingers that long in D'Espérance. People come, they go. They bring their own damage with them, every time.'

'That's what Cookie says, too.' It was almost uncannily close, except that she didn't believe there was anything uncanny about that at all.

'Ah, Cookie. Yes.' The doctor seemed almost to be laughing as he repeated the name. 'You should listen to Cookie. There's a man who knows what he's talking about.'

'There's a man who lingered,' his wife added. 'He's the exception.'

'Yes. But never mind even Cookie, for now. Georgie, you were going to tell us what you did next.'

Was she? Apparently, she was. She'd been trying to avoid it, but he was relentless and she couldn't be bothered to duck again. She said, 'I . . . took Kathie into the water –' that hurtling memory, a tackle any rugby player would be proud of – 'and we went down deep. Deeper than I thought it would be, and colder too. I . . . I should have brought her up sooner, I'm sorry, but—'

'I don't suppose you kept her under deliberately,' Dr Dorian said, mild and inoffensive and deceptive all three. 'Is that when you hurt your wrist?'

She was fidgeting with the bandage again; he thought it was a giveaway. Which it was, but not perhaps the way that he was thinking. She said, 'Yes. Well, no, not the first time –' *not even the second* – 'but . . .' Her voice drained away, the strength of it. Next he'd be asking her about the night, about being in the same room as Kathie, what had happened to cause her collapse. That was an interrogation she really couldn't face; she gave herself away too easily, even after all this time. Years of practice, years and years, and she was still a shoddy liar. Even when she got the words right and the voice too, her body would betray her. Besides, she was so tired of lying. Lying and smiling, bright brittle words to hide the blood behind her teeth. Instead of lying, then, she told him the truth about something entirely other. 'Frank isn't wrong about everything. There's a bell in the water.'

'A bell? And that . . . cut you?' For once he was honestly bewildered. It almost felt like a score.

'Yes,' she said. 'Bells do that. To me. In the house, and round about. They open up old wounds and make me bleed.'

Apparently, they didn't even need to be striking, except in her mind. *Sound carries underwater* – she remembered that from lessons, long ago. A bell lying still on the lake bed shouldn't be sending out any sounds at all, but she had heard it, felt it, bled for it.

And had been half-strangled by hands rising out of wax, that too, but that . . . didn't feel internal. It wasn't *hers*, not her own, not hers to carry. She was her own worst enemy; she hardly minded being attacked by someone else's.

If he kept on asking about the night gone and Kathie, she'd tell him about the hands of wax. Better that than admit to being Kathie's worst enemy too. *I did that to her.* The more she thought about it, the more sure she was. She'd seen it coming, and been deliberately too slow. She'd let it take the other girl, sooner than sacrifice herself. How much more guilty could you be?

Weirdly, he hardly seemed to blink when she told him about the bells. She couldn't see Ruth's face in the driving mirror – she did look – but the only sound that came from the back seat sounded more like a murmur of sympathy than the cynical snort she was expecting.

'Why's that, then?' the doctor asked. 'D'Espérance will do any amount of strange, hard things to you, if you come primed for it – but why bells? What do bells mean to you?'

She didn't have to tell him. She could just say *mind your own business*, or – as he knew who she was – *work it out for yourself.* He was smart enough, and his wife perhaps was smarter, at least in the ways that women work. She'd tell him, now or later. Grace need only shake her head, refuse, sit silent, let the moment by.

But he had that magic that some priests have, some doctors, some vicars. Some men: she'd never felt it in a woman.

At any rate, he asked the question and waited, and despite her firm intentions she found herself telling him, flat and simple.

'They rang a bell for my baby, on and on. I haven't been able to stand bells since. And then I came here, and . . . and started bleeding every time . . .'

And here they were, coming up the back drive, the same

way that Cookie had brought her yesterday, only yesterday; and he parked in the yard behind the house, and now she could slip out of the car without saying anything more, leave him with that to mull over, not give herself away any further. She could smile brightly and thank him for the ride, thank them both; promise to tell the captain and Webb too that they were here; duck in through the door and disappear and be gone, before either one of them could ask her to show them up to where Kathie lay in waiting.

NINE

S he hardly knew the house yet, hardly at all. Nothing was instinctive; her body didn't know which way to go, and nor did she. All she wanted was to get away, to be not there, not with them, not facing Kathie.

Of course she got lost. She was lost from the beginning. She walked into the house and the first thing she saw was that the ship's bell had gone from the corridor – *thank you, Tom* – and the second thing she saw was a stairway, and she just took it.

The first room she'd woken up in, the room she'd shared with Kathie, was on the second storey; Webb's room was one floor below. He'd be in one or the other. Despite her promise, she wasn't going anywhere near him. Instead she kept on going up, and was straightaway in unknown territory.

Up and up, and here were the attics: long dormitories, mattresses on the floor, and hung about with gaudy fabrics. *We all sleep together*, but some people erected walls anyway; sheets of cotton and sheer satin hung from the rafters to make cubicles that offered something that might almost be possession, almost privacy, almost.

She walked through one dormitory and another, interconnected; and no bells rang, and no hands clutched at her out of shadow, and there was nobody up here at this time of day, and even so she felt haunted, she felt watched.

Here was a staircase, and she was only a little lost yet. She thought that if she went down there, she'd find her way to the main hall and the captain's room behind. Which would again give her a chance to keep her promise, and again she avoided it. Turned the corner and kept on walking: all the length of the house, attic after attic, until she reached another staircase and another right angle, into the wing she hadn't broached yet.

She thought they didn't use it. She remembered Webb's

announcement last night, that the electrics were out; she thought
she shouldn't take the house on trust, in the half-dark.

Wouldn't have done, except that there was light coming up
from below, down the stairwell.

Everyone she was avoiding, she thought, was most likely
behind her. Someone had said this wing was empty, and
someone was here none the less; and she was curious, and
stubborn, and hated running away.

Besides, she was here as a spy, wasn't she? It was her job,
it was her duty to snoop out secrets.

Down the stairs she went, then. Slowly, carefully, treading
as light-footed as she knew how. No one she knew would
believe it of her, but Grace had learned the hard way what
Georgie had always known: how to fade into the background,
how to be invisible in company. How to survive, that meant,
in prison. Before then she'd been all look-at-me, all the time,
and people always had. Since then she'd been faking it at
parties, doing what she was paid for, but trying to stay insig-
nificant in-between. Unseen. It didn't always work, it couldn't,
especially when she had to keep her face in the papers or no
one would hire her for their parties any more; she had to keep
notorious, but she did her best to sidle unnoticed from one
engagement to the next, even from one room to another. She
used to walk the iron stairs of Holloway so silently the other
women took to calling her the ghost.

These stairs, well-seasoned wood set into stone, and in these
simple sandals? Not a problem. Not a creak. She went down
and down again, into the soft glow of an oil lamp set on a
table in an empty hallway.

This was the ground floor; the double doors that faced her
were high and half-open, alluring to the spy. Dust and silence
both hung in the air. There was light beyond the doors, flickering, uncertain. There had to be someone around, but – well,
she had to look.

She tiptoed like a child across the parquet floor, ducked her
head briefly around the door, ducked back again.

A library. A house like this? Of course there was a library.
She should have thought; she should have looked before.

A library lit by candlelight, by a long aisle of candles laid between its alcoves, from one end to the other. They stood in saucers on the bare floor, a long way – quite a long way – from the high ranks of formal dark-spined books, and even so: it didn't look safe to her. Open flames and so much wood and paper; pools of molten wax all set to spill. Let one taper tip over, topple into its neighbour's saucer, splash burning wax on to the parquet, a spreading river seeking out the shelves . . .

She didn't even want to go inside, she really didn't.

Tony would expect her to, and Tony got what Tony wanted; that was a rule.

Too bad for her.

In she went, then. It wasn't bravery, just a kind of sullen determination. She'd do what she came for, if she could. She'd do her best to make Tony happy. She'd realized long since that she couldn't do that for herself, so why not do it for him instead? Leaving someone happy had to be better than the other thing.

She was still afraid, and not only of fire. Even after last night, hot hands reaching. High shelves jutted out into the room, dividing up the space like stable stalls, two facing rows of alcoves, walls of books. Anyone might lurk behind any one of those partition walls; someone surely must be lurking somewhere. Someone had lit these candles, after all.

Nevertheless. She stepped out from behind the door, into that broad aisle of lights.

She almost wanted to sing as she went, to keep her spirits up. She was still treading softly, though; and while she could tiptoe and make a wilful noise, both together – and make a case for both, Georgie struggling for silence while Grace sang, two impulses in the same body – it would still be stupid, and she wouldn't do it.

Wanted to.

Wouldn't.

It was hard to see even into the first alcoves, on either side of her, even with a clear line of sight. The bare thin light of these first few candles struggled against the shifting shadows cast by the lines ahead, could hardly reach the side walls at all. She peered anyway, this way and that: saw nobody lurking in the dark, wanted to huff aloud with relief, swallowed it down.

Sidled further down the aisle, past those first alcoves; peered warily into the next.

Still no one.

She could see now why it was so dark in here, why candles gave the only light. On one side, the back wall was shelved all the way up to the iron gallery, where more shelves climbed to the ceiling. Books swallowed light, she thought, as though they needed it to read by. To read themselves, to keep their own words fresh: like blood to the tissues.

On the other side there were windows between the partitions, and it should still be light enough out there to see by – but the windows were all shuttered against the day, against the world. It seemed . . . deliberate, like a statement, but surely not the captain's. Nor Webb's. Their visions were all about outreach, not isolation; opening up, not shutting out.

Confused, still frightened, she walked on. Thankful to find herself still alone after one more pair of alcoves, and one more; coming closer to the end of the long room, no closer to any answer.

She felt a brief tug at her ankle, as though her trouser leg had snagged a thorn. Instinct moved her two ways, both at once: jerking her leg free, and twisting her head to look down, to see what she'd caught it against. Knowing already that there was nothing there, because for sure she would have seen it, she was being so careful, watching her path between the candles as warily as she watched the alcoves; dreading what that meant – *nothing there, seized by nothing, that absence that's been haunting me, dead baby*; she really didn't want to see, but she was looking anyway, by instinct or long training, that thing you do when something snags your clothing.

She looked down and no, there was nothing, except that one of the candles was guttering wildly, the one she'd just passed. Perhaps that sudden savage jerk of her leg – against what? she didn't know, couldn't answer, one more question – had stirred a current of air, enough to disturb the flame.

She watched it; it held her eye. She saw it draw back into its own shape for a moment, the flame rising from a wick, as it ought to. Stirred no more than any candle might be, burning on the floor of a surely-draughty room.

For a moment.

Then she saw it stretch into a new shape, a tiny arm, a doll's arm, with a doll's hand at the end of it: reaching, clutching. Stretching towards her, thin and fine and deadly.

She screamed, perhaps.

For a moment, on a breath.

And then scuttled back, surely out of its reach; and felt another little tug, and spun around, and so jerked her other leg free of the snatch of another of those flames, those arms, from the other side of the aisle.

Bent down and slapped her hand against smouldering wax-soaked fabric, heedless of the heat of it, until it wasn't smoking any more and there was just a scorched hole in her trouser hem. And then straightened slowly and stood, legs together and trembling now; and saw how the whole double line of candles up ahead had turned into a thicket of arms, like two hedges groping in time-lapse fast motion across the narrow space that divided them. Too narrow, she thought, that space, remembering Kathie and how the fiery hands had gripped her, how the girl had burned. These were nothing, minuscule by comparison, pencil-thin limbs and frail fingers trailing into wisps of smoke – but it only takes a spark to start a blaze. And she knew now how easily her clothes could catch; they were like wicks all ready for the flame. And she had a blister on her palm already; she couldn't go on using her bare hands to beat out incipient fires.

Nor could she just stand here, until the candles all burned down. She might – just – be safe now, this moment, cramped heel-and-toe between the two lines of candles, just out of reach of each; but her balance was uncertain already, she couldn't keep this up for hours. She'd wobble and have to step to one side or the other to save herself from falling. Have to step right into the reach of those seeking hands. And as the candles burned lower, their wicks would droop and lengthen, not burn fast enough away; the flames would strengthen and grow fatter, reach further . . .

She tried blowing one out, she did try. That was all Grace,

tough-minded, taking action. She crouched down – carefully, carefully! – and steadied herself on one hand, bent low, blew hard.

Not hard enough. The flame guttered and flailed like a flag in the wind of her breath, but it didn't go out. And when she had to stop blowing, when she had to breathe, then it came snapping back like a whip, vigorous and vicious. It almost reached her, that time. She swayed back, almost into the clutch of another flame, another hand behind her.

They were working together, she thought.

Well, of course they were. Being worked, rather. There was one directing intelligence behind them, one antagonistic spirit. One mind, perhaps – except that that would mean magic, and she still didn't believe in magic any more than she believed in prayer. Even with hands of flame groping for her, the impossible turned all too real.

She believed in ghosts, absolutely. She believed in her dead baby, and the power of bells.

Somebody else believed in fire, she guessed: believed in some ghost of their own and the power of flames.

She thought she'd tripped over someone else's haunting here. Maybe Frank's. He believed in his own story about the woman burned long ago, even if the doctor and his wife had dismissed it. That might be enough; he might be right. For sure he was right about the house, that something lurked here. It had driven him mad. It might yet kill her. She hadn't – quite – bled to death, and they'd stopped ringing the bells that cut her; that might not be enough. She might have blundered into Frank's nightmare here. She might yet burn.

A flame licked at her foot. If she'd still been wearing nylons, they'd have melted on to her skin; plastic sandals would have done the same. These were rope-soled, hand-sewn. They might burn, but at least they wouldn't melt.

She'd burn first, she thought.

That gave her an idea: not a good one, maybe, but the best she had. The only one she had. Flames ahead of her, flames behind her; she couldn't run this gauntlet. Someone – something – had waited, she thought, until she was halfway down the aisle. Thoroughly trapped.

She couldn't jump to safety, either. Not from a standing start. The aisle was too wide.

She slipped one foot free of its sandal, cautiously, watchful of her balance. Watching the flame hands on either side of her. This way or that, one alcove or the other . . .?

Some malign spirit might inhabit the candles now, but a human hand had set them out this way. With whatever purpose in mind. It couldn't have been meant for a trap – at least, not to trap her: nobody knew she'd be coming this way, she hadn't even known it herself until she came – but there must be a reason for this long aisle of lights. Someone had laid them out and lit them all.

Someone was going to come back and find them not quite all alight, not laid out quite so neatly.

One way or the other.

Just for a moment, she imagined one way, the worst way: the person coming in to find a fire blazing around a sprawled burning body, herself, with the whole library set aflame around her as she'd rolled and kicked in her agony, doomed and disastrous . . .

But that was all Georgie, imagining the worst. Grace wouldn't do that. Grace had no imagination. She just got on with things and let what happened happen. And dealt with that too when it came. Dealt badly, for the most part, came out worse. That was Grace, all Grace.

So was this: crouched and careful and never mind the library, thinking only of herself.

Well, perhaps the care was Georgie's. Grace would have flung more wildly, all devil-may-care and determined. Not cocked her arm and taken aim just where the candles were closest together, thinking it through, hoping to get as many as possible with a single fling.

Grace would probably have flung both sandals, one after the other, not kept one on her foot against a certain need.

Unable to jump that far, Grace would never have thought of hopping.

Cock, aim, fling. From low down and almost sideways, so that the angle of impact would carry as many candles as possible as far as possible.

Their flaming hands, perhaps, tried to catch at the sandal at it flew, but there was almost nothing to them, not enough. She'd flung hard, all of Grace's stubborn effort behind Georgie's thought and purpose.

The sandal toe caught one candle, rocked it on its saucer, knocked it sideways. Spilled its wax.

The body and bulk and heel of the sandal took out three more, sent them skittering across the floor. Opened a way.

Spilled a lot more wax, all across the floor; and one rolling candle didn't go out, and spread its flame generously across the liquid streaks.

Still, there was a gap. Not wide enough: slender arms of flame reached to bridge it, from the last candle standing on the one side to the spilled one on the other where it lay burning in a pool of its own wax. They looked like two hands shaking across a gulf.

Still, she could hop.

Could, and did. All Grace, overriding all Georgie's anxieties: up on her sandalled foot and one magnificent effortful hop, to land splat in that spilled pool, on that fallen candle. Cutting off its reaching arm at the elbow, crushing out its flame, breaking that bridge at its source.

Making a gap broad enough, keeping her out of flame's reach as she hopped again, through the line, beyond the aisle, into the alcove.

She wanted to cry, 'Safe!' when she got there, like a little girl in a game.

Perhaps she actually did that, under her breath, as though she couldn't hear it. Perhaps Georgie did.

Grace was busy: looking around at the burning puddles of wax, seeing the danger in them, the hands rising, reaching.

It was Georgie who pictured her stamping foot coming down against them, entwined in them, their flame clinging to the splashed wax on her skin and clothes. Clinging and rising, greeting, welcoming . . .

Grace was busy: turning away from those reaching hands, reaching herself to the shadows of a bottom shelf, where she knew the biggest books were always to be found in libraries like this. Her fingers located a tall heavy folio, and dragged it out. Leather-bound, broad and solid: that would do.

She turned back to the spilled spreading fires and used the book like a giant candle-snuffer. More like a candle-crusher, vigorously, violently. Walloped the fallen candles and their burning puddles and their snatching hands together, crushed them underbook, extinguished them one by one.

And then straightened with a huff of satisfaction, almost a shiver of pleasure. It still wasn't over; she was trapped in this alcove now, by that long double line of candles between here and the door, covering all the open floor-space, leaving her no room to sidle free.

Trapped more or less, for the moment. Give or take.

Georgie supposed that she could climb over the bookcase that made the wall of this alcove and down into the next. And the next, and the one after that, until she reached the door. Or she could unbar the shutter here, open the window, climb out that way; that'd be easier. Or . . .

Grace had a weapon, heavy in her hands. She thought she could walk from here to the open door, sweet and easy, crushing as she went.

One good thing about being Grace: she wasn't going to wait for anyone's permission. Not Georgie's, not anyone's.

She took a step out into that gap she'd torn in the neat line of candles, ready to rip it like muslin, all the way back to the hem – only, just as she did so she heard footsteps on the stairs, bold and deliberate, a voice in the hall.

A voice she knew.

Grace ducked back into the alcove out of sight, pressed her shoulders against the wall of books, clutched the folio against her chest almost as though she were trying to disguise herself, trying to pretend to be a book herself.

Suddenly she was shaking again, and her skin was prickling with sweat. That wasn't all Georgie.

The candles, she saw, were just candles again, burning to give light, a little, to mark a path from the door to the far end of the library. Nothing more than that: no fiery gauntlet, no tiny deadly fingers reaching.

They were going to walk in here, walk all the way down

that aisle of lights, because what else would you do, what else could you do? It was an open invitation.

Except that there was a gap in the line, and they'd see that, and wonder, and look into the alcove – and see her.

And then what?

She didn't know; but she knew who was coming, or one of them, and she hated that. Whatever this was, whatever it was for, it wasn't anything good: it was creepy and scary and possibly worse than that, something deep down wicked maybe, and she hated that Tom was at the heart of it.

She stood there and listened for him, hiding like a child, eavesdropping like a child. She could feel her own heart beating, pounding like a child's against the rigid leather of the book; she could hear her own breathing and was sure that he must too.

She waited to hear him exclaim: *no, wait, this isn't how I left them. Someone's been here. They might be here still . . .*

Instead she heard him laugh, still in the doorway, well out of sight. She heard him speak a word she didn't know, something dark and strong and beyond her understanding.

All the lights went out.

TEN

They went away then, Tom and his companion.

She stood in the dark for a long time, still hugging that book. Maybe she was waiting for the candles to leap into flame again. Maybe she was waiting for some kind of understanding to come, or Tom to come back, or someone else, or . . .

Mostly, she thought she was just standing there because it was easier than moving, when she had absolutely no idea where to go, what to do with this, what this was.

She didn't, she *wouldn't* believe in magic. Ghosts were allowed, ghosts were inevitable; but to her mind magic was something else, something other. Insupportable, beyond belief.

And Tom was . . . an innocent, she'd thought. Sweet boy.

If she'd expected anyone, it would've been Webb; but there really wasn't any question. Tom had stood there in the doorway and spoken a word – in Webb's rational language, she supposed – and out went all the lights.

Which was magic, and impossible. And him, which made no sense. And . . .

And so she stood there, at least until she'd stopped shaking and nothing had happened, nothing worse. No more voices, no more lights.

That long, and just a little longer.

It was remarkably hard to move, in fact. That first little step, out from the shelter of this charmingly solid bookcase: really astonishingly hard.

Still, she managed it eventually, if only because the alternative was only to stand there until someone came looking.

One step, and then another: out from shelter, out into the open darkness of the library floor. Perhaps she should still feel sheltered by that darkness, but of course she didn't; ghosts could see in the dark. She felt brutally exposed. Even if nobody came.

She might have followed the line of dead candles, feeling her way with her foot, kicking it; but in fact she didn't need to. The doors were still ajar, and that friendly oil-lamp was still burning in the hallway. She could walk towards the glow and not worry about tripping. She could hurry, even: worrying as she did so about discovery or worse, a figure, a silhouette suddenly appearing in the gap between the half-open doors . . .

It didn't happen. She came to the doors and through them, and only then realized that she was still clutching the folio. And wasn't going to take it back into the shadowy library, so she set it down just there beside the doors, like a mysterious confession, *I did this*, without quite saying either who or what.

There was another door – less tall, more square – which ought, she thought, to lead out on to the courtyard, but it was locked. Back up the stairs, then: all the way to the top, where she was confident of her route even in this fallen darkness.

If there were light switches she didn't grope for them, with the electrics unreliable. She just wanted to be out of this wing, gone from here before anyone came again. Not to get caught. *Oh, Tom* . . .

She was suddenly afraid of him, rather. Which wasn't anything she'd expected, or anything she knew how to handle. Grace had been afraid often and often these last years, she was used to that – but never of a boy. Of institutions, yes, men in uniform, judges and policemen and prison warders, but those had been impersonal. They called her Harley, or they called her by a number; they had nicknames and legends of their own that were whispered behind their backs, all up and down the galleries, in and out of cells. They weren't *people*.

This house . . . wasn't like that. It wasn't a battleground. It shouldn't be.

Tom wasn't like that. He wasn't in authority; he had no power over her. He shouldn't have.

He's a magician. He shouldn't be, but she had seen it. That was power, strange and fearful. And she had seen it when she ought not, where she ought not to have been. There was power in that too, but only if she found a way to use it. Whoever he'd been showing off for – it had been a performance, a demonstration: what else? – it was not her.

Georgie thought he'd be angry, if he found out. She was very fearful of men and their anger. It was a simpler way to be afraid, but just as potent.

She should probably stop thinking of him as a boy.

Through long empty attics, back towards the dormitories – and here was someone coming, flashing a torch against the increasing gloom. For a moment she froze; but only for a moment. Terror faded, as soon as she realized: *not Tom*. Tom wouldn't use an electric torch, where he could use a candle. Wouldn't need to, if he could control flame with a word; but he wouldn't do it anyway.

This figure was shorter than Tom, and stouter. And female, dressed in something long. Long and white . . .

'Mother Mary!'

'Ah, there you are, dear. I've been looking for you.' For an instant, the torch beam shone into her face; then it was snapped off. 'Sorry. I made you flinch, didn't I? I don't like to come this way without a light, and don't tell anyone else I said so but frankly candles are such a nuisance, always going out, and oil lamps are too heavy. Florence Nightingale must have had shoulders like a navvy. Or someone else to carry her lamp for her. That wouldn't surprise me in the least. Behind every great man there's a woman, you know – so it's probably true about great women too. Now come along – our own great man would like a word with you.'

'The captain?' she said hopefully, not really hopeful.

'No, the doctor. You've met him, he said.'

'Yes. They gave me a lift back from town. The doctor and his wife.' The woman in her proper place, presumably, behind him.

'Yes. Sometimes I think Ruth knows this house better than I do, even. She was here in the war, you know. Well, they both were; but she nursed, and I know what that means. On her feet all day and half the night, in and out, up and down. Men don't have a clue, what we really do for them.' Of course, she'd been a nurse herself; natural sympathy came through. And she was herself the woman behind a great man, or she thought so. Georgie thought she did. 'I've had people running all over, trying to chase you down, since the doctor lost you; it was Ruth who suggested you might have wandered over to the empty wing. What were you looking for?'

Privacy was on the tip of her tongue, but that would be a killer. Grace kept quiet; Georgie said, 'You'll think me silly, but at first I was only trying to find my suitcase. Someone's put it somewhere, and what with everything that went on last night, and changing rooms and so forth, I've lost track of it completely. So I went looking, without really a clue where to start; and once I'd started, I just sort of kept going. To be honest, I think maybe I was glad to be alone for a little bit. I'm not used to so much company . . .'

'Hmm. That's what Ruth said, more or less: that you'd gravitate that way for the solitude. Well, take us slowly, by all means; there is no hurry here. But remember, dear, this house is a community. You didn't come here to be alone, and we won't leave you so. And don't worry about your case. There's nothing there you need. Things don't matter, only people. Now come along, the doctor wants a word.'

Perhaps the doctor did want a word. She wasn't sure, once they got there. He asked questions, and she answered them. But they were back in the room of her utter guilt, with the object of her great offence laid out there, stark and unremitting: Kathie pale and empty on her mattress, barely living. Swallowed.

Not to be rescued, even by the so-clever doctor. He knew that, she thought, as well as she did. He might not know the truth – *I fed her to my terror, to save myself; I gave her up to nothingness* – but he did know the house, that was clear. He knew what kind of things could happen to people here. Things had happened in the past that were nothing to do with her. Grace might have found that a comfort, might have offered it up as an excuse. Georgie couldn't do that.

It was odd, that the invented girl should prove to be the honest one between them. She thought she liked Georgie, a lot better than she did Grace.

She thought Georgie didn't stand a chance, though, here in the house or out there in the world. Grace at least was a survivor.

The doctor was really only going through the motions now. She knew, if no one else did. If he saw more deeply into her than anyone else did – if he saw her guilt, her distress just at being here – he said nothing about it. Showed no sign of it, made no accusations.

Let her go at last, wearily, like a confession of failure.

Georgie hesitated, like a nice girl would: 'Please, what will happen to Kathie now?'

'We'll order up a private ambulance and take her down to London. We have a clinic there.' He and his wife, apparently: a shared enterprise, an unexpected concession of equality. 'We can look after her, try some new drugs, other treatments just coming through . . .'

He didn't expect any of them to work. Nor did she. She nodded and left the room, like a confession of guilt that no one but herself could hear.

Time still marches slowly, even without a ticking clock to keep it regular. The evening closed in, and dinner came. She found her way to the great kitchen and asked how she could help; she found shelter among a troop of women carrying bowls of salad, jugs of water. The doctor and his wife sat with the captain, of course, and Mother Mary. No need to go near them. Tom was present too, but he could only be on one side of the hall; she could sit on the other when she stopped to sit at all, with her back turned to him. Out of sight, out of mind – or almost. She had no idea what to do about Tom, no real idea what to do about anything.

She thought the house was big enough and full enough to avoid him, at least for the moment, while she thought. She thought there were people enough that she could avoid anyone, everyone. It's what she'd been doing, more or less. Years now. Even at parties: shrieking people's names, air-kissing them, getting stoned with them, going to bed with them. Avoiding them.

But here she was washing up, scrubbing pots – and suddenly

here was Tom, beaming at her, bouncing at her like a puppy, nothing like a magician.

Except that that was what he wanted to talk about, exclusively; except that he wouldn't call it magic, he wouldn't call it anything, he wouldn't even say what it was. Just, this fabulously exciting thing had happened this evening, it was like a test only it had gone extraordinarily better than he ever would have expected, he wasn't allowed to talk about it yet and that was such a shame because it was just so cool, but it was like the scales had fallen from his eyes and he'd realized just how powerful the rational language could be, how it really truly was going to change the world and save the world, just as Webb had always said it would, and he'd been looking for her everywhere ever since and where on earth had she *been* . . .?

I was right there, Tom. Watching you change the world. Nearly dying first, and being left terrified after; and I suppose that was Webb with you, was it? Webb who set up your little demonstration? That makes better sense . . .

It was easier to see Webb as the true magician, setting his candles in place like he set his people, his network, all around the world. Setting them on guard, perhaps, like a snare for the unwary, her. What he'd been holding against her, guarding against, and why it was worth her life to him – or Kathie's life before her – she couldn't guess. She hadn't been his enemy, till now.

Now, though . . . Now she'd seen the power and felt the terror . . . Now she could be his enemy, oh yes.

Tom's too, perhaps. If Tom was knowingly standing with Webb, learning his magic. Understanding what it meant.

She didn't answer Tom's question directly. Instead, she just shrugged and gestured with the dish mop. *I've been right here, doing my share. Doing woman-things, cooking and cleaning.* It was an alibi, of sorts. She didn't think he was going to start interrogating anyone to find out how long she'd been there, when she turned up, where she might have been before that or what she might have been doing.

Webb, she thought, would ask such questions, maybe. Webb might have noticed the candles knocked aside, out of his careful flight-path; he might know that something – someone – had triggered his snare. Someone more than the colony's cat.

He might even know who. He might—

He might do anything, and there might be nothing she could do about it. He'd said nothing, done nothing over dinner; that meant nothing, of course. He wouldn't want to show his hand. Reveal himself to the whole commune for what he was: *magician*. Only to his favourites, his special people, like Tom . . .

Kathie had been one of his. She wondered what the girl had done, to have him turn against her so thoroughly. So viciously.

She didn't need to be vicious herself to get rid of Tom tonight. Only a little cold, a little distant, a little unkind. Just enough to suggest that she had better things to do than talk to him. Better things, like scrubbing out these pots and chatting over her shoulder with the other women, handing drying cloths around but not handing one to him. Not inviting him to be one of the women.

Poor boy. There he was all full of himself and his own achievement, only wanting to share – and maybe wanting to share everything tonight, thinking he had a chance: her body and his in a bed for two, behind a door that closed, the crowning triumph of his perfect day – and here she was bursting his bubble with a casual pinprick, a cruel lack of interest.

It took a little while to penetrate, but he did get the message in the end. She saw all the effervescence leak out of him, she saw him deflate, and at last she saw him creep away to – presumably – a solitary bed in a crowded dormitory. She hoped his disappointment wouldn't fester, but if it did, well. Again, there was nothing she could do.

Herself, she kept to what shelter these new companions could provide. When the kitchen work was done, she drank a companionable mug of barleycup with them and shared a companionable joint; when it was time, she went upstairs with them to her own solitary bed in her own crowded dormitory.

*   *   *

At first, she never thought she'd sleep.

It was like Grace's fantasy of a girls' dormitory at boarding school. No doubt Georgie would know the reality of that, but this seemed close enough, all whispers and giggles from one end to the other, muttered complaints and hisses from the sleepy, the constant shift of restless bodies in the dark.

Once her eyes adjusted, it wasn't that dark. Windows were open, uncurtained; starlight was light enough for a sleepless girl to see figures move between the beds, to understand that actually not all of them were as solitary as her own.

She saw one couple slip off towards the stairs and away. Hand in hand, she thought they went. She hadn't checked from one end to the other, but she did think that there were only women in this long dorm, that they divided for sleeping in a way they didn't for the bathrooms. Well. She'd lived a Soho party life for a while now, with prison before that and the country-house circuit before that; nothing was new to her any more, and she really didn't care so long as no one came to trouble her, to try to share her bed.

Honestly, between Grace and Georgie, her own bed wasn't that solitary anyway. Sometimes she really did think she was two different women; there really wouldn't be room for a third.

At first she thought she'd never sleep. Then she thought she must have done.

It was later, darker, quiet.

No, not quiet. Quieter, yes. No more voices now.

Something, though: something hung in the air, the memory of sound. Something had woken her.

In her head – in her dream, if she'd been sleeping, if she'd been dreaming – it had been the sound of bells.

Which was why she thought she must have slept and dreamed it. There weren't any bells now. Tom had silenced them, or taken them away.

There was the great sunken bell beneath the lake, but she didn't think she'd been hearing that. Not this time. She wasn't swimming, not drowning, no.

Bleeding, though – she thought she might be. Her arm ached

beneath its bandage, in that dull dreary way of a wound that wouldn't heal. She didn't want to look.

She didn't want to listen, either. Just in case. She didn't want to lay temptation in the world's way, make a ready victim of herself, be opened up to the possibility of bells.

Didn't want to; couldn't help herself.

Lay still in the hush of that room, and the world came in to her through the open window; and below the breath of the wind, behind the sough of distant trees . . . Yes. She was sure of it: the low slow murmur of a bell, slightly hesitant and barely there, like the unsteady tick of a great clock running down, almost at its end. Like the beat of a great heart, dying.

Everyone else seemed to be sleeping. Awkwardly, one-handedly, she pulled herself up off her mattress and went to the window.

It was set low, in the slope of the roof; she could lean right out, and her turning head could pinpoint the source. It was so soft and deep, it was hardly even a sound now, only a sense of vibration in the air, but it drew her none the less: her attention and her blood both, reaching for it.

Besides, it wasn't hard to find. There was the great dark mass of the wood, with the star-glitter sky above it; and there was a single orange spark of light, like a fairy-tale lure, deep among the trees.

She thought she knew already, where that was and how to get there.

There was another light that she could see and then not see and then see again, whiter and cleaner, paler, shifting and irregular. She thought she knew what that was, too. She thought it was coming here. Coming out of the trees and briefly steady then, moving with purpose; and then gone entirely, lost behind the bulk of the house. On its way.

She thought she was mad to go, but going anyway; twice mad to go alone, but still not waking any other of the women.

Fumbling into clothes, glad of their simplicity in the darkness; shuffling in sandals between the narrow pallets and the sleeping forms; feeling her way down the dark of the stairs, until her hand found a light switch below and blessed it, pressed it.

Now she could hurry.

Now she was aware of carrying her bleeding arm crooked against her chest, the way it hurt less; and of a dampness at her breastbone, where a dark patch showed how blood was oozing through the bandage and through the shirt it pressed against.

Hurry, hurry.

Well, she was hurrying. Into trouble, towards that hypnotic murmur; with no idea beyond getting there, being there, learning just how much worse this could be. It might kill her, she did know that. She didn't care. She'd stopped being afraid of death long since, just as she'd stopped looking for it. She only needed to know what bell and how and why it was rumbling. Except *for her*: she knew that much already.

She thought she knew one other answer too, what bell it was. There was only one bell in the woods. Surely, only one . . .?

She let herself out of the house as soon as she found a door she could unbolt. Here and there around the courtyard a window was still lit, by electricity or lamp or candle; she could find company if she wanted it. In this irregular household, of course she could. She didn't have to go alone.

Nevertheless. She knew her route out of the courtyard. Didn't want to go that way – didn't, in honesty, *want* to go at all – but the low drone of the bell was still rolling in her bones, roiling in her belly, beating in her blood.

It was her choice, and she made it.

Her back to the house and those promising lights; her face to the dark. To the stable block, and the narrow passage further, turn right at the dungheap; follow the path around the wall of the kitchen garden, and then into the wood.

None of that would be easy. She wished she had a choice; she wished she had a torch.

No matter. She knew the way, more or less, and there was light at the end. She'd seen it burning.

Light at her back, to see her out of the courtyard. Light overhead, that too, for a while. She hurried through the archway under the clock tower, almost holding her breath for that plunge into absolute black, and then the star-bright sky was back and welcome and enough to show her the way across the stable yard.

Here was the mouth of the passageway, an arch of brick, a tunnel. She didn't much want to go in; she wasn't wholly certain she'd come out again. That bell tolled for her, she was sure of that. Somewhere, her child must be waiting. Doing nothing, being nothing. Ready.

Still. She'd come this far; there was nowhere else to go. Except back, of course. To the house and ask for help, for company, like a good colony girl ought to do; or all the way around, down the drive and along the lane to Cookie's house and through the wood from there. With him if he was awake, showing a light, willing.

That would be ridiculous, but oh, it was tempting. Cookie would understand and not fuss. Stand witness, if she needed that.

But she could as easily find him this way, if she wanted to fetch him out. If she chose to. And she'd come this far, and – no. Not turning back now. She didn't dare, quite. When she glanced over her shoulder, hoping for one last reassuring glimpse of a light in the great shadow of the house behind her, she saw instead a hint of movement under the clock tower, as though darkness were something physical, a fabric that could tear under pressure and be sucked down in shreds.

Here comes nothing, she thought. And almost waved at her unseen baby, almost waited.

Almost.

Instead, she turned and plunged into the black of the passageway. Fear behind her, puzzlement and uncertainty and fear ahead; right here there was only pain, the throbbing in her arm, the pulse of wet blood drawn out by that endless bell. She thought her baby was drawn to her blood, perhaps. That ought to make some kind of sense, somewhere. Somehow.

It was like a march of inevitability, a single string of purpose: from the bell to her, from her to her baby.

She was almost not sure now, which one of them was the

ghost. She could feel herself fading; she thought she must look translucent inside these pale clothes. Unreal.

She went on, feeling her way along the rough brick of the tunnel wall, drawn as much as anything by the rich smell of the dungheap at the end. For a moment, emerging at last into what seemed the almost brilliant light of the stars, she only stood and breathed, drawing that smell deep in, something to hold on to.

She wouldn't look back again, no. Just keep heading onward.

Cool thick grass beneath her feet now and the garden wall to follow, down to the wood. The wood would be the worst of it, she knew that. No starlight under the trees, and the path difficult to find and harder to follow, thorns and low branches tangling with her ankles and lashing for her eyes. And that was . . . assuming nothing worse. Assuming no bells, no blood, no nothing.

No bodiless baby in the path, no nothing.

He was behind her now, but . . . Well. She wasn't running away, she was forging ahead. He might forge faster; she had no way to tell. It was up to him. Or the house, perhaps. The house gave him presence, she thought; away from here, he existed only in her head and in a hole in the ground, on paper, in memory, in despair.

Here he was actual, in the way that a whirlpool is actual: nothing solid, just a constant sucking void, deadly and inimical and there.

There behind her, she thought as she ploughed on. There in front of her, perhaps: what she ploughed towards. The bell and the baby were the same thing, almost, in her head. Intricately linked, intimately threatening. One cut her and cut her; the other would drain her and drain her until there was nothing left, nothing of her either.

To drink and drink and not be satisfied: it was like a curse from ancient times, a legendary doom. For her, another source of guilt. She had killed her baby inside herself; she had cursed him to this cruel half-life, afterlife, being and not being.

Really, she thought he ought to catch up with her. Track her down and suck her up. Or lie in wait ahead, lurk within the sound of a striking bell, catch her as she bled out.

Either way. On she went. What else could she do? She couldn't outrun it, or him. If she fled this place, she'd still know they were waiting here. Her baby, proclaimed by every striking clock, up and down the valley: caught in every shadow, trapped by the house, because she came here. Given something that was almost shape, but never substance. In a house of bells, dust draining into sand: eternal loss, form without purpose, a worse fate than before.

She couldn't do that to him, no.

Let him drink her, then; let them cancel each other out.

But he would need to catch her first. Grace wasn't going to stand still and take it, not for anyone. Maybe she was just showing off for Georgie, one last lesson. *You don't have to let them take you. Kick and scream, fight back. March on. Run away, if you have to.*

Not that she was running away. He might be behind her still; he might be ahead. She didn't know and wasn't pausing to find out.

The one arm still cradled close, pulsing blood, pulsing pain. The other hooked across her face, against the slashing branches that she couldn't see. Her feet found the path more than her eyes did, better than her memory. The way of least resistance: it was the way she'd always gone.

Here was a fork where she'd turn off to go to Cookie's cottage, to ask for company, for help. Or rather, where she wouldn't. Where she could do, if she chose to.

She chose to go the other way, alone.

Soon enough she could smell smoke in the air, alongside all the damp wood night smells. She was oddly short of breath herself, tight-chested already, before she began to cough.

Well, there'd never been any question of sneaking up on him. She was making way too much noise just getting there, city girl out in the country in the dark, no idea how to go placidly amid the trees and the haste and that relentless rumour of a bell.

Coughing and gasping, then, she came out into the clearing.

Her night-blind eyes were dazzled by the flare of light, despite the smoke that swirled and pooled and rose in stinging clouds. That was the charcoal heap, she'd figured that: something – or someone, whoever it was that she'd seen coming back to the house by torchlight – had broken the crown of it like an eggshell, shattering the baked turfs and letting in the air. Now the dry wood inside was blazing, flame leaping out of that hole at the top and searing upward like a beacon, like a searchlight, like a finger probing for the sky.

Like an echo in contrasts of the tower that it illuminated, all shape and shadow against the determined dark of the wood.

Where was Frank? He should have been here, busy to save his charcoal, blocking out the air with frantic mud. Too late now, she guessed, but still . . . He ought to be here and was not.

Perhaps he'd been the one with the torch. Perhaps he'd done all this himself: sabotaged his own craft to send some crazy signal to the stars, left it burning, headed off . . .

Headed where? Frank didn't like to come to the house even in daylight. He thought it was haunted.

Not wrong there.

Maybe he was still here. Maybe the fire in his charcoal hadn't been enough. Someone had been ringing the bell, she was sure. Someone still was, perhaps, a little. She could feel the throb of it in the air, in her aching wrist.

She could walk through the open doorway into the hollow of the ruined tower to find out.

Of course she could. It was what she'd come for.

Wasn't it . . . ?

The fierce light made the stones of the tower glare almost white at her; it made the doorway and the higher windows and traceries, the ruder holes and breaks where stones had fallen, all the many openings look worse, black and threatening.

If she thought she saw movement inside – well, perhaps that was only the light shifting the shadows as the flame guttered and roared.

She took a few slow paces forward, and that shifting spear of light tossed her own shadow forward from her feet, all the way to the tower's mouth, so that she walked a path of darkness.

Hesitated on that path, and more than once, but walked it none the less.

All the way: across rough and broken ground, bare rock and thick tussocks and the half-laid stones around Frank's subterranean home. Pausing briefly, wondering whether to call down, to check that he wasn't sleeping.

Feeling the thrum of the bell in her bones, the damp sticky warmth of her blood against her own skin.

He wasn't sleeping. Not through this.

Keeping on, then, all the way.

Standing just for a moment on the threshold, in the doorway, in the dark: her own body cutting out the light that might otherwise have shown her what waited inside.

Stepping in, then.

Shifting sideways, to allow that fall of light: not much, it seemed in here. Barely enough.

Enough, though.

She couldn't see Frank, or anyone. He wasn't there; no one was.

Nor her baby, either. Not that kind of no one.

Something moved in the darkness, none the less.

Nothing much: just a line without body, a swaying presence, a rope.

Overhead, the bell droned on, as if its clapper grated against the rim, grated and grated, never properly striking, never properly still.

She reached out a hand, her good hand, to grip the rope and make it still, make that dreadful sound just stop.

The rope swung with more weight than she could readily control, one-handed. She let her body hang against it for a moment, hauling down, wondering if the bell at the top were really that heavy; and then she let her eyes drift upward.

Couldn't see the bell, of course. It would have been too far, too high in any case, in the dark; but there was something in the way, between her and the bell.

Something else on the rope.

Something heavy and hanging, swinging, making the bell sound lowly.

Oh.

That was Frank, she saw, when her eyes at last worked

through the foreshortening and the moving shadows and the moving corpse.

Frank with his eyes a-glitter when they caught the firelight coming through the tracery, but yes, very thoroughly a corpse.

Frank staring down, or seeming to, because the rope was looped around his neck, strangling-tight.

He might have hanged himself by accident, but she didn't see how. He was too high up that rope, halfway to the bell; and besides, he didn't ring it any more.

He might have hanged himself deliberately, but – well, he would have needed to climb that high up the rope, with the bell all a-clamour above him as he went, and she didn't quite see why he would. He was mad, yes, but even so . . .

In the back of her mind, another picture was forming. Another kind of madness altogether, her own: a vision of two hands, hands of smoke, rising out of the charcoal heap because someone had broken the skin of it and let them loose. Hands that only strengthened as the flame caught, as the fire roared.

Hands that gripped Frank by the throat – coolly, smoke not flame – and lifted him, strangled him even before they twisted the rope around his throat to let his own body-weight finish the work if they hadn't done it already.

Left him swinging, sounding the bell and swinging, sounding his own funeral knell as he swung, as he died.

Sounding hers too, perhaps, almost, as she stood there swaying beneath him, as she bled.

ELEVEN

Georgie would have done that, perhaps. She would have let it happen: would have stood there and bled and waited for a rescue that would not come. The bell was barely speaking now, to call them; the fire had flared up, but what were the odds that anyone else would see it? See it and come, two things, one unlikely and one effortful?

Tom said someone usually came out, in the middle of the night, to sit with Frank . . .

It was true, he had said that. But someone had been already, and done more than sit; and perhaps that had been Tom by torchlight, making his way back, leaving Frank hanging?

He's a magician. Candles go out at a word from him. He wouldn't need a torch.

Perhaps not – but perhaps he'd have to carry a candle. He might not be able to make a flame dance from nothing. And if he had to carry a candle, why not carry a torch?

And he was a magician. He could have put Frank up there, had the rope strangle him and dangle him at a word.

If there was a word for that. If the language allowed it.

Yes. If. Neither Grace nor Georgie knew. She didn't know if she were making excuses for Tom or accusing him, or both.

What she did know – what Grace knew, beyond question – was that she wasn't just going to stand here and bleed until she fell over, until she passed out. Wait and hope for rescue. No.

So, then. She had done what she could, to still Frank's swinging and the appalling grinding of that bell. Now she set her teeth, clutched her bleeding wrist against her chest because it couldn't hold itself there any longer, and set off walking.

Without a free hand to fend off stray branches and groping thorns, she couldn't save her face, let alone her hair. With leaves dense above and the light soon lost behind her, she couldn't see the danger before she'd walked straight into it, again and again and again.

Bleeding, then, from a dozen scratches or worse – and from two fresh cuts that were far, far worse – she tripped and stumbled and swore her way down one path and up another, and so came after all to Cookie's cottage.

And was not at all surprised to find his lights still on; and hammered on his door with her fist, because she couldn't stop now to find the knocker, everything was suddenly urgent; and her one hand was clumsy while the other one was dead, except she didn't think the dead should hurt so badly. She hoped not. And she thought she should probably not have come here, because she was fairly sure her baby was following her, but it was too late now; the door was opening, and oh!

That wasn't Cookie; that was the doctor's wife. Ruth. And there was the doctor behind her in the little sitting-room, smoking a cigar, looking on with interest; and she didn't know where Cookie was, but here was she, falling over the threshold, going down—

—and coming up on Cookie's settee, with the air full of smoke – that cigar, and Cookie's rollies, and Ruth too was having a cigarette – and that set her coughing, which reminded her.

She told them about Frank, not coughing now, in his blazing charcoal smoke. She thought she got it all out, all the important stuff, and then she was gone again.

She came back again in a room she hadn't seen before, low beams and an angled ceiling, far too cramped for D'Espérance. She must still be in Cookie's cottage: a little bedroom up in the eaves. A lamp burned in one corner, shaded by a silk scarf so that it cast a dim reddish light. For a while she just lay there, looking. She was conscious of another presence in the room, though: the sounds of movement, soft and subtle and controlled. Someone else's breathing, that too. She supposed that was movement too, the movement of air and muscles. It was oddly reassuring, that whoever watched this night with her did at least need to breathe.

No woman should be glad, not to find her child with her; but still. Here she was. Still breathing.

Not bleeding, not now. Her one hand checked the other, below the covers: freshly bandaged, and quite dry.

Also, no smell of smoke. None on her, none in the air. She'd been washed when she was undressed, before she was put to bed. Washed unconscious like a child, like a patient. Now she was being sat over in her sleep and in her waking, like a child, like a patient.

She turned her head, and was utterly unsurprised to find a nurse there. Ruth was sitting on a straight hard chair beside the bed, working with a crochet hook and a skein of wool.

Without lifting her eyes from her fingers, Ruth said, 'Well, I know that's nothing I did. I didn't even bring my knitting up, because the click of the needles might have disturbed you. How are you feeling?'

She thought about it for a moment. 'Fine,' she said, a little surprised to find that true. Then: 'Tired,' because she was that too. Then she remembered Frank and had to think about him, and how she felt about that; and then of course she had to ask, 'Is Frank . . .?'

The question seemed to die half-spoken, but it carried weight enough to get where she'd meant it to go.

'Frank's being taken care of,' Ruth said carefully. Covering the ground. 'The menfolk are out there now, with the authorities, handling everything. It's not exactly the first mysterious happening at D'Espérance. And the local police inspector is . . . well, very local. He's lived around here all his life. He knows about the house, and he won't make difficulties. Edward can certify it as a suicide, and people will accept that. Of course they will; what else? It's fairly obvious that the balance of the man's mind was disturbed. There'll need to be an inquest, but the coroner's onside too. It'll mean a day or two of disruption here and some formalities – you'll have to be interviewed, I'm afraid, though one of us will sit in with you and make sure to keep things easy – but I don't think there'll be too much trouble, so long as we can keep it out of the nationals. A little local suicide, they shouldn't be interested, but you never can tell what the Sundays might pick up . . .'

'Don't worry about the papers,' she said. 'I'll make sure they leave this alone.'

A little beat of silence, of disbelief: and then perhaps Ruth remembered who she was, or one of the people she was, and said, 'Really?'

'Really.'

'I . . . would have thought that your name would attract them, rather than the opposite.'

'I can play decoy if I have to, if that will help. But – no, I shouldn't have to do that. Only a phone call.' Tony would be upset, to have this news come so hard on the heels of her earlier report: *I've found him.* But Tony wanted what was best for the *Messenger*, and for himself. It was never good when the newspaper became the story; the last thing he'd want would be for this story to break nationally. He'd have to come up here himself then, to answer the coroner's questions in open court: why he'd sent a reporter to the commune under cover, exactly when and how he'd lost touch with his man, exactly how and why he'd chosen to send a notorious and unstable woman after him to find out what had happened . . .

No. That was not a story Tony would want to tell, nor to see told. Neither would his father. Between the two of them, they had influence enough to deter any other paper that came sniffing around. Tony was everybody's friend, and if friendship wasn't enough then his father's money would carry the day, or else his political contacts. That was how the world worked, for people like that. She knew; she'd seen it from underneath as they came crushing down on top of her. Nobody could stand up, under that.

'Well. We'd be very grateful. But you may not need to use the telephone, if face-to-face would be better.'

'I'm sorry?' Ruth didn't understand. The idea was to keep Tony from coming. Or thinking that he needed to come, or sending anyone else.

'We've a private ambulance arriving in the morning, to take Kathie down to London. My husband thinks that it ought to take you too, and I have to say I agree with him. You've lost a lot of blood, dear, never mind the shocks of the night. A few days in the clinic will put you on your feet again.'

It was the perfect escape for everyone. Any nosy journo wanting to know where she'd been would never think to look up here if he found her still in London, taking bed rest in some fancy private nursing-home. He'd think terrible things, and likely print them too, and she'd have all of that to live through; but it would all be lies, and lies were easy. You just denied them and denied them, and let people believe what they liked, what they were comfortable with. They'd all think she had a drink problem or another baby to get rid of: one or the other, or both. No one would bother to look any further; why should they? It was the best kind of lying, where you got someone else to tell the lies and they were all true anyway, even if not actually now . . .

'Oh, hush,' Ruth said gently. 'What are you crying for, you silly girl? Don't you worry, we'll take care of you. I could wish I'd had the care of you before this, but—'

Somehow, effortfully, she managed to shake her head. 'I'm sorry,' she said, and that was true too, 'but I can't come to London with you. I still have things to settle here.'

'The coroner will wait, dear. The policeman too, if he doesn't get to you this morning.'

'Not them. Things of my own.' Frank didn't change anything. Or no, that was nonsense; of course he did. But he didn't change everything. Not yet.

Not that she was getting out of bed in chase of things, not yet. She slept, and when she woke Cookie brought her food; and then again, the sleeping and the waking and the meal. Tea and toast the first time, with a coddled egg, nursery food; and then soup again, a different kind of soup, thick and nourishing. Invalid food.

She looked at him through the steam of the bowl, and frowned, and said, 'Why do they call you Cookie?'

He smiled and gestured at her tray. The bread was his own bake, clearly, and she rather thought he might have made the butter too.

'That's what I thought. Your name's not Mr Cook at all, is it?'

'That's right.'

And then he was gone, leaving her with more questions than answers, and more irritation than either. Wasn't the big house enigmatic enough already, without those who lived in its shadow playing their own games with mystery and shadow?

Apparently not. No matter.

*   *   *

In the afternoon, she had a visitor. Voices down below; light feet on the stairs; a hesitant knock on the door. That uncertain tapping would have been enough to give him away, if she wouldn't have known him just by his tread after following him about ever since she came here, if she hadn't heard his voice quite clearly wafting up the stairwell.

It was hard to reconcile the self-doubting boy on the landing here with the confident young magician who could kill a blaze of candles with a single word, but there it was. Here he was.

She would rather have avoided him, but this did have to happen; and it was probably better here, now, where he was unsure of his ground. So she told him to come in, and he did that; and fidgeted awkwardly at the foot of the bed, waiting for her to tell him to for Pete's sake sit down in the chair there, where Ruth had been before.

Instead, she patted the edge of the bed, where he'd be just a couple of inches and a couple of blankets from her barely-decent bed-warm flesh. He could hardly help but be aware of that, aware of every shift her body made between the old worn cotton sheets. Right now she just wanted to keep him off-balance.

He perched obediently where her hand had indicated. Lying through her teeth, she said, 'It's lovely to see you, Tom. Thanks for coming.'

'Well,' he said, 'of course . . .' And ran dry, and stopped; and shrugged, and rallied, and tried again. 'I feel, you know, responsible. I was the one who found you in the wood and brought you on. I introduced you to the house. And you've had such a rotten time since you came, though you were a hero for trying to save Kathie; and then last night, and – well, some people are saying you're a Jonah, that you bring trouble, but of course I don't believe that, and . . .'

And *somebody has to come and see you*, he seemed to be saying, *so it had better be me. There really isn't anybody else.* She was sure that wasn't actually what he meant to say, though it might still be the truth. She just smiled thinly and said, 'Well. I'm sorry if people think I'm bad luck. I don't think I believe in luck.' *Only what's deserved.* And never getting that, never being that lucky. 'Things happen, things have happened, but it's really not my fault. You're not saying that people really think it is?'

'Oh, no, not really. No, I'm sure not,' he said, sounding anything but sure. *Yes, they do.* 'Only, well, everything's been so . . . so *dramatic* since you came, and now Frank's dead and we've got police all over, and some of the people here don't mix well with the pigs; and they do just want someone to blame, and I'm afraid that's you.' *Because you're still a stranger*, he was saying, *not one of us.*

She could have given him a better reason. *Because I'm responsible,* she could have said. In part she was, no question; and she could take it all. Why not?

Because he knew the truth, of course; he knew how much he was responsible for himself. Of course he'd let the house blame her, but . . .

'Tom? Are you seriously saying that nothing strange had happened here before I came?' *Didn't you have to practise?*

'Oh – no, I'm not saying that. Of course not. Some people think the house is haunted; some think it's blessed. The captain says it's a reservoir of power. When I came here, I thought I was following ley lines to a nexus. Webb says it's not the house, it's the people. He says wherever you get a concentration of people who believe, even if they believe in different things, you're going to get a sense of something happening – but I . . . I . . . I don't think he's right. I think places store things up, like batteries; I think they take energy in and release it. Maybe it comes from us, I don't know. Maybe it's inherent in the earth, that's what I used to think, but . . .'

But he was being heretical, taking a stand against his guru, and it was really difficult for him; and he really, really didn't sound like a magician today, or like he'd ever made anything happen on his own account.

She could be kind. Georgie could, always. She said, 'But either way, any way it comes, there was stuff going on before I turned up, right?'

'Little things,' he said. 'Feelings, mostly. Some people thought they saw a ghost or a wood spirit or a manifestation of the Goddess. And then there was Frank, of course. Frank . . . well, we don't like to say he was mad. He just saw the

world differently, and it was a struggle always to keep him
settled. He couldn't stand being in the house, basically. From
the day he came, things happened around him. He said it was
a poltergeist, but I know Mother Mary thought he was doing
it all himself. Whether or not he remembered doing it, after.
Either he was pretending really hard, or else he had, you know,
a split personality, or else . . .'

'Or else it was real. To him, at least. And people who are
pretending don't hang themselves, mostly.'

'No. No, they don't. Which is why, well, don't tell anyone
– but I just think he was mad. I have to think that. It's either
that or . . . or something supernatural. Something malevolent.
In the house, or in the woods. Which I'm not going to believe,
but a lot of people do, that's what I'm saying. They think
you're like Frank, a catalyst. A lightning rod. Something that
brings out the bad stuff.'

And the thought distressed him deeply, or else he was a
very good actor; and she didn't believe that for a moment.
She knew a thing or two about playing a part. She'd played
herself half her life, and now she was Georgie too; and
even Grace at her most cynical couldn't see Tom faking it
this well.

And yet . . .

She said, 'Let's change the subject. Please,' as though she
couldn't bear to talk about this any longer; and then, when he
nodded an immediate acquiescence, she went straight on: 'Tell
me about last night. I know I was distracted, and I'm sorry;
but I didn't realize until afterwards that there was something
you wanted to tell me, something you were really pleased
about. Tell me about that.'

'Oh,' he said awkwardly, shrugging, 'that was nothing.
Nothing now.'

'No,' she said, 'it's not nothing. Then or now. Never mind
what's happened since – tell me what you did last night. I
really want to know.'

'It's just – it was like a door opening, and all this light
spilling out . . . Which is kind of apt, in a way, because of
what happened. What I did. Except it's not me, not really. It's
the language. There's real power in it, just like Webb's been

saying. It doesn't just describe the world, it can shape the world. Remake it.'

'I'm sorry, Tom, I'm not smart like you. I didn't do well at school. You're going to have to explain that. What did you actually do?'

'I said a word,' he said, quietly proud, 'the word for *extinguish*, and all the lights in the room went out.'

I know. I was there. But he thought it wasn't him, and so did she, now. He thought it was the word that counted; she wasn't so sure. 'Who else was there?' *Apart from me. I wasn't the lightning rod for this.*

She thought he would just say *Webb*, and then everything would be clear and easy.

He didn't.

Getting out of bed was a hard thing. Not the hardest, not yet; but hard enough, for now.

Just the physical act of it, getting up and washing, finding clothes: hard effort and tricky doings, she had no strength and no control. It was like working someone else's fingers, from a distance.

Stumbling her way downstairs, when balance was like something her body had forgotten: she had to lean into the wall all the way. And then stand straight and tell lies, say that she felt good, thanks, perfectly fit, and fine to be leaving now. Just going up to the house, yes. To see a man about a horse, yes. No, she didn't mean that literally; she wasn't delirious, no. She wasn't being deliberately evasive, either; she just wanted to talk to somebody, and no, it really wasn't any of Cookie's business, and . . .

Oh, all right, then. She was being deliberately evasive, yes.

Even so. He didn't have any right to stop her, even patients could discharge themselves from hospital, and . . .

Oh. More soup, before she went? Well, if he insisted, then. Yes.

The doctor and Ruth weren't there, which might be the only reason she got away with it. She couldn't have stood up to all three of them. She could hardly stand up at all, to be honest.

Sitting down was better. More soup: that was better too. For somebody who mostly couldn't be bothered to eat, she did seem to be wonderfully hungry.

And she didn't honestly have to stand up to Cookie much, once she'd let him bully her into this respite. Indeed, she almost thought he was colluding. He satisfied himself that she was fuelled and primed, and then he released her.

Better: he drove her up to the house. She had never expected him to do that. Whoever he was and whatever position he held here – she still didn't know his actual name, had no label for him beyond 'Cookie', which he really wasn't, any more than she thought he was a janitor – she'd come to think of him as a neutral observer, holding himself apart. Even this much engagement was a surprise. Though she supposed he just wanted to see what she meant to do, the results of it at least, and he must have doubted she'd even make it as far as the house without his help.

Either that, or he didn't want to confess to Dr Dorian – or to Ruth – that he'd let their patient walk through the woods all that way. These potent woods, when she was short of blood already, and still open at the wrist.

Anyway: he drove her to the back door but didn't try to come in, didn't apparently want to fuss over her once he was sure that she'd been delivered. Didn't want to snoop.

Which was just as well, because what she did – whatever she did – she didn't mean to be snooped upon.

The sun was setting, but it was not yet dinner time for the house. The captain's belly hadn't proclaimed it, or else there was no one to announce it, they hadn't yet thought to arrange a substitute for Frank. People were milling in the corridors like school kids, perching on window sills and squatting in circles on the floor, smoking like bad kids, waiting for the summons.

She thought somebody ought to be taking control. She was quite surprised that Webb wasn't: the first mate taking charge, keeping the great ship on time and on course. Deferring naturally to the captain, but still making sure the crew got fed . . . Wasn't that his job?

Keeping the gangways clear, that too. He wasn't doing that

either. She was prepared to elbow and kick her way through
if she had to, no more sweet shy Georgie now; but actually
they moved out of her way, mostly, when they saw her coming.
They all knew who she was, or at least who she was here,
who she was now: *the girl who saved Kathie and then didn't;
the girl who found Frank and couldn't save him either; the
Jonah.* None of these knew her well enough to talk to, these
random hippies; and those who might have stopped her anyway,
out of duty or curiosity or sentiment – well, perhaps they saw
something in her face.

Perhaps they saw something at her back, and catching up.

They were all of them conditioned, apparently, like
Pavlov's dogs; the high doors to the dining room stood open
and people had gathered in the hallway outside, but no one
had gone in yet.

She went in.

She walked all the way through, around the long low tables
to the matching doors at the far end.

And opened one of those, and walked on through; and would
have closed it again behind her anyway, and never mind whatever might be following, only she felt it snatched out of her
hand by something materially stronger than she was, slammed
shut with a force that said there'd be no opening it now, not
from either side. Not till this was done with.

Candles were all around. Maybe it was only the draught raised
by the slam of the door, but for a moment they all seemed to
reach toward her, yearningly. Fingers shaped themselves in
the flames.

Joss sticks burned in the fireplace and at the window, all
along the windows. Again, their smoke twisted and eddied in
the shifting air, formed hands and fingers, groped for her from
far away. Georgie thought of Frank and charcoal smoke, and
shuddered.

Mother Mary sat alone on her sofa, and smiled to see poor
Georgie scared.

Grace met her eye to eye, untroubled. 'What, no captain?
What have you done with him?'

'The captain's doing grandly,' she said, soft and dangerous, eternally protective. 'He's off being official with the policemen, and dear Frank. Webb's away too, down to London with his precious Kathie. They can look after themselves tonight, while I . . . look after you.'

'Everyone knows I'm here.' That came out too quickly; it sounded defensive where she'd meant to sound only calm and ordered, as well prepared as Mary.

'People in the house know that Georgie Hale's in here with me – but who's Georgie Hale? Does anybody know? If she vanishes, can anybody find her, or any trace of her? Maybe she just left by another door, gone as mysteriously as she came. Maybe that's a confession.'

'People in London know who she is. Who I am.' One person did, at any rate. And he'd come looking. She thought he would. He'd come for the story. *Sorry, Tony. You're too late.* Too late for Frank, he'd be too late for her too. If he came.

If he didn't, there'd be no one to tell her story. Except Mother Mary, who everybody listened to.

'Oh, I know who you are,' she said dangerously. 'I've always known. Everyone here has their head in the clouds, those who haven't smoked their brains entirely; they struggle to know nothing, and they frequently achieve it. I keep my eye on the world, as I do on everyone here. I knew Georgie Hale, even before she lied to me about her name.'

'Well, then. You know that people will come looking for me.' For almost the first time in her life she really wanted a cigarette, and of course she didn't have one. Grace used to carry them routinely, but only for the benefit of men. Georgie never would.

Besides, she really didn't fancy bringing flame and smoke quite that close to her throat. Not with Mary's eyes darkly on her, broodingly. She wondered if it were possible to be strangled from the inside.

'Of course, but again: if they find nothing, nobody, no body – then who's to say what happened? Grace Harley's tried to kill herself before. Say she went mad and hanged poor Frank, then came to me to confess; and I tried to keep her for the police, but she wouldn't stay and I couldn't hold her, she went running off into the woods and over the moor and she might be anywhere by morning. Her body might never be found. For certain sure it would never be laid at my door.'

There wasn't another chair, and she wasn't, was *not* going to squash up on the sofa next to Mother Mary, but she really needed to sit down now. So she did that, sliding her back down the wall, hoping that it looked cool and self-confident and not at all as though her legs were giving way beneath her.

Here was one mystery solved: the ship's bell that used to stand by the back door had been removed here, for the moment. Set right here on the floor like she was, out of the way but in the captain's eyeline when he was sitting in his place.

She said, 'You really think you can do that? Just make me vanish altogether, in a puff of smoke and nothing left behind? You can't afford another body.'

'Oh, not me, dear. I can't do anything of the sort. Of course not. I'm no magician. I don't even speak their precious magic language. The gods, though – oh, yes. I reckon the gods could take you away from me, little nuisance that you are. Or burn you right up where you sit and leave nothing but a smear of grease and the smell of overcooking. I'll ask them in a little while. Then we'll see.'

Was that how she justified it? Not her work, but the gods'? 'That must make things easy,' she said, smiling, relaxed. Nothing to it: this was the face she wore night after night, man after man. 'You just put it to them, and they decide. No kickback, no responsibility.'

'That's right. They take all the responsibility to themselves. They can do that; they're gods.'

It wasn't right, of course. It wasn't even sane. She really wasn't one to talk, but she knew sheer bloody madness when she heard it: out of her own mouth or someone else's, no difference.

Besides, it wasn't how this house worked. Mother Mary might believe it, she might *choose* to believe it, but she was fooling herself. It wasn't gods that stalked these high rooms, working strange miracles.

Grace knew. So did other people: Cookie, the doctor, Ruth. And at least Cookie knew where she was, and that she wasn't about to go running off into the wilds of the land in chase of some wild abstracted death. He was a sensible man; he'd want a more sensible story.

She tried to find comfort in that, that someone at least would want to dig deeper in search of her.

Tried hard.

Meantime, maybe she was only buying time but that seemed fair enough, a reasonable thing to do; she said, 'What's it all about, though, Mary? Frank, Kathie . . .' *Me* . . . 'What's it for?' *And why should the gods oblige you?*

'This is Leonard's great task,' Mary said, with just a hint of that breathless awe that said *he is my guru,* even while her smile said that she worked behind her guru's back, moved him around like a chess piece: *as we do, my dear, with our men; you'll know, you of all people, how could you not?* 'It's what he's meant to do, his work in the world. Of course the gods want to see him fulfil his purpose. It's what they want for us all.'

And he's happy, is he, for you to pave his way with corpses? Aloud, she only said, 'And, what, Frank stood in his way, did he?'

'Yes, of course. Frank was a spy; he worked for one of those Fleet Street rags that you make such an exhibit of yourself for. I expect you knew him, did you? So he changed his clothes and came up here and made like he was one of us, but I never believed him. He was never right. I looked through his things and found the proof. Notebooks, a camera. Spy stuff. I didn't mean that he should die, I only wanted rid of him, but the gods knew better. They tried to accommodate me at first, they tried just to scare him away; but he wouldn't go. He only moved out of the house and bedded down in the woods, and watched us all, and waited.'

And went mad, but it was no use saying that to someone squatting that same territory. She hadn't quite known till this that a person could be calm and competent and entirely crazy.

'What do you think he was waiting for?'

'For you. Obviously.'

She might be mad, but she was almost right, that too. Of course Tony would send someone else, when Frank disappeared; it meant only that the story was getting bigger.

Somewhere in the giddy maze of his head, Frank must have known that. He really might have been waiting.

Which made his death her fault, probably. One more blow to her conscience, one more stiffening in her spine. She was going to need it.

She said, 'And Kathie?' *Never mind me, I know about me. So do you.* The assault on Kathie bewildered her.

'She wanted to take Webb away from us. Nice little rich girl, Kathie – her dad owns half of Buckinghamshire. She was working to set him up down there: in his own institute was what she called it, with all the communications that are difficult here, and none of the distractions that our colony affords. She would have . . . diminished what Leonard is working for. I couldn't have that. People should come to us, not move away. I prayed for intervention. That's all.'

No, that wasn't all. She deluded herself, she took refuge behind her gods, but somewhere inside her she must know what she was doing. She'd gone out to Frank – using her torch, which perhaps nobody else in the house would have done; there were hurricane lamps for going outside in the dark, but Mary had never quite bought into the simple life – and no doubt she'd say that she'd gone only to witness, and perhaps she even managed to believe it, but that had to be fragile, crêpe-paper thin.

Grace wanted to tear through that, just to see what lay deeper down. She wasn't sure it would help, but it might make her feel better. Georgie thought that might be important.

Poking gently, she said, 'But now you've lost Webb anyway. You said he'd gone with Kathie . . .'

'Yes, but he'll be back. We still have all his work, his records here. And his faithful lieutenant. Tom can take over, if we have to do without Webb. I'm making sure of that.'

A little demonstration, the power of the rational language: yes, Tom had bought totally into that. Never doubting that it was his own achievement, never thinking that the woman who stood behind his shoulder might have been playing with him. Praying to her gods, no doubt, to kill the candle flames at the moment that Tom spoke his potent word. Deceiving him, and deceiving herself, that too.

She said, 'Why do your gods play with fire?' Trying to
sound a little naive, a little curious, nothing more. A girl at
the end of her tether, who only wants to know. 'It's all been
fire and smoke,' and nothing to do with gods. Even the hands
of wax had been flame at one remove, in either direction:
molten by fire, candles without wicks.

Mary hadn't been there, but that didn't seem to matter. The
house took what it wanted, used that as it chose. For her, from
her, it took the cold sucking absence of her baby; for Mary
and from Mary, hands made of flame. *And you went to Frank
and made that happen, Mary, didn't you? Broke his charcoal
heap deliberately to let the fire roar, and then I think you
stayed to watch your gods at work.*

'That's how we communicate,' Mary said, 'between the
world below and the world above. Fire and smoke are the tools
we use, the gods and we. The gods and me, at least. Though
I'm not alone. Other believers have other ways to talk to
heaven and to hear, I am sure; but fire has always been a
tradition. From burnt offerings to altar candles. And smoke,
incense, that too. From Catholic thurifers to Chinese joss. I
use candles and joss in my own worship, of course, to catch
the attention of the gods and speed my prayers on high.
Sometimes they choose to use the same means, to bless me
with an answer.

'I've always felt a special connection to fire,' she went on
musingly. 'From a child, I knew there was importance in the
flame. More significance than simply warmth and light. The
people here let the distinctions blur, and I'm sorry about that.
Even the captain doesn't see what seems so obvious to me.
Even though he's spent so much time in the east, far more
than I have . . .

'That's where the scales finally fell from my eyes, you
see. That's where I saw what fire really means. The captain
sent me to India, where people live closer to nature and closer
to their gods, both at once; where fire is still a clear messenger,
as it used to be for us. More than a messenger, indeed: where
people use it to convey their very souls to the next life. I
saw a young woman, newly widowed, dressed in her wedding
clothes and seated on her husband's funeral pyre. I saw the

fire lit; I saw her burn beside him. She never stirred to flee the flames, she never raised her voice. Only her hands – I saw her lift her hands to heaven as she burned. That, yes. That has stayed with me all these years.'

She was sure that it had. Hands, clutching out of flame: how not? Never ask if the girl had been tied to her chair, perhaps, or drugged. Or both. Mary had the image that she wanted, with the meaning that she chose. In this place, that was enough. More than enough. Fire and smoke, and hands to do her work for her, oh yes . . .

Mary didn't need her own hands, apparently, not any more. She spoke a word, and all the candle flames stiffened in response. 'Blessed be the gods,' she said quietly, her gaze calm and settled. 'Now, I have prayers to say, but I can do that quietly in my head and still listen to you. I've told you my story. Why don't you tell me yours? Oh, I know who you are, Grace Harley, and I know what the public knows, what the papers say about you. The party girl who put the Tory party in bed with the Communist party, or might have done. Found guilty of taking money for sex, from the men who were acquitted of paying it. That's always the way. But I think there's more to you than that, isn't there? You've made some devil's pact with the yellow press, I know that too – that you're here like Frank was, to spy for them – but it's more than that too. You may as well tell me, you know. No secrets now. It's just you and me and the gods in here. Nobody will be coming through that door until we're done.'

A sudden fierce light stood to confirm that. She had set candles in jars on either side of the double doors – but that was no candlelight that leapt out of them. They were pillars of light, rather, cold and tall, as broad around as her arm, thrusting up full-width from the mouths of their jars and then criss-crossing like laces, back and forth across the space between them. She couldn't imagine what would happen to anyone who forced the doors open and tried to come through. Perhaps the light would hold the doors closed, against any human strength; or else nobody would dream of disturbing Mary while they remained shut. One or the other, she supposed. Or both.

Well, then. No reason not to share her secrets. She never
had, with anyone – but one way or the other, it wasn't going
to matter here. Whoever eventually walked out of that door,
they were going to do it alone.

She said, 'I was pregnant, when they sent me to jail before
the trial.'

'Yes, dear, I know that. The whole world knows. Pregnant
and unmarried and couldn't even name the father, there had
been so many candidates.'

Couldn't, or wouldn't. But she didn't interrupt; Mary had
a head of steam and was forging onward.

'What better proof could you offer that you were guilty of
everything they said? No wonder they locked you away. But
then you lost the baby, and the judge took pity on you.' *I
wouldn't have done*, her manner said. *Never mind what's
happened since, or whatever's happened here. Hippy morals,
never mind those either. Guilty as charged, and you met your
just deserts.*

No. Never that. No punishment enough: not even this raw
confession, made in raw light to a woman who was mad, and
who despised her.

She said, 'I didn't lose my baby. I killed him.'

She said, 'While he was inside me still, while I was inside.
They were going to make abortion legal, but I couldn't, you
know. I couldn't *wait*. He wouldn't hold still and not grow
and just wait until the law let me get rid of him.'

She said, 'It would've been easier on the outside; I could've
managed it better. I knew people, outside. Of course I did.
But that didn't help me in Holloway. So I asked the women
there, and one of them got me something. I don't know what
– a powder, green and bitter it was. I mixed it with water and
swallowed it, and she said it'd make me miscarry. It . . . didn't
do that.'

There were tears leaking down her face now, but she
ignored them and so did Mary. 'I was ill for a few days, I
bled a little, but that was all. Only, then I didn't get any
bigger, and it didn't move any more, it didn't kick; and the
doctors said it was dead, my baby, but I still had to carry it
until. Until . . .'

That was it, apparently. A word that grounded on a memory too dreadful to discuss, a door she wouldn't open, a place she refused to go: the day she'd given birth, if that was what it was, to the son that she'd killed weeks before.

No punishment enough. Certainly nothing that Mary could do to her now, maybe not even anything the house had to offer. She had a terrible respect for the house, its own judgement, its insight; more than she'd ever had for the systems of law, the man who had sat in judgement over her. She'd seen too many judges with their trousers off.

Mary was something else again. Not constrained. Not sane, perhaps, but powerful even if she wouldn't admit it. And lethal, of course, that too.

Even now she might claim that she was praying, but what she was really doing, she was setting up to kill.

Where Grace sat – and she was all Grace now, all full of that self and what she had done, full and spilling over – there were candles on either side of her, and their lights were rising: nothing like regular candle-flames, and nothing either like the interlaced pillar-lights that kept the door. These rose like string and stretched like wire, bright golden fierce wires that bent back on themselves and twisted around, scribbled lines in mid-air that burned and burned and would not go out.

Lines that made shapes, yes.

Lines that etched two hands in light, right there in the air, between her and Mary: two hands of flame, each drawn from a thread of candlelight, too big and too bright and too potent, far too near.

Hands that twitched and stretched, that folded their fingers close and stretched them wide, that learned their reach and strength – and then reached out for her throat.

Georgie might just have sat there and let them take it. Take her. Crush or burn or both, she had no idea.

Grace, though? Grace was a survivor.

Full of guilt, overflowing with confession: even so.

Grace ducked and dived. Ducked under the fiery hands as they groped for her; dived sideways, past the candle in its jar, to where the ship's bell stood in its frame there on the floor, bulky and awkward and out of the way.

Snatched at it with her right hand, her good hand; gripped the rope and swung the clapper, struck the bell.

Struck it again and again, clattered it back and forth, sound and fury.

Felt her other wrist rip itself open against whatever stitches had been set there; felt the blood pulse out one more time.

And she had so little to start with, hardly enough; and even so.

She rang the bell for herself, wildly, raucously. And bled coldly, achingly; and heard Mary's puzzled laugh, and heard her say, 'You don't imagine that's going to call people in, do you? Those doors won't open for anyone, whether they try or not.'

No, she didn't think it was going to call people in. If it did, she didn't think they could possibly come in time. Those hands were feeling for her again, and never mind the nonsense of the gods: Mary was frowning in concentration, her own fingers stretching and curling as she pictured them around Grace's throat. The immaterial hands she'd conjured matched her moves exactly, following Grace down, stretching, curling . . .

She wouldn't burn as Kathie had. These had only the heat of two distant candles behind them, not the concentrated impulse of a bonfire. They looked hot, but their touch was cold, an icy wire against her skin as one brushed across her shoulder. She flinched, and tried to roll underneath their sudden grab. But Mary was quicker now, getting the hang of this unexpected puppetwork, or else Grace was just too slow. Weak and hurt and afraid, not fierce enough, not quite.

One of those hands had a grip on her arm, like a tangle of bitter wire; the other was insinuating itself around her throat. She flung her own hand up to fend it off, tried to tuck her chin deep down into her chest; but there was nothing there to fight against, nothing but the tight wire feel of it around her neck, nothing for her fingers to scrabble at.

She'd seen a rabbit in a snare one time, on an early country walk with one of her squires. She must look like that to Mary, she thought: snared and caught, eyes bulging and legs kicking helpless across the floor . . .

Not so helpless. Grace was no ready easy victim. Her foot

caught what she was kicking for, the candle in its jar. Caught it and spilled it and sent it spinning across the bare boards, breaking the thread of flame at its source, unravelling its whole hand so that its grip melted away.

Too bad that it was the wrong hand, the one that had held her by the arm, not the one that was choking her still.

Too bad also that it was only one candle out of dozens. The flame of another immediately rose like a snake on a string, questing towards her, starting to weave itself into another hand.

She could see that in the corner of her eye, just where her vision was starting to blur and sparkle. She couldn't breathe, she could get no air; all her neck was sore already, and this constriction was worse than the waxy strangling hands of before, like half a dozen wires cutting deep into her flesh.

She couldn't fight what she couldn't touch. She couldn't reach Mary either, safe on her sofa, too far away. But the bell was still humming, resonance throbbing through her head; blood was soaking the bandage on her wrist. She couldn't do more to summon her baby. He always came to the sound of bells. It was what she was banking on.

It was all she had.

It was nothing.

It was there, he was there: a nothingness so profound he seemed to suck down light itself, a darkness that glowed more vivid than any candle's flare.

Mary hadn't seen it yet. She had risen to her feet in the tension of the moment, taken a step or two away from the sofa; her hands worked as though she wanted to squeeze and crush Grace's throat herself, to feel soft flesh and tough cartilage buckle and yield beneath her rigid fingers.

She wasn't actually close to actually touching, but she was very close to getting what she wanted else; no more Grace and just her body to dispose of. Grace was dizzy in her head, and her sense of the world was diminishing, black curtains closing in. The pain in her chest was fading, even; air didn't seem so important any more. Nothing worth fighting for.

Maybe she was giving up at last. Not a survivor after all, not any longer. *Sorry, Tony.*

She could do that, she thought. She could give up now – if

it had only been her. She needn't hang on for ever, waiting
for things to get justifiably worse. If she could never be
punished enough, why be punished at all? Why not just be
free of it, out of it, gone . . .?

But it wasn't just her. There was Georgie too, who didn't
deserve any of this; and Mary, who shouldn't be allowed to
get away with it; and Kathie, who was the truly abused innocent; and Frank, who deserved more than smoke and suicide;
and . . .

And above all there was her baby, here was her baby, who
hadn't come all this way just to stand witness. Poor baby, never
had a chance of life, never had a chance to *do* anything . . .

He could do something now. He could claim Grace, the
way he'd been coming to do, coming and coming: given shape
by the house, given purpose by her own conscience. Or he
could save her. After all, she still hadn't been punished enough,
and what else could he be interested in?

He could save her, and save Georgie, and justify Frank.
Give something back to Kathie, even – even if it wasn't enough.

Punish Mary. Even if it wasn't enough.

That had to be how it worked. Didn't it?

Really, Grace couldn't decide.

Which was when Georgie took over. Not for long, just a spasm
of stubborn refusal to die like this, for someone else's fault. If
Grace didn't think her own life worth saving, Georgie absolutely
did. Stubborn and scared, she could turn the encroaching,
engulfing baby. *No, not me, not us; her, take her . . .*

Mary didn't know, she couldn't see. Intent on her target,
she never thought to look behind her.

The baby . . . was really not a baby any more. He almost
never had been. Not even dead a-borning, he'd never had the
chance to grow – but he had grown anyway, hand in hand
with his proper time, in his absence. That absence was toddler-
sized now, squat and solid. Not really toddler-shaped, no real
hint of human: no waving arms or stumping legs, no eyes or
dreadful smile. No personality: what chance had he ever had,
to be a person? Only the fact of him, the simple hollow absence
that he made, indisputable and deadly. Like a whirlpool in the
dry, sucking and sucking into nothingness.

If he had a name, Georgie had never heard it; but he must have had a name, he'd had a funeral.

Maybe she should ask Grace – but not now.

Now was only using the moment, the cold and brutal fact of it, using the dead. Grace had called him, and was bleeding herself away to draw him here; she'd done her bit. Georgie could direct him, without guilt. *There, the woman who's killing me. Us. Take her, she's yours. I give her to you, freely.*

No need to ring the bell again, it was only that she wanted to, one passing knell. She wasn't even sure who it was who passed, as the last of her little vision closed into black: only that she could see Mary toppling into a dark swirling shadow at her back, she could feel the pressure slacken at her throat, but thought it was probably too late; she thought Grace had gone already and she was going now, sliding away, gone . . .

TWELVE

I t was something of a surprise, then, to wake up.

Twice a surprise to wake up whole and singular, particular, herself.

Sunshine on her face; sheets so clean they were still rough from the laundry; a proper bed beneath her. She was oddly pleased to find herself here, but really had no idea where she was. *I don't think we're in Kansas any more.*

The third time pays for all, but she wasn't quite sure whether it counted when she surprised herself with a sudden out-loud giggle, hard and painful in her throat. She really was surprised, as well as sorry; her eyes flew open, nothing faked.

A proper hospital bed, in a private room. Her one arm lay outside the covers, bandaged more thoroughly than before; a vivid crimson tube disappeared into it. She tracked that back and up to a bottle hanging from a hook above. Someone else's blood; her baby would probably not be interested in that, not come for that.

Her baby would probably not come at all, this far from the house. She did have to be far now, she could feel it. Time and distance both; she had a vague sense of days and miles gone.

She turned her head, and maybe that was the third surprise, because of course there was someone sitting there in the shadows – she was getting used to that: again, the third time – only this time it was Tony's flatmate Robbo, and she really had not expected that.

She frowned, just fractionally, which seemed to take an immoderate amount of effort.

He grinned at her. 'What am I doing here, is that it?'

She didn't seem to have a voice just now, but her head at least was working. She nodded, carefully. Her neck – well, she knew it was there, and she could feel that it had been badly wrenched, but it was hardly more than sore now. Days, then; days for definite.

'Just sitting in. Relax. I'll fetch him for you in a minute. I sent him off an hour ago, for a cup of tea and a biscuit; I expect he's fallen asleep again. I keep telling him to go home, and he won't.'

Home. That meant London, didn't it? She frowned again, tried a word this time: 'Where—?' It came out as a croak, and as sore as the giggle.

Robbo interpreted. 'Where are we? The Dorians' clinic. Harley Street. It's nice here, though I wouldn't want to be a patient. We came up and fetched you, before you ask. Drove up overnight, with Tony in a panic all the way; that car of his is stupid, but it can't half motor. I got to drive it all the way back, while Tony rode in the ambulance with you. That was, what, two days and two nights ago, and he hasn't been to bed. Mostly he's been sitting here, watching you breathe. Making sure. Getting cross with them when they wouldn't take any more of his blood; not sure if that's his or not –' with a nod at the bottle – 'but you've had a couple of pints from him. That's the other reason for the tea and biscuits; he needs topping up. Fetch him for you, shall I?'

'Please, Robbo.'

'Sure. Here –' he worked a pedal out of her sight beneath the bed, and she felt her head and shoulders rise – 'you sit up a little, not to scare him more than he's been scared already. Try to look alive. Drink this.' He pressed a glass of something into her good hand; she sipped dutifully and tasted welcome sweetness. Glucose, she thought, stirred into water. 'At the moment you sound worse than you look, even. Dead and buried and dug up again, that's how you sound. That's no good to Tony. He's been in a bit of a state . . .'

He looked it, when at last he came: haggard, with deep shadows under his bloodshot eyes and his hair wild. Where was her sleek groomed Tony gone? Left behind, presumably, on that mad drive north. He couldn't keep up. Never mind; they'd find him again. Polish him up, dress him pretty. That shirt he was wearing now – well, yes. Two days and two nights? She could believe that. It was just that she couldn't *believe* it. Not on him.

'Tony, love.' He'd taken time to splash cold water on his face – or Robbo had told him to, more likely; his hair was damp at the edges, and his collar too. She'd used that same time to do what Robbo had told her to, sipping and swallowing with her difficult throat, getting her voice ready for him. It still sounded jagged and rusty to her ears, it still tore at her on its way out, but she'd done what she could. Made an effort. Much like him. 'Robbo says you came racing to the rescue.'

He shrugged awkwardly. 'Nearly too late, though. It was the police getting through to me, when they'd figured out who Francis was; they wanted to know if I'd sent him up there on a story. That sergeant's probably still on the line. As soon as I understood, I just dropped the phone and ran. Got Robbo to ride shotgun, and drive when I couldn't do it any more. God, I was so scared for you. Francis was dead, and I'd sent you after him . . .'

'You weren't to know.'

'Yeah, I was. It's my job to know.'

'No, it's your job to find out. Which is why you have people like Francis. And me.'

'Not you. Not you ever again.'

Only days ago, she'd been hoping that maybe he would hire her properly. Now he sat there on her bed and held her hand in both of his and promised that he would never ever do that, and her heart surged with warmth.

At the same time, she cringed from what she had to tell him next.

Still. She could do it, now. Not the same confession that she'd made to Mary – once was enough, surely? Sometimes one time paid for all – but this one mattered as much, or maybe more; and yet she could manage it at last. She thought she could.

She said, 'Tony—' and stalled all unexpectedly, not as brave as she thought after all.

He squeezed her hand and misunderstood her entirely, and said, 'You don't have to worry. Not any more, not about anything, but especially not that mess back at the house. By the time the police got there, Dr Dorian was thoroughly in charge. He says Mary died of a heart attack, and I'm sure he's right.' Which meant that he wasn't at all sure, he was just riding with the luck of it. 'Leonard's not challenging him, anyway, which seems to be what matters. The police are happy enough with a suicide and a natural causes. At any rate, nothing comes back to you. You weren't even there.'

'Wasn't I? Who's writing it up for you, then?' *Frank's not.*

'Nobody,' he said, one word that shook her world. Tony was forgoing the story, letting it lie. For her sake.

Now, perhaps, she could do it. She could tell him. If she did it fast.

She said, 'Tony, my baby . . .'

'Hush,' he said, 'don't. That's long gone.' *Dead and buried.*

'Tony, he was yours. Your baby. Ours.'

'Hush, I said,' he said. 'I know.'

'You know?'

'Of course. I've always known. Who do you think it is who leaves the flowers on little Anthony's grave?'

She didn't know that anyone left flowers on his grave. She'd never been, since the day of the funeral. She didn't dare. Someone was sure to see, and take a photo, and sell it to one or another of the papers, maybe the *Messenger*, maybe to Tony himself. And besides, she couldn't bear the bells.

It had never crossed her mind that somebody else might actually go.

She seemed to be crying again; and her one hand was no good, all numb and bound up with bandages and drip, and her other hand was entirely tangled up with Tony's; and besides, she didn't have a hanky anyway, so what was she going to do, blow her nose on the sheet?

She sniffed instead, disgustingly, and tried to rub her eyes against her shoulders; and felt his hand disengage from hers and made a little noise of protest before she felt it coming back with something soft, a nice big hanky, 'There you go, love. Give you a drink, shall I?'

He was still Tony, after all; he didn't mean water. She sniffed again and shook her head with a smile at the quarter-bottle of vodka he produced from a pocket, and blew her nose and wiped her eyes and said, 'I'm in *hospital*, Tone!'

'I know it. We'll get you out, soon as the doctor lets us.

Home with me, where I can look after you.' Something had shifted in him, something radical. Of course he didn't want to say it – he was still a man, after all, even under all the artifice – but it was there, underwriting this sudden determination to take charge of her. A new balance, different priorities, a changed understanding. Nothing had changed in his feelings, any more than it had in hers; only his recognition of them. His confession, perhaps.

Even so: 'Tony, no.' She wouldn't do it. Not now. Something had maybe shifted in her too.

'What?'

'You need to ask? Seriously? Remember your father, over dinner? Over *breakfast*?'

'Oh, lord. No, darling, not the family pile. I'll never take you there again, if you don't want to go. The flat, I meant, for the moment.'

The flat, as she remembered it, was rather full of Robbo. *Your factotum*, and there was his father again. Sneering, in a really nasty way. She said, 'I don't think Robbo would like that.'

'Robbo can lump it. He can move out, if you two keep tripping over each other. He'll be fine; there are half a dozen boys he can stay with, pro tem.'

'Pro what tem?' She didn't know if you could really say that, but it seemed to make sense for the moment. Pro tem. Maybe this was why she liked the phrase so much, because she'd learned it from Tony?

'Until we find the place you'd rather be. I think you're done with Soho, aren't you, pet? It's not been kind to you, and it's not an obligation. There are other places we can live.'

'What about the paper, though?' This was all too hectic; he'd regret it, as soon as he calmed down. If Robbo couldn't calm him, it must be up to her. Down to her. Funny how they both meant the same thing, when they sounded opposite.

Funny how her mind was tripping over words. Maybe there were drugs in the drip, as well as blood. Maybe it was just him, he'd infected her. She had him in her bloodstream now, soaked through all the way to the bone.

Nothing new in that; she'd always had him right there, deep

down. Blood and bone. It was only that he seemed to know it now. Maybe that was all that had shifted. Maybe it was everything.

He said, 'Don't worry about the paper. We won't go miles and miles away. A little house in the country, maybe. Somewhere I can still run up to town, but you don't have to if you don't want to.'

A little house in the country? Him and her? She thought about cottages, all she knew. Chickens and eggs – or was that farmers' wives? Roses around the door.

'I don't think I'd be very good at gardening, Tony.' Mud under her fingernails. Her *broken* fingernails. She couldn't see it.

'We'll get a bloody gardener.'

She realized suddenly – giggling suddenly – that he knew no more than she did. Never mind his dad's big house: servants and horses and cocktails on the terrace, that wasn't the real country. Well, they could learn together. It would be an adventure. If they hated it, they could move back to the city. Not to Soho. He was right about that.

'We could get a kitten,' she said, playing along. 'I've always wanted a kitten.' Something to hold her down, to keep her in. Make her sit still for a while.

'We could make more babies,' he said. 'If you'd like that.'

Would she? She wasn't sure. 'We'd have to get married.' That would mean church. Bells. Photographers.

'Well, yes.' He was counting on it. Taking it for granted. 'You'll want to change your name, after all,' he said.

Yes, but not in a way that brought everybody out to watch; that took away the point of the thing. Tony Fledgwood marrying Grace Harley? That would be news beyond measure. She could think of a way to blunt it, though. Pro tem.

'Tony?'

'Mmm?'

'. . . Do you think you could call me Georgie?'